Cailleach~Witch

Jane Gilheaney Barry

Acknowledgements

First and foremost I have to thank my wonderful husband Adrian for being a source of unfailing support, understanding, and encouragement from day one.

My beautiful daughters, Shaylyn, Saoirse, and Sadhbh, who make me so proud and happy every day. My siblings, I'd be lost without them, Brenda, Colm, Laura, and Martha.

A special thanks to Martha who has been my constant reader and re-reader of the book. Thank you for reading, for never doubting, and for talking to me endlessly about it.

To my childhood friend Clare McGovern, also for reading, for her excellent feedback, and for her friendship. No one could have a better friend.

To my editor Sheryl Lee and my cover designer Mirna Gilman. It was an absolute joy to work with you both. Thank you for your patience, skill, and dedication to my vision for Cailleach~Witch.

To all my friends and followers at That Curious Love of Green blog/fb page. Many of you have been on this journey with me from the beginning. The number one thing you all said through the process was 'keep going.' Turns out that was great advice.

To my parents John and Nora, to whom this book is dedicated. Thank you for giving me the love of books, nature, history, and the mountain. Thank you for giving me strength, passion, and the gift of storytelling. Thank you for always making home a haven, and for telling me to write.

Lastly I have to acknowledge both sets of grandparents. Madge and Tom Gilheaney, Miskawn, Aughnasheelin. And Mary Susan and Patrick Fox, Coragh, Corraleehan. So much of their influence is alive here, like the legacy of storytelling, inherited from my mother, and from her father before her. And the legacy of the people themselves. The people most of all.

Thank you

To my parents, John and Nora Gilheaney

Contents

Chapter 1...1

The Waiting

Chapter 2...10

Letters

Chapter 3...27

The Lost Ones

Chapter 4...37

The Sisters Return

Chapter 5...47

First Impressions

Chapter 6...54

Honor

Chapter 7...59

The Cailleach

Chapter 8...63

Return to the Mountain

Chapter 9..74

The Funeral

Chapter 10..84

Mary - Memories and Regrets

Chapter 11..90

Sliabh Earrach 1969

Chapter 12..108

In the Graveyard

Chapter 13..117

Mary Mannion - Marry in Haste

Chapter 14..126

Caer - Revenge is a dish best served Cold

Chapter 15..133

Memoirs & Memories

Chapter 16..149

Her Kind

Chapter 17..155

Called to the Quest

Chapter 18..174

Jaen and the Cailleach

Chapter 19..178

Journal of Devin Cleary - September 1995

Chapter 20..183

Ellen Cleary

Chapter 21..189

Gifts

Chapter 22..195

Ellen - Part 2

Chapter 23..203

The Stranger

Chapter 24..210

Erin

Chapter 25..215

Drew – October 1995

Chapter 26..226

Honor and Dealan – October 1994

Chapter 27..237

   Going to Town

Chapter 28..245

   Hot Whiskey – November 1995

Chapter 29..254

   A Murder

Chapter 30..262

   Revelations

Chapter 31..270

   Parting is Such Sweet Sorrow – 1960

Chapter 32..277

   Journal of Caer Cleary – August 1960

Chapter 33..287

   This is Goodbye

Chapter 34..293

   Journal of Dara Cleary – April 1995

Chapter 35..302

   The Lovers

Chapter 36..325

Origins

Chapter 37..332

In the Chapel

Chapter 38..340

Diary of Dara Cleary – Bilberry Sunday 1985

Chapter 39..353

All Change

Chapter 40..371

May Day's Eve 1995

Chapter 41..384

Full Circle

Glossary...394

Pronunciation Guide 397

About the Author 398

Before You Go 399

Chapter 1

The Waiting

Erin

Summer was passing us by, growing heavy. I was in the garden with Honor and too many butterflies, too much gravity, and a cool glass of wine, when the black dog came shuffling up the lane with the sky on his back.

'The girls are returning,' Honor said.

I followed her gaze to the mountain. This time we were ready. She went back to her deadheading, me to my wine, but everything was different now.

The family comings and goings are marked always with one form or other of storm. On the day the girls came, dark clouds rumbled low in a sky turbulent since dawn. *Dark things to come*, I thought with interest as I gathered some interest myself among the throngs at Dublin airport. I'd been standing, hands on hips, my face turned to the maelstrom above.

Ten years before, we sent them away – after the incident, when the people turned on them. This kind of thing happened sometimes. It wasn't the girls' fault. They couldn't help what they were, and the townspeople couldn't help but take their chance for rage when it came along. A combination of fear and need is a difficult one.

It wouldn't have lasted, of course. They'd never drive us out, not that we could go. We were tied to that place as the mountain itself and with the wisdom of ages we knew – when modern medicine failed them and they couldn't find comfort or cure, it was back to us they would come, eager for the charms, the healing herbs, the water, and the hands.

Ours was a last chance for many, and no one would forget it soon, but Aunt Mae had been right. There was no need for the young girls to suffer it. Their time here would come soon enough and the mountain would have its way, but not yet. We sent for their father.

As light broke on the appointed day, grey morning mist morphed into swirling clouds, as if stirred by an angry invisible hand, and the wind cried with bone chilling eeriness. We worked calm and fast to batten the hatches, greenhouse, garden, animals, house, nothing new. Marius was our concern, driving in these conditions and still hours away. We were close, much more, you might call it, attuned to the elements than regular folk. We'd invoked protection from the Cailleach's wrath, but there was still a chance he wouldn't make it.

All we could do now was wait, and we stood, the old aunts Ellen and Mae, my twin Honor, our nieces and me. My chest tightened with pain for the waiting, the silence, and what we must do. The clocks struck one.

'It's time,' said Mae.

We made our way through the rooms, a quiet determined procession, while all around us the house creaked and swayed as an old ship forlorn for the parting. Living here, I often imagined, was like living at sea, though none of us had ever seen it. I thought too of the difference; a ship is free.

In the hall the volume of elements rose, and the temperature dropped along with my resolve. What if he wasn't there, hadn't made it? And what if he was? Were we doing the right thing? But without so much as a glance for us or each other, Mae and Ellen, like gladiators meeting the crowd, heaved and threw open the door. In rushed the darkness, the stinging rain, the monstrous wind. I was aware just for a moment of so much hair, jet, gold, slate and vermillion, filling the air then falling in waves of slow motion. But there was no time to lose in dreaming. Honor led Drew and I led Devin out and down the treacherous steps to the lane and their father there, waiting.

We turned for Dara, tight lipped and pale as a changeling but steady and coming alone. Looking up to the house, the mountain above, the sky on top, it felt as if any minute the whole lot might come crashing down. No words were spoken, the handover swift, brutal. What could any of us say? We stepped back to the wall, back up the stone steps, like sentries who know the drill well and are weary of it. When we got to the top we stopped, turned, and watched them.

'There go the roses,' said Ellen.

As the car pulled away Devin and Drew looked back. It had comforted them, to see our calm exteriors illuminated in the doorway, and they watched for as long as the forest would let them. We didn't move or bow our heads. We were used to the storm, to that life in the shadow of the mountain. I supposed that Dara heard the sound as we did, that she steeled herself against it much as we were doing. She was strong for her age and not once did she turn around. I admired her grit. Someday she was going to need it, we all would.

We watched the car as it slowly snaked the road, sometimes visible, sometimes only the lights through the forest. Once we knew not only that they'd made it down but that they'd crossed the bridge at town, we invoked the elements into a banishing.

For how long, we wondered? Not forever, we knew, but our hearts were still broken. It was a strange thing to send and to wish them away when we needed them with us so badly.

'Safe away little birds,' said Mae.

The air was still now.

After that was a hard time for us, and for Honor especially, but life soon went on as before. We were strong enough, the two sets of two sisters, Ellen and Mae, Honor and me. But it was a terrible thing to lose the girls and especially Dara, because you must understand, this was not the first time. When Dara was one year old we stood in the same place, watching her and her mother, our sister Caer, leave. And now, by choice, we had sent her and her sisters away. We were losing again.

...

Making my way to the gate I thought how quickly the years had come in. In many ways, it seemed only yesterday my sisters Honor, Caer, and I had been the young ones. Sometimes I'd forget Caer been gone from the mountain for twenty-six years and had been dead eighteen years. Honor and I were 'the aunts' now.

Not the *old* aunts, perhaps, but at this rate it wouldn't be long.

Twenty-six years since Caer had left with baby Dara. She was the first Cleary woman in living memory to leave this place. We knew we'd never see our sister again, but we understood she had to go. We, Honor and I, stayed on at our mountain home, minding the farm and the people as the women of our family have done for generations.

We are *Bean Feasa*, wise women, healers, or witches. It depends on what you need, it depends on who you talk to. People travel from across the country, even from out in the world for our help. Charms, cures, curses, though we don't deal in curses now, that's in the past.

...

Caer left with a man who'd come from Cádiz in Spain out of interest for a book he was writing on the healing traditions of Europe. Marius had the openness and sensitivity of an artist, one of those rare people you don't meet very often, secure in his own skin, a free spirit. He saw in her eyes the destruction and pain and found he wasn't afraid and wouldn't break himself against it. From the first moment he saw her he knew he'd never love again.

At the time Honor said, 'Caer has all the luck.'

We were working in the garden. There'd been a glut of crops that year and it took a lot of saving. Our backs were sore, our baskets heaving.

'You can't be serious?'

'I'm only serious about the fact she gets two great loves, and gets away from here.'

'Three great loves,' I said. 'You forget Dara, Dara makes it worthwhile for all of us.'

'I know, but I can't help it. Look at him, he's beautiful, he's crazy about her. I envy her escape.'

'Even so, how can she do it? How can she leave us?'

A pained look passed over her face. 'I don't know,' she said. 'Strength I suppose. She's been through the fires but she's still strong.'

'Yes, yes, I know,' I muttered, kicking over a basket. 'Stronger than our mother was, stronger than we are. How often did we hear that growing up?'

'You're worried about the quest? Of what will become of us *weaklings* without her?'

'I know life goes on but her time on the quest is done, a *Bean Feasa* can't practice with pain in her heart, you know this.'

'I seem to manage.'

'You're only bitter, it's hardly the same!' We laughed at that.

'What about the child? I mean, she will come back one day, won't she?'

Honor nodded. 'One day.'

'So is there nothing we can do now except wait? Rot?'

'Waiting is so long... I wouldn't say *nothing*.'

She had a flair for mystery and I wasn't satisfied yet. I wanted assurance, something. I wanted her to tell me that our time wasn't done, our chances gone. After all, it mattered more to her than it did to me, but I was just as bound as she was. Would *she* take the quest now? Could she? Did I even want her to?

I pushed her.

'Well that tells me a lot, Honor. The quest abandoned, and after everything we did. You're not forgetting?'

'*Forget?*' she snapped glacially. 'How could I forget?'

We worked on then, seeking solace in the black earth, peace for the peace-less. You could find it there sometimes, but forget? You could never forget. I was sorry I'd said it. In truth, I was more content here than she was. This fate, it wasn't so difficult for me. Our sister's laughter came to us in waves, languorous as the air itself.

'Maybe she can make it,' I suggested. I meant it as encouragement, as hope.

But without pause she replied, '*My envy of escape and love are foolish, for strong or not there'll be no escape for her, and maybe no escape for us.*'

'Why? What have you seen?'

'I've seen nothing. It's too hot now, I'm going in.'

Honor hadn't seen a future for our sister, though at the time she didn't tell me, and yet, for all of that still she envied her.

Chapter 2

Letters

Espinho, Porto, Portugal, 1974

Dear Honor & Erin,

I'm writing to tell you the news that Dara and Devin have a new little sister. I've called her Drew, the dawn of a new circle.

Dara remains the one. I miss you both, but we've made a good life here. Sometimes I see groups of women and it fills me with such nostalgia. I miss that in my life, aunts, sisters, allies. I miss other things too, things I never thought to miss, like the stiffness of the heather as it holds its ground against the cold north wind, the winding lanes of fuchsia, the scent of the pine, the colours of the mountain. I even miss the rain.

Here Porto's all faded grandeur, blue, white, and the sea. The smell is one of salt and heat and something else that is strange to me. I don't know what it is, but the sense of freedom is intoxicating.

We eat bacalhau, the local fish specialty, and drink port wine and Mateus rosé. We walk sandy beaches, buy fresh fish from the little boats that dot the port and looking up we marvel at the bridges over the Douro, the colourful houses that cling to the rock and we laugh at the sun.

Marius is well and we're happy. I have my moments, but he is so strong and so passionate he makes me forget, for a time at least. This is a good place for family and it's easy to have children here, though I suppose I won't have any more.

The night this child was conceived I was returning home from the market. There was a blood sky, the scent of bougainvillea filled the air, it reminded me of you, Erin, but it was missing something. It didn't have the aliveness of our mountain air. I was outside the church of Santa Rita Agorio and I heard a man's voice behind me say, 'Boa Noite.' 'It's a beautiful night is it not, señorita?'

I turned to see who had spoken and it was a young priest, very young and very fair against that fiery sky. He was smiling at me, and I froze, staring, I couldn't speak to him. So I did the only thing that I could do, I ran. I ran to Marius, the only one I thought could save me. I didn't want to think about he who was lost. I wanted only to think of the present, the way Marius did. I don't know why I tell you this now, I tried so hard to erase it, but that evening, the colours, the scents and all that they conjured stayed with me, like countless other days and nights have stayed with me. Only now I know you can't erase what you haven't made peace with, what you cling to.

Well, my other news is that soon we'll be leaving. Heading south for Spain first and then Africa. Our route will take us to Lisbon, Seville and Cadiz, to Marius' home for a while. We'll take the boat to Morocco. Beyond that I don't know, but as much as I like it here now I'll be happy to go. I've come to depend on an ever changing horizon, if you can imagine.

Caer

...

Erin

We sat back slowly, taking it all in. Could our lives be any more different? All Caer's talk of freedom, travel and *endlessly changing horizons* must have been killing Honor, but this was good news, the very best news. A new circle meant new hope, best to focus on that. Honor was still as the grave for a moment but I knew her, and like earth in winter it was only a surface thing. She looked greener than normal today, and she jumped when I patted her bun.

'How about a teapot of gin?' I suggested. As I rattled the cups, a mournful wind shook the casements and she paced, full of longing. Her bones were no match for her restless heart. And her mind still moved in that future she wanted, the steps that were needed, how long it would take her to get us there. 'Here, sit, drink this, you'll feel better.'

We drank a toast to Caer's news then sat silent, watching the shadows and flames, the stories being told there.

I was thinking how strange it was, these children we'd never met, our own blood out there in the world and yet tied to us, to this place. I said as much plus several other things, not one she heard. In the end she just left like a great rush of wind, all at once. Curling up in the chair I pulled an old blanket about me, and watching the fire I finished my drink. I was in no hurry. It was comforting to sit here, safe from all storms. But soon I went back to my stillroom, my heaven. To my tinctures, my herbs and my medicines. I could lose hours here, and often did. It was not in Honor's nature to enjoy things but I was a hedonist. I loved my world and took pleasure in it.

Sliabh Earrach, our home in the North West of Ireland, is not a place many would think of for pleasure. To the west lies greater mountains, stretches of coast, places of wild and outstanding beauty, the *'must see'* list makers. We share in the wildness and weather but we're off the beaten track. Like the castle in the fairy tale, wild, overgrown, forgotten. This is witch country.

No one here is waiting on a prince.

...

Erin

Two years passed, and if anything we grew apart, Honor and me. It's normal, I think, for adult siblings, to grow apart without malice, and to come back again. Like waves in an ocean. She continued on her self-appointed quest and I continued with my healing work, until one day, another letter came.

Tetouan, Africa, 1976

Even in Africa I can hear our mountain. It never stops calling me home. After some soul searching I've decided to start teaching the children, but that is all. I'll be teaching them to keep things hidden from the outside world that will always turn on them. I want them to have a chance at a normal life. We never had that chance and now it's too late for us. I would wish something different for them. Erin, I know you and the aunts will not agree or even think it's possible, but we will see. I am still the most powerful. No one knows yet what will come.

I want to tell you about my girls. Drew is just a baby still, two years old, my bright one I call her, her power will be second sight.

Devin is five. She will be a great healer, like you Erin, and you Mae. She has that ultra sensitivity and has been showing signs of healing hands since eighteen months old. Without knowing it she's practicing already. I can see her power will be very great, perhaps even greater than yours.

Dara is seven. She's the main reason I've had to face up to reality and begin proper training. She shares mine and our mother's power, I feel sure she's the one.

I know it's wrong, that it goes against the proper order. You, Honor, should be guiding Drew, and Erin guiding Devin, and maybe one day when they're older, well you never know, do you?

As much as I would like to keep them from that place forever, even I know the only way for them to be free of their fate in the long run is to embrace it, to know and to face what they are. They may yet have that chance but for now, at least, the mountain will not have its way. For now, they are mine only.

Love Caer

We read the letter with varying rising and sinking feelings for it wasn't true, the mountain would have its way and soon. For now, we remained focused on thoughts of the children and the knowledge she had begun their training. That night we made three Celtic knot pendants, one for each of the girls, to protect them from otherworld ministrations and sent them off without delay.

Seasons turned, Honor and I, the aunts too, we grew older, we waited.

...

Erin

It was two more years before we received another letter, not from Caer this time but from Marius. The post woman, Bridget, met Honor at the gateway to the forest. She was standing stock still watching the road as if waiting for Bridget, or god knows what. Her long loose hair almost covered her face, and under her arm she'd a crow, wrapped in a tea towel.

'Jesus, Mary and Joseph,' said Bridget, clucking to herself, 'saves me heading up there anyway,' then rolling down the window, ignoring the bird who cocked his head balefully at her she called, 'Morning Honor! Just the one item today.' She handed over the letter. It was rich cream parchment, sealed in a blood red wax.

'A lovely letter, from your sister, maybe?' She was mad for news. 'How is she, anyway? Any sign of her to come home? Ye must miss her... and the baby? I suppose she's not a baby now, what was her name?'

'Dara,' they both said at the same time.

Honor turned away quickly into the forest, leaving Bridget shaking her head, muttering, 'Oh, she's a strange one, that one.' She was disappointed to have gotten no gossip. No other houses past this point, thanks be to god. For the rest of the day and for days later the scene followed her, the black crow, the pale face, the wild hair, the weight of the envelope, the blood red wax.

Rushing into the kitchen Honor tore the envelope open and devoured its contents before passing it to me...

Tetouan, Africa, 1978

Forgive me, I know it is strange that I write but after all this time the fog around your sister has become much harder to reach through. There's no easy way to say this so I'll just say it, I'm losing her.

I know what you think. You think I never had her, and it's true but we've had our own happiness. She's had her dark times always, but now, well, I can only describe her as haunted.

I don't know how else to explain, so here it is, she's in communion with the mountain.

Just the other night she woke me in a desperate state, she wanted to go home she said, had to go right away. 'Is it the mountain?' I asked. 'Yes' she said, then, 'No, it's me, it's me,' and she wept.

Then a while later, 'It's Seán,' she said, he's there, he's...' and she made the most terrible inhuman sound. I leapt towards her, I tried to tell her this would pass, that she was safe here.

My voice was calm but it wasn't calm I felt. She'd never mentioned him like this before, never been this upset. All the years I'd shared her with his memory, it wasn't a problem or a secret, but she has a great capacity for happiness, did you know that? She'd never had to speak his name before.

I tried to hold her but I don't think she knew I was there. 'Don't leave me,'...she wept again. As if I would ever leave her. I was wretched, I insisted I would never, and though I knew it wasn't me she meant, I meant it.

Everything changed again after that. She was calm the next day, unpacked her things, assured me she was fine. No, she didn't want to go home now, yes she was sure. It was just a few bad nights, nothing to worry about, she was over it she said. If anything, I found this more sinister. As if she'd decided or done something final.

So I asked her straight, 'What about Seán?'

She paled but never faltered. 'Oh that, just a dream... a bad dream, you know how I get. You mustn't worry, it's over now, believe me, it's over.'

But I am worried, gravely so, and I have to ask if you can do anything? If you can help?

We didn't have to go very far from Sliabh Earrach to realise she couldn't get away from it and now it's like she never left.

Marius

...

Erin

We couldn't say what had happened, it was not of our understanding, but it was cruel was it not? Caer had been ready to return. If she had come back then things might have been different. As it was they were about to get a whole lot worse.

We replied to Marius quickly:

Sliabh Earrach, Co Leitrim, Ireland

Dear Marius

19

You must bring our sister home. We want to help. Together it's possible we can do something but we can't come to you. Please don't delay. Did the children get the pendants? Can you make sure they wear them? They will help keep them safe.

Honor & Erin

We wrote to Caer too:

Dear Caer,

Remember who you are. You are the strongest Cleary there has ever been, the only one who has ever been able to leave. You found the strength for that, to resist the curse and more besides. Can you not now find the strength to come back and help us end this thing once and for all?

The world has been cruel to you but you are not alone. We are three, remember?

Please come.

Please come.

We will be strong.

And there will yet be a reckoning.

Your sisters in fate.

Honor & Erin

That was all we could do and for a while we let ourselves think she'd come back. She was older so we'd always looked up to her, were stronger when she was around. Now we willed her return, prepared for it. Ah, we couldn't help it. We, the house too, we brightened a little. Secretly we made plans, all the things we would do when she came. We hadn't seen our sister in eight years and here we were all in our thirties, still young, young enough for another act?

We wondered if she would be different, pictured her coming back through the forest, over the lane and up the stone steps to us. We wondered a lot of things. The thought of being three sisters again had excited our spirits and if you were to analyse it all it was hope. We had renewed hope that our chance hadn't passed, that we might still be the ones who would break the curse once and for all and be free. Was that not a heady fantasy?

Mae and Ellen watched and were silent. With foresight and sadness or with envy for their own lost chances? We couldn't tell, but for some reason we tried to hide our feelings from them, though they knew of course, they always knew.

And then the letter came.

Before we even opened it we knew she wasn't coming, the fuchsias I'd picked that morning had withered to dust on the table. With heavy hearts we sat down and read her last letter.

Tetouan, Africa, 1978

I had a dream once. I dream all the time, but this was different, in this like in so many other dreams I was with Seán, but we were old. I'd spent my life with him.

I never wanted to wake again.

The warmth of that dream stayed with me for days. But she was jealous of the dream. SHE wanted me just for her, and she told me terrible things. None of it was true. It was all to get me to give him up but that was the one thing I could never do.

Even when he was lost to me, even when I knew. Still she wouldn't leave me alone, and all this time she wants me back, but she'll never get me back.

But Honor, Erin, I've never been able to ask and I don't want to ask now but, do you know? Did the Cailleach take him? Or is it worse? What she told me, it couldn't be true? And I was never able to accept that he just changed his mind, didn't want me. I knew it had to be more but not what she said, not that.

The night Dara was born, you remember? That day I went to her. I couldn't stand it anymore, I had to see her face to face. Ask her to give him back to me or tell me what had happened at least. The journey was slow, treacherous. I admit I was foolish to go.

I don't know for sure but think I fell, and I must have passed out for a moment. When I woke I realised my waters had broken. I got up slowly and thinking better of my mission headed back in the direction of home, but every so often the waters came again in a rush and a dull ache had started to spread and squeeze like an angry fist in my back. I was trying not to panic but there was no getting away from the fact I was alone on the mountain and in labour. Mae had been going to deliver the baby. She'd been ready. I myself had not thought about it, I'd been thinking only of him and I whispered his name now, Seán, Seán...

Caw, caw, caw, caw, the crows answered, circling above. Startled and shaking I considered the odds. It was a mild night with soft rain and wind but the chances of making it home? There were no other houses around and soon night would fall. I scanned the horizon in hope of seeing someone but who'd be out here at this time, this high? My eyes fell on the hawthorn tree, our old friend. I set out slow but determined to reach it. Do you remember? This was mine and Seán's place. We'd played here as children, hid as teenagers and then later as lovers in secret. I cried out as I reached it, the pains coming harder with less space between.

Day turned to night and the night was profound. The air seemed sweet, almost sickly. The forest, a rich thick curtain, surrounded the mountain and me. Why had nobody found me? Where were my aunts? My sisters? How long had I been here? Exhaustion consumed me. Something was wrong. Maybe we'll die here, I thought, and the thought seemed good. I could feel my strength like a river deserting me and I thought I was ready to go. I willed it, but I opened my eyes one last time and to my shock, he was there, coming towards me.

Had I already died or was I dreaming? Trembling, I spoke, 'Are you real?' He nodded and knelt with me. 'But...I thought you were dead, I was sure...all this time...where were you? Everyone's been looking...they...' I had to stop. I couldn't ask him anything else, besides I didn't want to die now. I wanted to fight! To live! For his part Seán still didn't answer me, in fact he never spoke, not once.

Even in my suffering I knew it wasn't right, that there was evil in it. But I was just so happy he was there, that even in this terror we were two. His eyes were sad, and they were dark, darker eyes than I knew, had known all my life. I told myself I'd make everything better. And I promised him too.

When she was born at last I watched him hold her, a tiny girl, adding her cry to the dark. And as he carried us both down the mountain my mind travelled back to other times of peril we'd shared, and times of love, and I clung to him. It was almost dawn, the silver mists were parting slow.

'Do you remember, Seán? The happy times. We can have those again. We can go away, just like we planned.'

He didn't bring us to the house but to the barn beside. We'd heard the voices in the forest, seen the beam of searchlights. He laid us down gently, but then he went to leave. And I lost it, I screamed,

'You're not leaving me again, NO!!!' My fingers felt bony and useless but I held him as tight as I could.

'Look at me,' I commanded feverishly, my whole body shaking with intent. If I could only search his eyes I thought, have him see me, make him speak.

'Say something... For god's sake, Seán, what's happened to you?' It seemed hopeless, but every last shred of my will concentrated on keeping him with me. And then, as if a fog had lifted, the light came back to him.

He was the boy again, the man I knew. Fierce grief and tenderness flowed from him.

'Caer,' he said, 'I love you, I want to stay here with you like we planned, forever, but I can't... I have to go.'

'No Seán, it's an enchantment, it's the Cailleach, we can get you back, but you have to fight, just wait, please, my sisters, we...' He pulled me to him and kissed me.

We had kissed many times, in life, in this place, and every kiss was right, but this was different. This was the end, was goodbye, and I felt it, a terrible severing. It was death. And he left with the dawn.

I thought he must have made a deal with the Cailleach and she let him come back to me just that one time and that meant she still had him somehow. I tried to find him, I searched everywhere. I went to the Cailleach, but she of course was indifferent.

'Come back to me where you belong,' she said, 'you and the child.'

Still I searched, I questioned all and everything. I thought I might die with longing, for what the mountain knows. All the joy went out of living for me after that. Turns out everything fades away in life, except the sadness of lost love. I won't be coming home. He was home to me.

Caer

Chapter 3

The Lost Ones

The devastation of reading her words was complete, we knew all was lost. We remembered that night as if it were yesterday. By the time we found them she was out of her mind with fever. It was a miracle they'd both survived the ordeal. She'd talked and talked about how Seán had come to her, had delivered the baby and how we had to go right away and get him back.

Our poor sister, it was the hardest thing we'd ever done not to tell her the truth. I'd found Seán's body that day. It was while we'd been searching for her on the dark side of the mountain. A lonelier place you will never see. It had lain there some time but one thing was clear. In his death locked fist he held a sheaf of human hair. Hair black as a crow's, wavy and long. Only one person we knew had hair like that, Caer herself.

I could have tried to remove it, could have gone to the guards and his people for help, but what other secrets might an autopsy reveal? And besides, the investigation alone would lead straight to our door after all that had happened between him and Caer, especially that night in the chapel, the last time he'd been seen alive. And so I'd done what everyone in this family does in a crisis, I called on my sister.

Honor and I placed the body where no one would ever find it, not without sadness or regret, you understand. We had loved him like a brother and maybe never fully realised until we closed his eyes, tenderly closed the earth over him, making sure to leave the grave unmarked in any way, making sure it would never be found, unless one of us told it, and we would never tell it. His mother, our sister, they would never know the truth. To deny him a proper burial, it was hard to do.

We stood there a long time. It was a lonely place to have died in, where the only sounds were the ever blowing wind, the calling of the curlew.

'We are truly damned,' I'd said at the time and over the years we'd felt it, always questioning our action, our veils of secrecy, but never our vow, we never questioned that.

We didn't discuss whether we thought Caer had done this or not, and if not her, who and why? There was some talk that he'd been involved with the IRA but we thought the Cailleach most likely, not that we could prove it. It didn't seem possible that Caer would have done it, but it didn't seem impossible either. The quest did strange things to people, we'd learned that the hard way, and people weren't entirely wrong when they said she'd gone mad. But we remembered what the aunts told us all those years ago, about what our great aunts had done, and we wouldn't second guess our own or anything she'd done in the name of the quest.

All we knew was what the people reported they'd seen and heard that last evening and that Caer had no memory of it. That and the fact she had loved him. At the end of the day we had to protect our sister on the quest, protect the next generation. We were healers and helpers and in a way we were servants of the people, but our first duty was to the house.

...

One year later Caer had left with Marius and the child, never to return. Now eight years had passed and she was in danger again, close to death. We had to think of the children, not one now but three. Honor had thought someone should go to Caer before something terrible happened, but who? Reality was we had no one to send. We'd sent the pendants and now we sent rowan berries and twigs of elder with instructions to place them in the children's clothes to protect from bewitchment and pain. The Cailleach wouldn't hurt them exactly but we didn't want them exposed to anything that might jeopardise their future.

...

Marius

On the night of Caer's death Marius was sleeping, a fitful sleep full of dark and terrible things. Twice he'd woken, thinking she was calling him. He'd reached out but her side of the bed was still empty. She was late tonight, but she had said she might be. It was raining heavily and its rhythm carried him away in dreams again.

'Marius,' she said. He went very still then, a ghost of a smile on his face. In his dream it seemed they were back in the woods at *Sliabh Earrach*, on the very first day they'd met.

'Marius, you must listen. The children. I was wrong about everything. The answers, the freedom, everything is there. You have to bring them to my sisters, you have to do it now, promise me that you will, Marius?'

'Where are you?' he whispered. 'Why aren't you here?'

'I've gone back. Back where I belong. You will bring them, won't you, Marius? Promise me, promise me.'

Deep in sleep he answered quietly that he would bring them, yes, he would, and come to bed. But there was no answer, only silence, and then he thought he heard her say,

'*I did love you.*'

Did love him. Did love. Past tense.

And then the dream changed. She was falling back and down into the forest bed. Marius woke in a sweat, his heart thundering in his chest. A knock on the door startled him further, and looking out he saw the police car, and knew it was over, he knew his lovely haunted girl was dead.

…

Honor

At the same time, half way across the world, Honor was out on the mountain. She'd been on a house call with old Molly and Jimmy Prior. She had just finished and was getting ready to leave when Molly sidled up to her.

'Aren't you ever afraid? Out there?'

Honor looked at Molly who gasped and recoiled, for in those eyes she saw no colour or even the absence of colour but the whole room around them reflected. She hesitated, but age made her brave.

'A woman, walking alone like that, even one with your,' she paused, 'abilities. There are still things to fear out there, even for you,' she'd added, pleased with herself.

Everyone in these parts knew of the Cailleach, the paranormal landscape figure, an otherworld creature, and stayed well away from her cave on the mountain, a known gateway to the otherworld and no place for man or beast. Fear of her made the Clearys a convenient scapegoat for anything that went wrong. Whether the cattle were sick or the hens not laying, or the weather too wet or too hot or too cold, it was their fault.

Many theories abounded, had been whispered for centuries, that they were one and the same, the women and her. That they lived in fear of her as much as anyone else was another, after all not only did the Cailleach's cave lie directly above the Cleary house but the house too was built into the mountain, or so it seemed. Who knew the truth? Who could? If you had cause to step inside the house you weren't likely to speak of it, and if you grew up around here you lived in fear of the Cailleach. You might think you didn't, but the superstition ran deep.

This was always the way of it, thought Honor, and one reason she left most of this work to Erin. They, the people, went around the place afraid of their lives, of her, avoiding her gaze, avoiding her. But as soon as they needed help, as soon as they'd witnessed her work as a healer they thought they knew better. They let their guard down because now in their minds she seemed softer, more vulnerable, just because she would help them. What fools they were. They thought they knew pain and what fear was, what she was. They knew nothing.

'And what have I to fear? The night? The people? The otherworld? You have it wrong, Molly. I am the one who is feared.' As if in answer a blood chilling scream pierced the air, the banshee, the messenger of death.

'Jesus, Mary and Joseph,' cried Molly, making the sign of the cross. She grabbed Honor's arm. 'It's not for himself is it?'

'No,' said Honor, removing the old woman's grip. 'I told you, he'll be fine now in just a few days.' The old woman looked doubtful. 'It's not for him,' Honor repeated, heading for the door.

'Goodbye Honor, thank you.' It was almost a whisper, not the confident tone of before. From the window Molly watched her disappear and shivering turned back to her husband and the certainty of the fire. She sat close to Jimmy, placing a hand on his. She was uneasy now, maybe she shouldn't have said all she'd said to Honor Cleary, shouldn't have looked in those strange eyes of hers, and she was strange that one, not like Erin who seemed almost normal, or Mae either. She hadn't said who the banshee was for and they did say she had the gift of sight but she sure was in a fierce hurry to get out in that night and a banshee calling in it. *God help us all,* she thought.

Honor, sure of foot and purpose, hadn't gone very far before she heard that terrible sound again. No mistaking the banshee's wail. She was just coming up to the pass when the ghostly figure appeared before her, a soul wandering, making its way to the otherworld. And she watched in horror of recognition as she saw that the ghost was her sister. So it was as she'd foreseen. She hadn't seen Caer in person since she'd left with Marius all those years ago, but there was no mistaking that long black hair, no mistaking one of her own. 'Caer,' she called, *'Caer.'* She tried to follow, but in vain. In despair, she watched the lonely figure on its long march. 'Caer.'

Caer hadn't seen or heard her sister, she was searching. She'd been searching for a long time. She didn't know how long. Didn't know Honor kept silent vigil with her, for as long as she held her in sight, and for a long time after.

Walking home, Honor wondered if fear would be better than pain, if you had the choice.

Erin, Ellen and Mae had heard the banshee too, they were waiting, all three standing together, pale as statues in moonlight when Honor walked in. Honor looked to her aunts in turn and then to Erin.

'Our sister is dead.'

Erin rushed past her, down the stone steps. The three women followed, formed a circle around her. Through rain and tears she reeled, and raged with herself, with her fate, with the mountain, and calling her dead sister's name. Mae's heart ached for her nieces, the latest generation to come to this. Ellen, as always, betrayed nothing, she just stood, no expression, just watching. And Honor?

Honor cried no tears but inside she felt something so sharp she thought at first it might be a heart attack. She felt her physiology change, every cell and fibre seemed to tear and rearrange itself as her mind played a high speed replay of their lives, glimpses of future and past, and then just as suddenly she was back, just in time to see Erin extend her hand to the mountain. She was about to lay down her own curse, was opening her mouth to speak it.

In one swift motion Honor gripped her sister's wrist. '*STOP.*'

Stunned, Erin looked at her a moment then said, 'You're right, you should be the one to do it.'

'No.' Honor shook her head. 'Erin, no. No more curses, but a promise. Whatever it takes, whatever happens now, we are going to end this.' Pain, she'd decided, was better than fear, there was power in it.

Chapter 4

The Sisters Return

For a long time the sisters had known they'd be going back. It was the law of the wild that was there and they'd stayed away for as long as they could, but now the pull was strong. They knew the mountain was where they belonged.

They'd started life in far flung corners of the world, as far as their mother could take them, and had never seen or even heard tell of *Sliabh Earrach* until after she died. From then on they'd spent the best part of every year with the aunts. Their father came less and less. Over time his grief had morphed into hate of the place and worse, every time he came the children seemed less his and less of the world somehow. Caer had been right, they belonged there, and eventually he stopped going.

Last thing he ever expected was to hear from the aunts, to be asked to take the girls away again. They were sixteen, fourteen and eleven and already bearing the scars of that cursed place. Whatever she'd wanted them to find at *Sliabh Earrach*, they hadn't found it. He was glad to do it for them, and for the memory of the woman he'd loved. From that they'd spent ten years, first with Marius then out in the world, a happy wandering existence. But lately, something had changed. They'd become restless, and filled with longing for the mists of the green place, for Ireland.

Journal of Devin Cleary, July 26ᵗʰ 1995

Today we return to *Sliabh Earrach*. I want to go, it's where I'm meant to be. All my life I've been quietly learning and sometimes practicing. At first my mother taught me and then after she died we came back here and the aunts took over for a while. In the beginning it was easier with them because they didn't hide it. I was young and for a long time didn't know this openness would bring harm to me and my sisters, the aunts and the house too. After what happened with Dara and the locals I felt my mother had been right. I never practiced openly again.

There's going to be a funeral, our great aunt Mae's. You'd think she did it on purpose, Erin did say she planned it. We needed a final push and Mae's death provided it. She was old but vital, healthy. People in our family die young or live long. We don't do medium anything.

It's strange to think of the place without Mae. Will the house feel as sheltering? She was the rock it was built on. Strong, capable, kind too, and the most like a mother to us after ours was gone. Her sister Ellen, now there was a strange one. Wore white always, and she carried a small axe at her waist, for chopping fuchsias.

'Why fuchsias?' I asked her once.

'They're no wild thing,' she said, as if the reason were obvious.

'So, they're here now, what harm are they doing?'

'They don't belong.'

Ellen didn't say much, but when she did you were left more confused, or with more questions, not that she'd answer them.

Of the two young aunts Erin was closest to us. Honor was just not the type. They were all except Mae... distracted. Work was a part of it, their healing work and running the farm and house. There was always work to be done, but it was more than that. It put me in mind of Dara now. She is increasingly forgetful of everyday things. I see a lot of her in my memories of them. Intense people who live in the interior, full of wistfulness and furious longings.

First Ellen and now Mae died before we came back. That was a shame, but maybe they'd known we would come? Erin and Honor knew. The púca had walked up to the house in the guise of a dog with a storm on his back just to warn them.

And when I asked Erin what she and Honor had thought or said to Mae about these death plans she'd said they paid her no mind. Well, that's our family for you. Make open plans for your own death and no one pays any attention.

Speaking of plans, this part of the country is shelter-less scrub, known for its wet black stone. It's a pure wild place where nothing will grow without hardship. But *Sliabh Earrach* is lush and green and will grow anything the aunts want to grow. The people say it's otherworld magic, but of course not. It's just what comes of being intimate with the land, of ancient wisdom, and necessity. I suppose that is a kind of magic, maybe the only kind. They, we, are natural witches, kitchen witches, and solitary witches, but there is something of the other kind too, something dark.

But that's not my path. I'm one called to heal and help, my power is protection. Still, I'm hoping in time the aunts will see that for the family to thrive we need to become more open, more vulnerable, however risky or strange the prospect. I am more of the people than my sisters so it's easier for me to think of such things. I know that none of this will happen overnight and I know we have enough with just going back for the moment.

Fact is, I'm twenty-three, and though I'm not without fear it's time for me to do the work I was born to do. I'm going to learn everything I can from the aunts and then I'm going to practice openly again. And who knows, maybe one day we'll know peace. That's what I want, the freedom of peace, more than anything.

Journal of Drew Cleary, July 26th 1995

I'm on my way to Ireland, to the home of my mother, where my aunts Honor and Erin still live. I'm traveling with my sisters of course who've been weird all day, more than normal that is. I don't know what's wrong with them. After all, it was their decision to return now. I was eleven when we left my aunts' home the last time. I do remember some things but not I think, as clearly as they do. Okay, I'm the normal one, there I said it, ha! Though normal is an elastic idea in our family.

We are descended from *Bean Feasa,* wise women, healers going back further than anyone knows. But the rumour is we've always been there. Some say we have a connection to the mountain and the legends of a fairy woman or witch, one of the Tuatha, the mystical race. We call her the Cailleach.

When people in Ireland talk about the fairies they're not speaking of those candy coloured pictures like the kind you find in children's books. They're talking about the Fae, otherworld creatures. They can take the form of an animal, of a woman, or a man. They look just like you or me, only rangier, with small intense light coloured eyes, like sea born jewels. And they have a strangeness about them, an otherness, that attracts and repels, and can't be defined. Perhaps that's what the people see in us. I don't know, but I've always liked the stories.

My own power is a cool if creepy one, second sight. In theory it means I can see into the future or the past. I may foresee a death, even my own. I couldn't just get the shape shifting power, could I? I don't think it's happened me yet, though I dream a lot, fragmented dreams mostly, of dark things and death.

The only thing I remember clearly about *Sliabh Earrach* is the day we left it. When I think of it now the tips of my fingers ache. There was a hurricane.

The steps from the aunt's front door are treacherous at the best of times, especially to a child. But that day they flowed away from us like water over wood and moss. It rushed over my hands and rendered them useless, it poured into my eyes and my mouth. I clung to the watery house on one side, and on the other side to the only thing that felt certain, Erin.

I wanted to see her but she was up in the sky somewhere, reaching down to me. I was frightened of losing her, and myself, in that watery land. When at last I could steal a glance I saw that her hair had come loose and was whipping the sky like forked lightning. She smiled at me and I gasped, because I knew then she was a part of it, and maybe I was too. And I wasn't afraid after that. I stopped holding back and rushed on down and down, into the water and black.

As the car pulled away and the aunts began to fade from sight, I looked back. Four shadows stood illuminated in the doorway, Honor and Erin, Ellen and Mae. There was something in the way they stood unmoving, the shifting sky above their heads, the towering mountain behind them. I had a sense again that all of it was alive and that the aunts, the house, like a ship and its crew, were protecting us. Only then did I notice my fingers were bleeding. And when I looked back again they were gone.

Journal of Dara Cleary, July 26th 1995

In just a few short hours we'll be back in that place. How I despise it. My mother's home, *Sliabh Earrach*. I don't want to go but I don't feel there's a choice, I'm being pulled.

In spite of my feeling I try not to curse that I feel cursed by. A long time ago, while my mother taught my sisters how to use their powers, she taught me how not to use mine.

'The power of life and death is in the tongue,' she'd say.

She and I were the most alike so perhaps she was afraid I would inherit her madness. You see that betrayal there? I feel guilty to have said it. We shouldn't speak ill of the dead who can't defend themselves. I loved my mother for the short time I had her in my life and it was short, just eight years. Eight years of mostly happiness, the only happiness I've known. It was more at least than my sisters had.

Things I know about my mother. She was very powerful, the most powerful in her family. Like all the Cleary women, she grew up an outcast, but she did have a friend, a boy. Unfortunately for everyone, themselves especially, they fell in love. This, for some reason, didn't stop him going for the priesthood of all things, which took him away a few years. By the time he came back she had changed, gone mad is what the townspeople said. These are people to whom mad is anything different. Whatever the truth they were deathly afraid of her. It didn't stop them tormenting her. In spite of all this my parents found they were still in love and secretly had an affair. The products of that affair were scandal, broken hearts, disappearances, and me. As you can imagine, this legacy greatly affected my life, especially from the age of eight to sixteen when we lived with the aunts.

The aunts and the house, though wonderful, rarely spoke of my mother, only sometimes in whispers, and only to each other, never to me. Much of her remains secret and what's more, just remains. Her presence, her influence, her legacy, she colours everything, and the town never let me forget it. After the day on the mountain the aunts sent us away. I was glad, and I swore at the time that I'd never go back again.

Now at twenty-six I've been a world traveller, a healer, a lover, a friend, and a sister of course, but inside I've a soul that can't rest, a heart that can't heal, a mind that won't forget, and my powers are growing. The question is, what am I supposed to do with all of that?

My powers are elemental. I can shape and shift the weather, plus I have the power of breath and words, incantations, spells if you prefer, and I can communicate with the otherworld. Yes, I know it *sounds* crazy, and there's more; I can put a curse on you. Some call it the evil eye and where I'm going everyone believes all of this so you'd think they'd take pains not to cross me. Perhaps this time will be different. The only power I use is the elemental one, but it's mostly unconscious. I can't help but wonder if being away all these years has held me back and if being back there will make a difference and how? I guess we'll find out.

Looking at my sisters I can see they're happy. Drew's her cool self, and Devin has all these ideas and plans, well I have plans too. I have unfinished business with the town and I have questions, like what really happened to my parents? Why am I being pulled here? This darkness I feel, what does it mean? Am *I* cursed? Can I change my future or is it already set? I don't intend to end up like my mother. I want revenge, yes I admit it, and I want to live. Somehow, someplace, someday.

The aunts and *Sliabh Earrach*, they hold secrets of mine, links to my past, keys to my future. I will not be swayed from my quest for answers and revenge. Revenge for my parents and how they were treated, revenge for me and my sisters.

Aunt Mae will be buried tomorrow. The rumour mill will have kicked in before then but that's where we're going to be seen for the first time in ten years, and I for one am looking forward to the stir that our return is going to make.

Chapter 5

First Impressions

Erin hadn't taken her eyes off the gate for so long they were starting to burn. The wait was unbearable. Heat, the crowds and the closed in feeling, she tried not to dwell on it. It was hard to be in these places, a lifetime of living in wilderness will do that to a person, less will do that to a person. Honor wouldn't agree of course. Her twin would, she knew, have lived happier anywhere else but Erin loved her wild home, her mountain.

She thought of her house now, and the garden. Of her stillroom with its neat rows of bottles and jars, the scent of herbs, of healing trees and flowers. The wide open landscape that held only wind, sky, and the changing colours of the mountain, while below her the valley, like a canvas, stretched out over endless miles.

Like a mantra or prayer she whispered, 'Rowan, ash, alder, oak, lilies, roses, sage, whin, whitethorn, lilac, meadowsweet, dandelion, vervain, woodbine. Sow and gather by dew or by moonlight, lift with the left hand and lay with the other.' The music of the words slowed her heart, she could breathe again. Soon the air would change. It would be autumn, and she'd have lots of work to do. Preparation for the long winter to come, and it was going to be a long and interesting one.

She thought about the girls. Devin, the healer, held special interest. All her life Mae had been her teacher and they'd been close, quite like mother and daughter. Now she would be teacher to a niece who shared her power and passion. The thought made her happy. While the other powers called for great restraint the healing power called for years of study and hard work. The gift alone was not enough. Once she'd thought she might teach a child of her own, but it wasn't to be. The others wouldn't agree but of all the powers, healing was most important for it put life and death in your hands.

The eldest, Dara, the dark daughter. She'd inherited her mother's vast array of powers, cursing, shaping the elements, communicating with the otherworld, which basically meant interceding with otherworld beings on people's behalf. This had been more central to the *Bean Feasa's* work in the past. The belief was any human problem that couldn't be solved by human efforts was because the person had, usually unwittingly, done something to offend otherworld beings or fairies.

The dangers of these dark powers for Dara and for those around her were great. It had been the same for her mother and grandmother before her. From a young age Caer had known at least something of what it meant to be this way, but what of Dara? How much did she know? Would she be as strong as her mother had been, or stronger? She hadn't always had the support or guidance she needed but what use to dwell on that now? Such a practical thought, worthy of Mae, Erin mused. Fact was, from this day on, whatever Dara did would affect all of them.

The youngest sister, Drew. Hers was the power of sight, visions of past and of future, same as Honor. Erin wondered if she'd had any visions yet. Of all the powers it was least consistent or controllable. It came when it would, not often before adulthood. What age was Drew now? Twenty? Twenty-one? Soon then. In the meantime, her role was in the power of three. This could be felt any time the girls were together, like a crackle of energy, a force of strength. All sisters and to some extent all sibling groups have something of this power, which is why sibling groups are always so very affecting.

Three *Bean Feasa* siblings and three girls are especially powerful, for when all are together their combined powers grow. This made the third child special in a way they rarely felt themselves. If she had not been born her sisters could never reach their full strength and if she was lost, died, or if she left, their powers would severely diminish. Even as twins this was how it had been for her and Honor all these years without Caer, and for their aunts Ellen and Mae without Jaen. Dara was destined for the quest, and Devin for the healing tradition that was the protection and stability of the family, the community too. But neither could be fully realised without the vision, and the presence, of the third sister. Of three sisters living their truth, and fulfilling their purpose in life, that was the holy grail of life. And there had not been three sisters at *Sliabh Earrach* for twenty-five years, until now.

So deep in her thoughts was Erin that this time when the doors parted and it was finally them she was almost surprised and then shocked at the sight. She had been prepared she thought, no. In that moment Erin knew she was old in a way she'd never noticed before. Not in any value or envy of youth, she was a woman who loved life, who had, in spite of her own disappointments, grown happier with the passing years. It was only the shortness of it all that was the painful thing.

Out in front strode the youngest, Drew, but she was so tall. They were all so tall. Erin pulled herself up to her not inconsiderable five foot eight and squinted at this youngest niece to fully assess her. This one had the look all right, no mistaking the slight frame, the high planed face and slanted eyes. These fairy like people are usually very dark or very fair, but Drew, like Honor, was red as the fox. There was an energy to her that was more than beauty or youth. Light, but with a hectic quality. Erin frowned, bringer of light or bringer of death, she wondered?

Devin followed. What a contrast. Serene, she seemed almost to float. Slightly smaller in height than the others, her eyes were slanted too but were not the cold flint of her sisters. Hers were moss green with corners of amber and warmth, like sun dappled ground in the forest. While Drew's skin was pale with a green tinge, and framed by unruly hair, Devin's skin was like cream and her hair fell in gold velvet folds. Wisdom and knowledge radiated from her, confidence and sensuality. Erin felt her soul leap in recognition of the niece who shared her art. *What a healer she is going to make*, she thought.

But Dara, now there was a stab to the heart. Surely this was Caer back to life? Here was the same black hair and eyes, not black as they seemed but pure emerald green. She was taller, as they all were, but while her sister's energies were open and clear, Dara's were mercurial and closely guarded, her presence striking and unsettling. She was like electricity, always moving, ever out of reach. There was no earthly way to describe her. *Well that explains the sky today,* thought Erin, delighting in her analysis.

The frightened children who'd stood before her all those years before, who'd lost their mother, and then suffered so much at the hands of their peers growing up. Those children were gone. A new chapter in the Cleary story was about to be written.

Filled with pride and anticipation, tempered with grief and regret, Erin hugged them in turn, pausing longest with Dara.

'Our dear girl,' she said, pulling her niece close again before holding her at arm's length. 'You are so like them. I see them both in you, Dara,' she sniffed.

'Well,' she continued brightly, 'this is truly the best day of my life.' She extended her reach to Drew and Devin, and pulling each of their hands in to hers felt a rush, a long forgotten sensation.

'Erin? Are you all right?'

'Yes,' she said slowly, 'I was just thinking about Honor. She's been looking forward to this day for so long but is still unprepared, I think. We should get going, we've a good drive ahead. I want to hear everything about your lives this past ten years, don't leave anything out, we are starved for excitement here.'

'Really?' Dara asked. 'No drama since we left?'

'Not so much,' Erin said lightly. 'Though I expect that will all change now you're back.'

Chapter 6

Honor

Night crept in and shadows long at *Sliabh Earrach*. To the outside world the house was devoid of life, but deep inside I stood, impatiently waiting. And from the way the storm battered the windows I knew it had come from the north, from the mountain.

'I'd have thought you'd be happy,' I said, as a flash of lightning revealed us. And I looked to the bed where Mae was laid out, before we were plunged again into darkness. 'You've a strange way of showing it.'

I shivered, not with fear or cold but with anticipation, and looked to the clock again. Soon they'd be here, all the Cleary women at *Sliabh Earrach,* for the first time in twenty-five years.

I would have liked to go for them myself but someone had to stay, and it was better that I be the one. If I had gone there was always the danger I might not return and I couldn't think like that now. I lit some candles, more to pass the time than anything, and resumed my restless vigil. Every now and then I'd pause to look over at Mae, half expecting her to sit up and say something.

Instead I spoke warmly to her.

'You did this, Mae, you brought them.'

I was a changed woman these days, only in part since Mae's death. And in our last moments together the knowing that this was the end got the better of me.

'Are we strong enough for this, Mae? Tell me what you think?' I had never spoken like this before. It was so out of character that Mae, who'd been sinking alarmingly fast, brightened suddenly.

Placing a care worn hand on my face and fixing me with a clear gaze she said,

'Yes. You always thought Caer was the strongest, but she was the one who left.'

'That wasn't easy, that took a lot of strength,' I said, defending my sister.

'Not as much as it took for you to stay. To be the one who stays, the one who sacrifices freedom...love.' The words hung heavy between us.

So she knew, for how long, I wondered.

'Listen to me now, Honor, no one could do more, you hear me? You've never been one to run, that can be bad or good, but no matter. You've never been one for rules or tradition either and that could be your greatest asset. Forget the world a while longer. You're needed here. I know it's hard for you, being needed, but I know you and you'll handle it. You're going to live a long time, Honor Cleary. Stay the course.'

I'd felt bad for asking but had to admit, the words helped me.

'Honor.' She was fading again. 'It's all going to change, Honor, it's all going to change. Be ready.'

'Yes,' I nodded, 'yes.'

I sat back in the armchair, my skin prickling with heat and hoped she was right, about changes, about everything. I wished she would tell me more, and wished Erin would come. Anyone else might have dismissed her words as the ramblings of a dying woman that didn't have to make sense, but we were inclined to ponder significances.

I thought about this and all Mae had done, not just for the family but for so many of them, out there. The thought of her life of service without freedom weighed heavy. I wanted to tell her everything. Mine and Erin's secret plans, the progress we were making. Hearing Erin's footsteps in the hall I was preparing to go when I noticed Mae watching me, her eyes full of language and understanding. She knew our plans. And I was glad she knew. There were enough secrets in this house. It felt like a blessing.

'I'm here.' Erin breezed into the room, welcome as air.

When I looked back to Mae she had closed her eyes, faded again.

On a hot and heavy July afternoon she left us. The sky went dark as if in mourning, and it rained a while, the summer kind. Warm and arousing. The loss was harder than expected. We thought we were used to loss and death, what with Caer, and the others. We knew the natural and the unnatural order. Knew that every loss is different, and you never know the space a person held in your life till they were gone.

Never had the house felt so lonely, or we so alone, as in those days before the girls came home.

'We're the aunts now,' said Erin, as she stirred some concoction.

I lifted my head from the books.

'Fucking great,' I said, and she laughed. Then she couldn't stop laughing. She looked beautiful, I thought, and even youthful. It's because she's happy.

'You even laugh like a witch, you know that.'

'Takes one to know one.'

Forget the world a while longer, stay the course.' I reminded myself of Mae's advice, before going back to my work, as had Erin in her way, into work and preparation, for a farewell, and a homecoming.

She'd also said a change was coming, and now at last above the crying wind, the fire glowed, flames soaring, the clock ticked time, and the table was set for nine. Their faces stared down from the walls. Our mother Jaen, aunts Ellen and Mae, our sister Caer. The house had held an air of death a long time that alone might explain our love of the mountain, of the wild places that remembered nothing and didn't care. In many ways it explained us too.

Now at last the house would be filled and excited by life again. I went to the window, eager to see them arrive. I had waited so long for this moment and was thinking how everything was ready, perfect, when I saw him. I wasn't sure at first, but a flash of lightning revealed him. He was looking at me, asking me to see him. My hands shook as I closed the curtain. But moments later I went to the door and stepping out into the night whispered, 'Dealan.' But only the mountain answered.

Chapter 7

The Cailleach

Honor was right about one thing, I am contented. I've called and the sisters have answered. They are coming back to me.

I've waited years, but years mean nothing. I've been here thousands of years, our fates entwined, they are bound. Every mountain holds darkness and those closest to me, Caer, before her Jaen, and now Dara, are part of it and me. Some, like Honor, Ellen, and the young one, Drew, are the restless wanderers, who live in the shadows between worlds. The healers, Erin, Devin, Mae; with these women my connection is not strong, their powers the furthest from my own. They are less otherworldly than their sisters, their lives more easy, but the dark ones, they are mine, and will yet be more mine.

It is they who deal in curses, who hear, who see, and can communicate with other worlds, and with me. The girl's mother Caer, we met many times, despite Mae's best efforts to keep us apart. After all the trouble she tried to leave, she went as far as anyone had ever gone but still she could not escape me. I was everywhere she went, in warm waters of foreign seas, in golden sands on distant shores. She found my cold hard presence in every gentle breeze she felt. Because she carried me with her.

But she was strong. She resisted more than anyone had before. It was the hardest time any of the women have ever given me. Their duty is to be here always and always three sisters. If one leaves it weakens us all, and Caer, she had the child as well. I couldn't take the risk. I didn't kill her exactly, I just didn't make it easy for her to live.

After she died and the children came back I got a sense of them for the first time. Drew was too young, but it was clear Devin would be healer, and Dara my dark one. She was only eight years old when she began coming to me. She'd walk right out the door, follow the lane and then leave it, crossing fields and bog, dotted with bog cotton flowers. She'd sit on the old mass rock that hung over the valley and we'd talk and laugh and make the winds roar. Her eyes, bright with tears of sun and wind would flash as a wild thing. She was not easily frightened, what a Cailleach she would have made. Her powers were already strong, perhaps more so than her mothers had been. I had a feeling for her as to a child of my own. A feeling I'd not had since the time before. It amused and saddened me as some lost memory. I wanted to keep her with me, but I'd let her go back to the house of the aunts.

She struggled with her fate in those early years but that was her mother's fault, her father's too. What they call love had been Caer's downfall. It signalled the end of the game for her, and yet in Dara I saw a fire so great, I had to wonder. Caer's power, her feeling for the man, and the pain that came later. Perhaps it was for some good that he and Caer had been destroyed, when she was the result.

Years later, on that day with the town spawn, Dara summoned me. Because of this Mae sent them away. I was so angry we had weeks of storm, starting the day they left, but Mae would not be moved, as was her way. She reasoned they were still a group of sisters at the house. Honor and Erin, she and Ellen. Two different sets of sisters, but a group of note all the same, she said. They could hold things together until the girls came back again. I had to accept it as much as I raged. But I enjoyed the hardships they endured after that from the townspeople, and how it affected them, being without the girls.

I turned away from the aunts for a time, and that was a mistake. I was too focused on Dara, the next generation, and when they'd come back. They are a part of me, these women. I knew in time they'd answer the call. And I vowed that once they did return, they'd never leave again.

Now at last the day has come. Dara's mood growing closer is affecting my hand. I could resist but I like to let her have that. Not many things have sway with me and it's little enough. My glory days are coming back again. So yes, Honor, yes I am content. It's not I alone who calls the weather. And it won't be long before she comes to me. You will never be able to hold her.

Chapter 8

Return to the Mountain

The house, unchanged, was as the girls remembered. To see the house was good, it had always been a haven. What you might expect was an old cottage of the type, mostly derelict, that dot any Irish mountainside. But this was no ordinary house. Being too tall, and too high up, were it not held tight in the mountain's grip, you'd imagine it floating, or falling. Perhaps taking the landscape, trees, mountain, and sky along with it. It had a curious air, even to those who knew it. It spoke of mystery and darkness. It repelled and attracted, belonged and didn't belong; like all living things, it was complex.

The house could only be reached on its west side with a steep drive from town. To the rear and north the mountain soared above its highest points. To the east, a death drop to the forest. To the south, a garden ran down to the river, beyond which bog, trees, and patchwork fields flowed towards town. Now add to this scene if you will, a flight of steps, steep and crumbling, green with moss and lichen, that ran from that west side up, along the house wall to the door.

Reasons to come knocking? Need or menace, love or loss, or fear. Life is hard here, for the women too. They live a rich life within but have to think of protection. The house must serve many purposes beyond that of a normal house. For centuries it has kept the women safe within its walls while keeping dangers out.

It was late when the girls and Erin arrived at last, but the rain had stopped and the pale moon rising clearly showed the house and Honor, standing by the door. It was the same way she'd stood when they'd left ten years before, only this time she was smiling. She seemed unchanged bar streaks of white in her hair. Between her and Erin, she was the one people feared. They avoided her path and her eyes. From a young age she had cultivated an exterior armour of stillness that was deeply unsettling to others, because of the fire she held inside.

In her dress she was somewhat austere. She was tall and she walked tall. Her hair she wore either loose, sometimes rolled at the nape of her neck, or else piled on top of her head, which only made her taller. Up was best for thinking and work, and she worked most of the time. With her pale skin that seemed almost green, and a penchant for long skirts, she had a look that could have been from any generation. They were a well matched pair, the house and Honor.

As her nieces arrived Honor felt an almost forgotten sensation, a quickening in her veins. As they started walking, awakening memory in the damp earth, echoes in the forest, a small breath escaped her and was picked up by the wind. They all felt it then.

By way of greeting Honor spoke each name in turn and then ushered them in. Erin stood with her sister a moment, noting the change in atmosphere, letting it wash over them, and looking towards the mountain. If anything, it seemed to stand out more sharply and strangely than ever, in the glow of that post storm evening.

Inside, the ancient house of Cleary held a cornucopia of rooms large and small that offered many good comforts and surprising delights. Callers would little know that beyond that forbidding front door the house shrank and expanded by turns in every direction, from pools of light to corners of dark. And at its heart, a large kitchen, where an old range that never went out huffed and glowed under various pans. Hugging the range, an assortment of armchairs, mis-matched and faded, and a menagerie, cats, dogs, a fox, and various birds. All around, the walls were lined with dressers, shelves, and secret presses of indeterminate origin or age, that held countless jars and jugs and curiosities. Overhead hung branches and herbs, baskets and lanterns. A low slung central light gave orange glow to a heaving table with spoils from the garden spilled as far as the eye could see. A decanter of wine, candles and glasses, and great sheaves of herbs, a wild tangle of flowers and books, propping other books, notebooks too, no end to them.

Off the kitchen lay a key to their survival. An internal stillroom, or green room. From here came precious seeds for herbs, vegetables and flowers, for medicines and the garden. It was a garden in itself and many things could survive here that would otherwise not survive in these parts. With its glass roof, the heat gain, along with the range, warmed the heart of the house, and provided the women with food all year round. With its rich green growth and sultry atmosphere you could conjure far flung exotic places, but looking up above the vaulted glass you'd see the grey sky and the mountain soaring.

The rest of the house held various rooms, tucked here and there, not one of standard proportions. Because the house had been moulded to the site and not the other way around, you were always either coming around, climbing, or going down.

When the girls stepped inside that evening, for the first time in ten years, the house seemed to sigh in contentment. Fires burned more brightly, doors opened before them, even the darkest corners seemed lighter as they moved from one room to the next, their talk and laughter filling every space.

Honor poured the wine. 'A toast,' she said. 'Tonight, everything is perfect, everything is as it should be. To freedom.'

Five women held their cups aloft.

'To freedom,' they said.

But in the time it took to clink and sip, something changed. The candles flickered, the door blew open, and Honor jumped in her seat.

'I guess not everyone liked your toast,' Erin said.

Honor paid her no mind.

'Let's eat.'

...

In the supermarket Marie Kelly, like a hound with the scent of blood, was breathlessly telling the news.

'They've come back!'

'Who?'

'The Clearys,' she hissed.

'Where?' they gasped. 'When?'

'I saw them, just a few hours ago, with Erin. Headed for the mountain.'

So the bitch was back, thought Una McGovern, pretending interest in stock. She should have known. Only that morning she'd noticed strange light on the mountain and wondered. A frisson of excitement edged with fear gripped the people, and they huddled together for more.

'I couldn't see very clearly but it was them all right, looked straight through me they did...'

'All of them?' Una asked. They turned to look at her.

Marie, savouring the moment answered, 'Oh yes, all grown up, put you in mind of the aunts, back in the day.'

'We'll have to watch our backs now,' someone added.

'That's right,' Marie agreed, her mission of old reignited. 'We have the community to think of, the children.'

'Ah, go along with yourself, that old nonsense,' offered another, by way of encouragement.

Marie continued, 'Those women and their ways are not welcome here, and the sooner they realise that the better.'

'Surely to god they've only come for the funeral?'

'Never would have thought they'd come back, even for that.'

'Aye, not after all these years, and they didn't come for Ellen's?'

'She didn't have one, remember?'

'Ah yes, another mystery. Hard to keep up.'

'Never would have thought they'd come, considering everything that's gone on.'

'Never expected to see them again.'

'Maybe they plan on staying this time?'

'Hardly, three young women, living up there with the aunts in this day and age, sure what would they do with themselves?'

'The same as that family have always done I'm sure,' said Joe Wrynn, who had just arrived and was rifling the newspapers. 'Take care of the community of course, what else?' he offered, when no one else did.

Marie folded her arms and snorted, 'Take care indeed, a curse on us more like.'

'Is that wise chat? After everything that's gone on,' countered Joe.

But his words fell on deaf ears and undeterred they went on stirring. 'The best thing those girls could do for everyone is stay away from here.'

'No doubt this is just a visit and after old Mae is laid to rest they'll be gone.'

'They'd better be, that's all I'm saying.'

Una had turned away and pretended interest in her work, she already knew Dara Cleary had come back for more than just a funeral.

'How long has it been since they left here?' someone asked. 'Let's see now, this is, and then there was that, and then...'

'It's been ten years,' said Joe carefully.

That was enough to shut everyone up for the moment, even Marie, who'd been chief instigator of the campaign for their last departure, but it didn't temper her righteous intent.

...

At *Sliabh Earrach* the disturbance of before was forgotten in the aroma of so much good food filling the room, eliciting a mood of warmth and sighs of pleasure in the near dark. The girls had almost forgotten the pleasure assault that was the aunts' food, infused as it was with passion, with skill, and with magic. When they'd been little, every ill and sadness had been treated in this way. Mini soda cakes on the range, mushrooms picked at dawn, then sprinkled with salt and herbs, dotted with butter and roasted to bursting, floury spuds, fresh eggs, sweet tea, and boxty. Here in the house it was easy to remember only the good things, to forget the world outside the door.

Later, when the girls were alone, Devin said, 'Well that was lovely, and weird of course.'

'I know, with Honor,' said Dara.

'What happened there? It's not like her to lose her composure, is it?'

'There was a presence.' Drew had said nothing to now.

Her sisters turned to her.

'A presence? So that's what Erin meant?'

'Yes, there was something there, or someone.'

'Mae's spirit? One of the others?'

'No, a stranger.'

'In the house?'

'Yes, but not threatening I think.'

'Drew! You felt all this? For real?'

Drew grinned.

'Tell us more.'

But there wasn't any more to tell. She had felt it, that was all.

Later that moonlit night, tucked up in their old rooms and beds, they watched familiar shadows move across the walls. These they'd almost forgotten, remembered only in dreams, were here now. Shadows of trees filled the room and among them other shapes too, the unmistakable swish of heavy hair and dresses, the curve of waists, the turn of faces. Benign, evanescent, some familiar, mostly women, children and babies too. And they fell asleep, lulled by the whispering voices.

But Drew's sleep was fitful and full of birds. And just before dawn she was woken by something rattling her window. It was a magpie trying to get in.

Going to the window the words *one for sorrow* came to mind and she asked of the creature, 'Who are you?'

The bird stopped abruptly, cocked its ebony head, and there in its eye she saw herself reflected. It stared a moment longer and was gone. Looking out she saw there no sign of the bird now, but a pale moon clearly showed a large dog that looked more like a wolf in the street, watching the house.

She pulled back but quickly realised it was not her window he was looking to but somewhere higher. What rooms lie above this one? She frowned, trying to remember. The wolf's gaze never faltered but his body was restless, he was troubled. What did he want? Was he looking for help? She supposed these were the kind of things that happened here.

Feeling tired she turned back to her cosy bed. What did all of this mean, she wondered, sinking gratefully into the cool sheets. Was she even awake now, or dreaming? It felt real but then it always did, she thought, drifting off.

Meanwhile, high above Drew's window, Honor stood at hers watching the same scene.

'That's seven days in a row he's come,' said Erin coming into her sister's room.

'Yes.'

'And now he comes into the house too? Aren't you going to do anything about it?'

'I already did.'

Chapter 9

The Funeral

The morning of Mae's funeral dawned soft and mild. Dara was up and dressed early. She'd slept well and felt rested. Comforting scents and sounds were wafting from the kitchen, as was always the way in her memories. She took one last look at herself and smiling, headed down.

On her way she saw that after all the house was not unchanged as it had first seemed. And what had been hidden in darkness was now plain to see. It was threadbare, faded, and crumbling. And no wonder, she thought. Years of storm had taken their toll. But at its heart it was solid, and the air was one of calm and quiet fortitude. In the kitchen Honor and Erin were sitting at the table sharing a large pot of coffee. Their eyes widened when she walked in.

'You get a fright, every time you see me?'

'We'll get used to it,' said Honor.

'Nice dress,' added Erin.

'I like red.'

'I like red too.'

'Here, have some coffee.'

Dara took the cup and went to sit by the range.

'So Dara, how does it feel to be home?'

Home. A strange idea that somehow hadn't felt so strange since they'd arrived. It was easy. Easy to be here, to dream here. She felt safe here, she realised. They all did. It was not as she'd expected.

'It feels right.' She nodded.

'That's good,' said Erin, pleased. 'This is your home, will always be your home.'

'If you want it to be,' added Honor, then seeing Erin's face she conceded, 'The house has always been good.'

Devin and Drew breezed in looking for coffee and food. Dara sat quiet, enjoying the scene, the banter of nieces and aunts.

'And what about the mountain?' Erin asked. 'Did you miss it?'

Dara took a long slow taste of the coffee. She thought back to the day of the incident that had taken her away from here, and to the days before that. Before the aunts sent them away. All these years she'd been longing for something. But not a place, she thought. And not this place. The way she was feeling now, it was memory stirring desire and comfort, nothing more. They were watching her, waiting for her to answer.

'I never dreamed of the mountain.'

A look of relief passed over their faces.

'It dreamed of you,' said Honor.

Getting up to pour herself another cup, she thought how lucky they were to have these things. A safe place for dreaming, sisters, and inside the walls, freedom. She thought of her mother and all the moving around they'd done as children, so far away from here. Had her mother done the wrong thing by leaving, she wondered? Or had there been no safe harbour for her, even here?

'Is it strange no one has called to sympathise?' asked Devin.

'God no, they wouldn't dream of calling to the house, but they've been leaving cards and flowers out by the gate these past few days. She was popular, you know, unusual for a Cleary.'

'Maybe things are changing?' suggested Devin hopefully.

Erin laughed. 'I doubt that, not so long as your aunt Honor's around, and now Dara too.'

'I feel as if I was born to trouble, to provoke.'

'We're women, and witches, it's our duty. But it's always like that when people are different,' said Erin.

A short time later the five women and undertaker, not without difficulty, carried Mae's coffin from the house, down the steps and through the rustling woods to the hearse. The air felt heavy and close. It smelled of rain, and earth, and turf smoke. The cortege, all two cars, wound its way down the mountain and was joined along the way by other cars, well-wishers, neighbours, and news seekers. Here and there one or more people dotted the roadside, blessing themselves and bowing their heads. Like all the Clearys, Mae was a pagan so there was no church service. Their destination was the graveyard.

Today it was thronged with people. As Erin had said, Mae was more 'of the people' than the rest of them. Of course, the crowd was there for another reason too. Five Cleary women arriving at the graveyard was an event in itself, a rare spectacle. Alone any one of them would command attention but five, with their history, and the controversy that surrounded them, was not to be missed. The truth was, everyone held a stake in that story. Now they clamoured and strained for a glimpse before parting before them. None dared start with the whispering here, but thoughts ran rampant.

Honor Cleary might look at you and where would you be then? Not long after this one for the ground perhaps.

The look of that young one. No denying that face or who her father was. No getting away from the truth.

Evil the lot of them.

She'd kill you soon as look at you that one, just like her mother.

So like her grandmother, Jaen Cleary.

Look at the cut of them.

Fine things, even the older ones.

I wouldn't mind a go.

I'd say they'd be something.

Jesus.

I wonder if the rumours are true?

Great bodies.

Bitches.

Rides.

Full of themselves.

Think they're special, think they're better than us.

The height of those heels.

Is that fur?

Red! Who would wear red to a funeral?

Why did they have to come back here?

No respect.

God bless us and save us all.

Devil women.

Stunning.

No denying they have something, even with those slanty cat eyes.

Wow.

They should never have come back.

Jesus.

Funny triangle shaped eyes, and that white skin, almost green.

Those eyes.

Don't look in those eyes if you know what's good for you.

Middle one's the spit of Erin.

Imagine wearing your hair like that, at their age.

No sign of the twins to let the water in a bit yet. How do they manage to stay so young looking?

A bit like the nuns. No men, none living with them anyway, or living.

Drugs. Something Erin's cooked up. Look at the bitch. Still flirting with every man alive, at her age, the whore.

Sluts.

None of Seán Mannion's family here anyway... Mary won't be liking this. Terrible business.

Oh they were behind it all right. Sure I was there when she cursed him, in the chapel of all places. The awful words that came out of that mouth, those evil eyes of hers, and the look in his, it broke him. It did.

Shocking.

Sure we'd all known the truth for ages and her, as if butter wouldn't melt. It was her led him astray, away from his god and his people. He never stood a chance whatever happened to him. Poor lad.

Fr. O'Reilly stood patiently watching and sighed. He'd long given up on fighting these women, and as a result, hadn't they developed an understanding of sorts? He didn't interfere in their business and they didn't interfere in his, well most of the time. Generations of priests before him had fought them and lost, they had all lost one way or another, the women, the community too. But this was a different time and he was of a milder and more modern disposition than some of his predecessors. The people of the parish would do better if they'd remember all the ways these women had helped them through the years and give up the superstitions and gossip. After all, they were a part of this place too, and had as much right as anyone else in it. He supposed it must be a big ask, especially now, looking at this spectacle unfolding.

The women stood up to the grave. Fully aware of the thoughts that surrounded them, each adopted her own mode of transportation, of armour. Drew marched forward, cool and unmoved by the scene. And looking back, she smiled at the others, her sharp intelligent eyes bold with humour.

Devin followed, measured and steady. Her brow furrowed with thought she looked around her with such a warm, earnest and troubled expression, that many averted their own eyes, out of shame or embarrassment for their behaviour. She spoke warmly to anyone she recognised, and nodded to those she didn't. Her tender heart was very much evident.

Honor appeared to grow taller, colder, and more intimidating with every passing second. Only her eyes blazed, from green to grey to black, reflecting the colours of the landscape, betraying her inner fiery depths. And anyone who met that shifting gaze got a cold chill for the price.

Erin channelled a different power. Every man and every woman too watched spellbound, as she moved in a slow and mesmerising fashion. Her eyes brimmed with just the starting of tears making everyone sad, without understanding. They flushed and shifted uneasily, loosening collars and swallowing hard. And as much as they tried or wanted, they couldn't tear their eyes from her.

The girls watched, impressed. They had not known this about her before. She smiled and everyone smiled in response, everyone except Honor, the only one immune to her sister's power.

And Dara? Later, when the people talked of the day, over pints of beer, ironing boards, firesides, roadsides and tea cups, they all agreed she must have been the most glamorous person ever seen in a graveyard. And there was the usual chat about her parents, and what had gone on before. But not one could admit that her presence was deeply unsettling. That what flowed from her was much too alarming to describe or even think about with any ease. While Honor was fearsome in the fullest sense of a witch, that was easier, something separate from them. Dara was a walking reminder of all that was darkest in all of them, in this place. And they didn't like it.

Fr. O'Reilly had called order and finally got down to the business of burying Mae. He had offered to do this, to say a few words, as a goodwill exercise. He had thought it might help things if some elements in the town saw a peace between church and *Bean Feasa*. Still, he'd been surprised when they'd agreed. He assumed they were thinking of the nieces coming home, of making things a bit easier after all that bad business before. Now he saw he was perhaps still naive about it all.

He talked about Mae's great service to the community, her kindness and generosity, her hard life.

Only the poorest in spirit could argue. The people stood thinking of death, their feet sinking in the clay that was waiting to claim them. For once they were glad of the soft rain, the winds of autumn that swept down from the mountain. It reminded them they were, for now at least, still in the land of the living.

Chapter 10

Mary - Memories and Regrets

At this very same time in a pristine house across town, Mary Mannion was thinking of death too, the death of her son. She'd never doubted he was dead, and more often now she thought of her own death that must be coming soon. She'd been given the sentence, nine months, a year at most the doctor had said. Would she ever learn the truth? As she looked at old photos of Seán she felt the loss as keenly as she'd ever felt it.

'What happened to you?' she whispered, but Seán didn't answer, just smiled a frozen smile from long ago.

Getting up, Mary walked to the window. From here she could see clear to the mountain, across the rooftops of town. Ribbons of lane showed here and there in the forest, along with the peaks of that house. It shared a name with the mountain, *Sliabh Earrach* the people called it, Spring Mountain. A strange name for any house, especially one without hope she thought. And she wondered the same thing she'd wondered all her life, what secrets lay behind those walls?

Twice she had gone there looking for Sean, she thought back to it now. The first time he was very young and hadn't come home, again, despite her dire warnings to stay away from the house and that girl. Marie Kelly had offered to go with her, or in her stead, but she'd said there was no need, she'd handle this her own way for now. She and Marie, they were friends of a sort, more acquaintances, through the church.

As much as she wasn't a fan of the Clearys, Marie was over the top. Mary had asked her once what it was about them that bothered her so much and she'd said, 'It's the way they walk, and the way they talk.' Mary figured she meant everything about them, everything about them bothered her. Not too solid a reason, even if she did have a point.

No, it was best she handle this herself. Marie would only make things worse, and she still cared about her own reputation. She'd driven in anger, nearly crashing into Con Ryan's cows at the mouth of the forest. He'd waved and come shuffling over as she'd cursed under her breath.

Pushing his cap back he leaned on the car and said, 'You're in a fierce hurry there Mary, you going up be-yont?'

'Yes, I have some business with the Clearys,' she said curtly.

'You shouldn't go up there, no one should go up there unless they have to. Should have built a wall here years ago and blown the head off anyone who as much as sticks their neck over.'

He smelled of tree sap, peat, and sweat and leaning in he said, 'Strange things afoot on the mountain, Mary, always was, always will be. You'd do well to keep that youngster of yours away from here, his head's been turned.'

'He's just a boy,' Mary snapped, wrinkling her nose.

'Aye, mebbee so, mebbee so.' Con tapped the roof of the car with a peat lined hand. 'Good luck to ya Mary,' he called, before shuffling back into the trees.

Even more incensed she'd driven on until she could go no further. Leaving the car she went the rest of the journey on foot, which wasn't far. Within minutes she stood in the clearing by the gates and high walls of *Sliabh Earrach*. This was the closest she'd been since her teens. The house and family were often the centre of dares. How close would you go, were you brave enough to take something with you? A stone, or a twig perhaps? She herself had broken a branch from the whitethorn, the one people hung hopes on. Rags and scarves fluttered from its twisted branches, each one representing that hope, the cure for a sickness. The belief was the tree would absorb the disease. Many people claimed it had cured them, but many had died too. Breaking the branch all those years ago, Mary had turned to find herself facing Jaen Cleary. She'd been scared but holding her head high she walked passed her.

'You'll pay for that, Mary,' Jaen had said.

Jaen Cleary, her old rival, dead now, dead a long time. The passing years had not made the place less forbidding or strange, she noted. High and pointed, clinging to the rock face, it was hard to tell where the house ended and the mountain began. The old people said it held a secret way into the mountain and looking at it now that was what you'd imagine.

On this occasion she'd had no cause to go any closer as right at that moment he appeared, startled to see her. Stone faced but relieved, she motioned for him to come with her.

Once they were back in the car she'd said, 'You're never to come here again, Seán, do you hear me? Do you understand?'

'No, Mam, she's my friend, what's the big deal?'

Not wanting to get into talk of paganism, witchcraft, promiscuity and madness with her child she'd replied,

'You have other friends, you don't need to be friends with the likes of her, and you have me.' She looked at him hopefully but his arms were folded, his eyes fixed on the road. She'd noticed that having 'her' held less value lately and it pained her, feeling redundant already. 'And you have your church friends, what more do you need?'

Seán didn't answer, just sighed.

...

Years later she'd asked him, if he remembered that day. She'd been shocked when he told her that in that house the whole town was against, he had felt happier and freer than anywhere else. He'd never had to watch his words, or his back. He even liked the work, he said. Farming, gardening, and in the kitchen. He'd never even admitted to Caer but he loved working with the aunts. Sowing and weeding, chopping and stirring. They never criticised him or were cross, it seemed. He was a bit afraid of Ellen with her white clothes, strange pronouncements, and that axe in her belt. But even that just added to the intoxicating wildness of the place. It was so different to anything else he knew. They accepted him.

Most of all, he said, he liked to listen to them talk. He'd always loved words and it was lyrical talk, full of mystery. He'd been young then and under his mother's rule he knew, but he'd long decided that not even she could force him to give Caer up, her or the house.

Chapter 11

Sliabh Earrach 1969

Weeks had passed with no sign of Seán, but still the searches continued. To the people the facts were simple and delicious. She'd cursed him, they'd seen it, and now he was gone. That they'd been having an affair was no secret and now pregnancy gave them all the evidence they needed. The old people said he'd gone the way of the men who'd built the Cleary house, into the bowels of the mountain, to the Cailleach who lived there and fed on their bones. Some even blamed her, his own mother. They said he'd gone to get away from her. *Poor Seán Mannion, his whole life controlled by women and see what it did for him? He was soft, he was weak for them.*

All the talk, it was too much for Mary, and in grief and anger she'd gone to the house for that second time. Everything looked the same but how things had changed. On that first day the sun had been shining, her boy had been twelve, his whole life ahead of him. This time the house floated in grey mist and rain, the air was heavy with wood and turf smoke, and he was missing. Her boy, her only joy in life. She'd stood on the same spot, thinking over these past weeks, willing him to appear, pictured him walking towards her. The guards, along with volunteers, were combing the countryside but so far nothing, no sign. It was a horrible thing. She felt sure the women knew something and the whole town thought the same.

She'd stood for so long that finally Mae had come out to meet her, wordlessly ushering her in.

Once inside she found her tongue. 'Where is he? What have you done with my son?'

'We don't have him, Mary, I'm sorry. We were very fond of Seán always. If we could help you, we would. Come, you'll have a drink now you're here.'

'No.'

It was unsettling to be in this house, to feel their eyes, their stillness, and worse, their pity, but thoughts of Seán drove her. She rounded on them coldly.

'Where is *it* then?'

'Where is what?'

'You know well what I mean, the way into the mountain.'

'You don't believe that old nonsense.'

'Very well, I'll have to go to the cave then.'

Ellen and Mae exchanged glances. The last thing they needed was more heat on the family.

'That would not be wise, Mary,' warned Ellen and then quickly, 'and it won't bring him back.'

'Oh really, is that a fact, Ellen Cleary. I mean, you know this do you? You know it won't bring him back if I go there, but back from where, Ellen? BACK FROM WHERE?'

Ellen's words had ignited her fury and she shouted again, 'Where is he?'

'We don't know.'

'Yes you do, I believe you do know.'

'Mary, please forgive Ellen, she's very, alarmist and not used to...company, but she's right about this, you know it's not safe there, you know this, Mary.'

It was true. No matter what people believed about these women, the Cailleach or the mountain, there wasn't a person alive would go near the Cailleach's cave. Young people had been known to from time to time and the best you could say about that was for the rest of their lives they would startle more easily by day, and dream more uneasily by night. The close call, the realisation too late, the brush of the Cailleach's presence.

A stranger, too, might go without knowing, but never a local. They'd say it was because of the pits, the loose rocks, the old mine shafts, of which there were many. If you fell in you would never be found, and all of that was true, was sensible, but truer still was that they believed. They believed it was a gateway to the otherworld. It never had to be spoken, to be proved. To go there? Nothing would compel them.

Firmly and gently, Mae led the exhausted woman to the kitchen. She put her sitting in one of the large chairs that seemed to swallow her up instantly, and gave her a warming drink. Then sitting back, she regarded this most unlikely of visitors. They didn't have friends, the Cleary women, didn't have the time or inclination to be social with people. But people, and women especially, were interesting, thought Mae. Even those who wanted to kill you. It was passion, raw and complex, she could relate to.

Here was a creature she had always known. Who lived so close and yet, so different a life. Mary had community, a husband, religion, a child, a good reputation. Everything that society approved of. And this hid a dark reality. No one had to see the unhappiness, the wasted life, or the abuse. She, on the other hand, was single, childless, independent, and skilled in healing, and this ensured she was a pariah, even without her particular family history.

And this was how Caer found them. She'd seen Ellen first, standing with hands tightly clasped, watching someone or something. Her obvious discomfort had alerted Caer to something different, but nothing could have prepared her for the sight of Mae and her lost lover's mother sitting in not uneasy silence, drinking tea by the fire. They had never met before. Now Mary's eyes moved down her body, to the unmistakeable swell of pregnancy. Laying down her cup she rose sharply and walked towards her.

'What have you done?'

'Mrs Mannion. I swear, I've done nothing. I love him, he loves me too.'

'He doesn't love you!' she sneered. 'You don't know what love is, you *WITCH.*'

The blood drained from Caer's face. Mae shook her head sternly at Ellen. To wait, her silent plea.

'Soon you will, though,' she went on bitterly. 'Soon you'll know the pain of real love, the love of a mother for a child. A child you would do anything for, would die for.'

'Your grandchild,' said Ellen.

'I don't think so. It could be anyone's couldn't it.'

'Get out,' Ellen said.

'Yes,' Mae agreed, 'that's enough, Mary,' taking her by the elbow and deftly steering her away.

'I'm sorry we couldn't help you, Mary, truly I am. He's a lovely lad, always was. And he was never able to leave

Caer for any length of time, despite your best efforts. He loved her.'

Stopping by the door she looked at the woman once more; Seán's controlling mother, old adversary of her sister Jaen, long time critic of the family, and continued again not unkindly, 'If I could help I would. We loved him too.'

Mary glared at her coldly. 'If it's the last thing I do I'll see her hang for this... and maybe you too.'

'You stay away from Caer, now Mary, I don't want her upset any more, and, mind your step.' She nodded to the pitch black drop. 'It's a long way down and no way back for those who don't heed the warning.' She closed the door firmly, leaving Mary alone to make her own way down the treacherous steps, clinging tight to the house as she went.

Curse these walls. Mae had threatened her. What was she hiding? Was Seán in the house? In the Cailleach's cave? Or was he down there somewhere in that ravine? Fallen perhaps, in an accident, or pushed? But if they knew something why wouldn't they tell? They had to be protecting Caer. She felt sure Caer had not done it on purpose, but an accident, a mistake, that was possible.

On reaching the gate she looked back. The figure of a woman stood illuminated in an upstairs window, watching her, she didn't know which one. For the first time she felt out of her depth, even frightened. She wanted to get away as fast as possible but feared for some reason she wouldn't. Everything seemed to threaten and mock her, the house, the mountain, the old tree with its rags and relics of illness flying in the wind, the one she had broken that day long ago, the day she'd met Jaen Cleary. Jaen had said she'd have to pay.

Driving away she felt more certain than ever that something terrible had happened to her son. The Cleary women were involved in more ways than just ill fated romance and now a baby coming. Only she couldn't shake the feeling that they weren't really evil, not them all, anyhow. Whatever the answer, these women were not what she'd thought. Hadn't she felt a connection with Mae in the warmth of that kitchen? In spite of Ellen, before Caer had come in? The thought was poor comfort.

First thing the next morning she called Detective Shane Cogan. She told him she needed to add to her statement about the last day she'd seen Seán and asked when they were going to interview Caer Cleary. Already arranged, first thing in the morning he'd told her.

...

Detective Shane Cogan had had to admit that standing on a crumbling stairwell in heavy mist, a lethal drop to his right, facing a door knocker shaped like a woman's hand, had been no normal day at the office. He'd looked down to where his colleagues stood tight to the wall on the steps below, a grey soup of fog undulating around them.

'It's just a house, right?' Tim joked. That was what Shane had said to them on the way up here, had said many more times to himself.

'We're not in Kansas anymore, Toto,' he grinned. 'You wouldn't want to be bothered by heights, would you?' *So why are you so uneasy*, he wondered to himself, before finally taking that cold iron hand in his, half expecting it to spring to life and throw him over the edge.

One knock and the door opened, heavy and slow, to a pair of green eyes.

'Please come in,' came the voice.

'Thank you, Ms Cleary, I'm sorry it's not under better circumstances.'

She smiled warmly at him. 'It's rarely better circumstances bring people to our door.'

He was stunned, straight to his heart the effect of her. *Never look a Cleary woman in the eye,* were the words that came to mind now, too late. He'd heard that often enough in this investigation.

'Miss… Ms Cleary,' he said, trying to sound normal.

'Call me Erin.'

'Erin,' he repeated. 'As part of our investigation into the disappearance of Seán Mannion we need you, your aunts and sisters to make statements of your whereabouts on the night of the first of May.'

'I see.'

He cleared his throat and went on, 'You're under no obligation, nor is any of your family to give us a statement, but if you refuse we will be forced to arrest and detain you at the station for questioning. Do you understand?'

'Yes,' she said again.

'You agree to co-operate and give a statement?'

In answer she walked away, leaving a powerful scent in her wake. The two men and one woman followed, transfixed.

Turning her head she said, 'You like what you see, Shane?'

He blushed.

'Everyone will want to know what it was like.'

'What's that now?'

'The house. It's very old, you know.'

The house, he'd barely noticed the house once inside.

She led them into the kitchen. 'Will here be suitable to your needs?'

'Yes, here is fine.'

'My sisters and aunts will be here any moment, so you can speak with me first. Shall we begin?'

...

Erin had been right, everyone in town had wanted to know what the house was like. It wouldn't have been his place or that of the others to say, but more the truth it was hard to explain. It was easy to imagine that all you'd ever heard and all the madness was true, but it was a very old house in a very wild place, so surely that could all be expected?

What was surprising was how it, and more, how she had made him feel. In the deluge of scent and confused sensation something had stirred and awoken in him. He was filled with strange desire. And all he'd wanted to do from that day to this was go back there. The faces, the eyes he'd looked into were full of secret longings and strengths. And one face, one pair of eyes above all had stayed with him, Erin. He'd been enchanted, he knew, and what's more he didn't care. Were they human women at all? They seemed more like the mountain itself, wildness in human form.

Maybe he should have interviewed them in town, at the station, the place of society and men. But the whole town was lit up enough without that excitement, though it might have to happen yet. The women had co-operated, but Seán Mannion was still missing and Caer Cleary was the last person to see him, plus they'd had a fight that night, witnessed by most of the town. It didn't look great for her at the moment. It would look even worse if a body was found. But so far nothing, no trace.

The talk was Caer had killed him, and along with her sisters and aunts, hidden the body. But why would she kill him? What possible motive could she or any of them have? Sure there were plenty of outrageous stories from the old days, other disappearances, mysterious deaths. There was even a documented case of a Cleary being killed by her sisters, that at least was documented, but the rest was only folktales.

So far he knew that Seán Mannion had practically lived at their house all his life. That he and Caer had been close always. The women seemed to genuinely care about him, and she loved him, or said she did. That was the only thing everyone seemed agreed on, everyone he spoke to. That he had loved her? No doubt. That she had loved him? It seemed that those who spoke fairly said yes.

'He should never have been a priest, he should have stood up to that mother of his. It was the girl he wanted always.'

'How do you know?'

'Sure I have eyes haven't I? Anyone with eyes could see that.'

The less charitable, the more superstitious, said she had bewitched and then cursed him, hadn't they heard her do it, heard her speak the words. Not that anyone could remember the words, and not that he could count feelings. And a few people had accused her outright. The problem was facts, facts were in short supply. One fact, thought Shane, was what he knew about love you could fit on a stamp, but he knew pain and he'd seen it in her when they'd spoken. She was suffering all right. Whether that was suffering of guilt and regret or love and loss remained to be seen.

Shane had always been devoted to his work. He'd seen some things over the years, terrible things, they haunted him, drove him too, and he was the best in his field. But he'd never had a case like this. There was something here that went beyond the case, Seán Mannion, or the women. The whole town was different to anything else he'd encountered. He was determined to get to the bottom of it. His room in the local hotel had a clear view to the mountain. And looking out he thought about Erin, if she was there now, what she was doing.

With effort he forced the rusted window open and breathed in the night air. There'd been women in his life, but he'd never been in love, never even had family, not like these women did. And he'd always put work first. He didn't regret it. Only sometimes he thought it would be nice to have someone. So maybe he envied them a little. Perhaps a lot of people did. Perhaps a lot of people would love to have the closeness that family had and even the love Caer and Seán had. He thought he wouldn't mind being bewitched or even cursed like the people said, not if it meant someone cared for you like that.

At the house Mae praised her niece. 'You did well, Erin. He didn't suspect a thing you know?'

'I know.'

'He likes you.'

'Don't they all.'

'Oh not them all dear, not them all.'

1995 - Journal of Mary Mannion

Twenty-six years later and the town was lit up with gossip again, bringing everything back, all the horror. The Cleary girls had returned, three girls, one my grandchild. Yes, I knew it was true. Any fool would know he had to be a candidate at least. Everyone thought I lived life in denial or didn't know the truth, didn't want to know, but my denial was a public act. Privately I knew everything except what happened him. All those years ago the talk had been about Caer Cleary and Seán Mannion, the worst kind of scandal. A priest having an affair would have been shocking enough for any small town but with a Cleary, a *Bean Feasa* no less, was unthinkable. Even before he disappeared it was the talk of the country. If only he hadn't been given this parish, if only he had never come back here.

What the town didn't know was the day he'd disappeared he'd told me about them. I'd guessed at the affair of course, but had been in denial about it, I'd had to be. After a lifetime of sacrifice, of abuse at the hands of my husband, his father, I'd turned to my son and the church for refuge. I'd put all my hope in them and he had betrayed me. It was a terrible blow to my sense of purpose and right, to my place in the community. Everyone knew Jack Mannion was a good for nothing layabout, a wife beater. I'd spent years hiding his handiwork as best I could and saving Seán from it. Seán had been such a good boy always, good at school, a sweet child, kind, always thinking of me. From the day he was born he'd made me so proud and I'd looked forward to the day that I could hold my head high again in this god forsaken town as the mother of Seán Mannion, a great man, a man who commanded respect, a priest. Once I'd set my sights on the priesthood I'd devoted all my energy to that end. As for him, he always found it hard to refuse me, he felt responsible for me and all I'd been through.

When I realised the truth of the affair I'd told myself it was just a youthful slip, the last fling of a man in his weakness. The thought had disgusted me as it made me think of him as being more his father's child than mine, so I'd turned my thoughts away from Seán and onto Caer. She was to blame. She had turned his head. Hadn't she always had a strange kind of hold on him, even as children? I'd wondered if there were some kind of magical forces at work. After all, what was in it for her? Did she think he had money, was that it? The land and the house would pass to him eventually. Or maybe it was just sport for her as some kind of pagan temptress to take a man away from his true calling to the priesthood? It would fizzle out soon enough and he'd see sense, I was sure of it, but then he'd come to me. God how I wished he hadn't. For the truth was worse than anything I'd have had to bear without it.

He told me he was in love with her, in love! He'd always been in love with her he said, and that it had been wrong for him to join the priesthood, wrong for me to push him that direction and wrong for him to let me. He said while I'd had some part he really blamed himself. He'd been young and foolish. It was true he had wanted always to make me happy, to make up somehow for the life I'd had at the hands of his father, but he'd realised he couldn't live a lie to do it and so he was going away now, with Caer, for good. Neither of them could have a life here. They wanted to live somewhere they felt free. I protested, cajoled, and I begged.

'She's pregnant,' he said finally. And in that moment I knew all was lost. My son, the priest, had fathered a child. I could never come back from this scandal, never hold my head up again. In desperation and blind fury I let fly about the fool he was. Didn't he know what she *was*? What her people were? God knows how many men she'd been with, the child could be anyone's, why did he think it was his? I called him weak, blind, stupid, taken for a fool by a slut, a pagan, a witch no less.

'I'm sorry,' he said. 'Sorry it has to be this way. No one else in the town knows, only her sisters. We've come up with a plan so that no one will suspect. I'm to meet her now outside the chapel. There'll be lots of people arriving for mass. We're going to have a row for all to hear. That will have everyone thinking we're on bad terms. We have it all worked out. By the time we're finished they'll think the rumours about us are just that, rumours. That at least should make things easier for you. We're going to Dublin, and I'm leaving the priesthood of course. We're to be married.' He lit up with happiness when he said it, and I seethed inside. 'And then we'll leave Ireland. She has to get away from here and I feel the same. I wasn't meant to tell you, but I thought I owed you that much at least.'

'You fool,' I'd raged. 'You think anyone will believe *that!* Why, the world and the crows know you've been carrying on with that woman. You've been *seen*,' I hissed, 'on the mountain, in broad daylight, no better than animals.'

'That's a lie,' Seán said hotly, his eyes blazing. He'd never spoken to me like that before, I had to sit down with the shock of it.

But he wasn't his father and taking pity on me he came over and hugged me though I didn't respond. His arms and shoulders were strong. I'd leaned on them long before it was so and now here he was, a man and a good man, but I couldn't respect that, couldn't see past myself. He looked at me then and said, 'A long time ago you gave me a choice, Mother. You told me to choose between you and her. I chose you. It was the wrong choice. I've been given a second chance and I don't intend on wasting it. I love her, why can't you understand that? I love her. This time I choose her.' He headed for the door. 'Goodbye, Mum,' he said sadly. A moment later he was gone.

I never saw or heard from him again and from what I heard later neither did his precious Caer. Well, not from after their 'row' at the chapel. He was seen headed for the mountain, but no one saw him again after that. Everyone blamed her for his disappearance. Heard her 'cursing' him they said, and that he'd seemed shocked, upset when it happened. When he didn't return home for the requisite number of days I'd reported him missing. The guards came for my statement and then of course later they went to see Caer as well. I gave them all I could at the time. I didn't tell them his plan for eloping with Caer, that he'd said her sisters knew, or about the baby.

'No, he wasn't depressed, didn't have any enemies I knew of. Yes, he had things to live for, he was happier than I'd ever seen him before.'

When I realised the truth of that, how he'd always been happiest with her and that I'd tried always to take it away from him, and the truth that even now it was me and my reputation I was thinking of by not telling them everything, I wept. I knew I was damned, as bad as a person could get and I knew in my soul and my heart that he was truly lost, because baby or no baby Mae had been right. Nothing and no one could have kept him from her had he been alive, and it was hard for me to understand a love like that.

Chapter 12

In the Graveyard

After Mae's funeral a few people came up to sympathise with the family. Here were some of the women Mae had delivered of children, now old people themselves. There were those she'd helped with their farms, or their health, kept from the grave, or the road.

Among them was Joe Wrynn, the local librarian, genealogist and historian, former schoolmate of Seán and Caer. Some years before he'd written a book about the family.

'Listen to this,' Honor had said at the time, before reading, *'"The Cleary women are also known for their considerable powers of enchantment and seduction."* He's talking about you there, Erin,' she said.

Erin shrugged. 'Go on.'

Mae laughed, enjoying it.

'And while they are essentially healers and will never turn away a person or indeed an animal in need, it has

always been considered prudent to avoid their gaze, and certainly to avoid prolonged periods in their company or any form of relationship. For it is said, that in them resides a force supernatural that can't be possessed. They are wildness. Like the mountain, the river, the forest, and yes, even the Cailleach.'

...

Today Joe had with him a student, his assistant, Dúlta McMahon. Joe shook hands solemnly with each of the sisters. 'Sorry for your trouble, she was truly an exceptional woman,' and, 'Welcome home,' before stopping to chat for a moment with Honor and Erin. Just a little something he'd been thinking for a while. He had a small budget for hosting a series of talks and he wondered perhaps if Erin would consider speaking on natural remedies or something along those lines? He was sure there would be a lot of interest, and a few pounds in it for herself? Of course, now wasn't the time to be talking, only when would he see them, so he thought he'd just mention it. He was so open and natural that Erin nicely protested, it wouldn't be something she could consider. She was sure she could not do it, but such a nice thought she said, so kind of him to think of them and how was he keeping anyway?

Meanwhile, a tad awkwardly, his now forgotten assistant followed his boss's path taking each sister's hand, feeling more and more dazzled at each new grip, as each pair of eyes turned and met his until when at last he came to Drew he slipped, almost back into the grave, almost taking her with him. They managed not to fall in, though Dúlta realised he was still holding her and she him. She released her hold first and then reluctantly, he did the same.

'Be careful, there,' Dara whispered.

Neither Dúlta nor Drew acknowledged her but just stood smiling at each other.

Dara and Devin exchanged looks.

'Love in a graveyard,' laughed Dara. 'Who'd have thought it.'

'Devin could do it,' said Drew, still looking and smiling at the lad.

'Yes,' agreed Devin, 'I'd love to.'

'What's that?' Erin frowned at the suggestion, and the unfolding scene.

'Devin could give the talk,' Drew repeated.

'That's a great idea,' Dúlta enthused. 'Will you come too? On the night?'

'Of course,' Drew smiled, 'wouldn't miss it.'

Erin paled. 'Who is this, person, Joe?'

'Oh sorry, excuse me for not introducing you. Erin, Honor, ladies, this is Dúlta McMahon, he's on work placement with me. Dúlta, this is the Cleary family. Erin, Honor, Dara, Devin I believe, and I see you've met Drew.'

'Yes,' came the still transfixed reply.

'My how time flies.' Erin signalled for them to leave. 'We really should be getting back, nice to see you again Joe, and, assistant.' She was already leading the march to the car, while Honor brought up the rear.

'That's great now,' Joe said cheerily to his young companion. In truth it had gone much better than he'd thought it would.

The two men watched the strange party make its way through the headstones. Even in her haste Erin stopped to pick some wildflower or other in her path, while Honor ran her hands firmly and reverently over the headstones, as one feeling their way in the dark, or in love with a stone might.

Joe shook his head. 'The townspeople would be fairly blessing themselves if they'd seen that behaviour. You know, I'd hoped but I didn't really think... Dúlta, Dúlta, are you listening?'

'Oh sorry, I wasn't,' he admitted.

'Your head's been turned.'

'She can have power over me any time.'

'Don't worry, she knows it,' laughed Joe, tapping his arm. 'Come on, it's freezing. I'll buy you a drink.'

...

Mary Mannion wasn't the only one staying away from Mae's funeral. Watching from a distance, John O'Brien had come to see Dara. He hadn't seen her since that day on the mountain, the day of the incident. The thought made him sick to his stomach now. He'd been young and stupid, but there was no excuse. He'd never dreamed it would go so far. Once it kicked off he hadn't the balls to try to stop it, either. He'd stood there watching like the coward he was. And the shame of that was nearly worse than what he'd been living with since. Every time he closed his eyes he saw her face, when she knew he'd betrayed her, and he hated himself.

They'd been friends, for a while. He'd fancied her of course, all the lads did, but the other lads, like the girls, tormented her, made her life hell and she didn't trust them. She was someone who had learned not to trust, with good reason, but he had convinced her she could trust him. He made her believe he was a friend, when really he was worse than any of them, a snake in the grass. He'd led her to it, and she'd made him pay the price, made them all pay. Hadn't he lived a life of regret and bad luck ever since? Everywhere he went it followed him, she followed him, and there was still more paying to be done. It was the anniversary this year. He knew that was the real reason she'd come. For revenge. And seeing her today only confirmed it.

...

Stirrings

Back at the house Dara was wondering what to do. They'd been back a few hours already, had eaten and talked, about Mae mostly. Now the others were curled up by the fire, but she couldn't relax.

'What will you do now, Dara?' Honor asked. 'Now that the funeral is done?'

Dara knew she didn't mean for the evening but rather, what was her next move?

'I think I'll explore the house,' she said lightly, but her eyes said don't push me and Honor knew.

'Try the library, that's the place for you.'

In truth, Dara didn't know her next move and if she did she wouldn't tell them. One thing she felt sure of, that was keeping her thoughts to herself. No mean feat in this family. She wandered the house, aimlessly at first, before ending up in the library as Honor so clearly wanted. Looking around the room lined from floor to ceiling with books she found herself drawn to one shelf in particular. The books here were different to the others, for one thing obviously handmade. All were well worn and faded, some more than others, but not dusty at all. *Someone's been reading or at least taking care of these*, she thought, breathing them in. They smelt of dark woods you've come to the edge of, that beckon you in. She ran her hands over their delicate spines, lightly at first, then more hungrily, until her fingers started to burn. Then, sinking to her knees, she read the names aloud. Dana, Darerca, Drew, Rachel, Seren, Jaen, Tuiren, Caer... she stopped. Her mother's name. Her mother's book. All around her the house was silent, except for a clock ticking somewhere. She stared a while before leaving the room.

Now what? She was supposed to read those books. Honor had been more than hinting, but her instinct already told her it was so. And she wanted to. So badly that she couldn't, yet. Her fingers still burned with sensation. It was a feeling she knew well, had suffered in times of stress and danger since childhood. Her mother had been the same. Clenching them tighter she left the house, and running down the steps crossed the garden, and out the yawning gate. Her plan was to stay in the woods, and she did at first, taking pleasure in its green and silent paths, more overgrown than she remembered.

But to her right glimmers of autumn light seemed to call to her. At first the briars and trees held her back. She could barely stand in places, it was as if no one had come this way in years. But she persevered and finally, freeing herself of their grip, made her way out to the meadow, and for the first time since coming back here, she lifted her eyes to the mountain.

Now again she had the same feeling she'd had on the journey here, and with the books just before, on the night they'd arrived, and even before that. It was a feeling of being pulled, only now it was stronger, clearer. The mountain was calling her, and strangely exhilarated she started walking towards it. She'd almost forgotten she used to do this as a child. This had always been the closest way from the house, with only trees and a few sloping fields separating them. Now the closer she got the better she felt. Restlessness, longing, they left her.

Next her eyes fell on the whitethorn, the fairy tree. And reaching its shelter she spoke to it. 'What is your story, whitethorn? Tell me yours, I'll tell you mine.' But the tree stood silent watching her. 'Ah, I see, you want to hold your secrets a while. That's fine with me, secrets I understand.' It was large for a whitethorn tree and circling it slowly, she ran her hand along the knotted surface, hoping to purge the last of the burning sensation. 'How old you must be, maybe hundreds of years, and how many Cleary women have stood here before me, I wonder?'

The tree trembled, its branches swaying mournfully, lightly brushing her head. 'That many,' she said, as her fingers met with a change in the bark. Carved letters, and she read the words also carved on her heart, Seán and Caer. She studied the shapes, searching, the way one searches a map or old photographs. But whatever the landscape knew it had forgotten, or kept hidden for now. 'But I will find out,' she said.

Chapter 13

Mary Mannion - Marry in Haste

Seán Mannion had known Caer Cleary all his life. At school they were outsiders who depended on each other, but at home their lives could not have been more different. Neither house had much money. Seán's dad was a drinker and a bully who couldn't keep steady work and had run his farm into debt. Caer didn't know who her father was. No one could figure where the Clearys money came from or how they survived in general. They weren't on welfare or people would know, they couldn't, or wouldn't take money for their healing work, and they never went any further than about twenty miles or so from their home. It could be said they knew that space like no one else, every rock and blade of grass in it.

Seán's home was traditional, religious, to all appearances a good Catholic family. Caer's was a house of healers, of sisters and aunts. His mother was against the friendship from the start. Mary Mannion was a very pious woman. She'd been reared in a strict Catholic household and now as an adult that was what she clung to. She had married her husband because she wanted to escape the stifling home she'd grown up in. The eldest of nine children, both her parents were devout Catholics from the old school. They followed the law of the church to the letter. Mary and her siblings led sheltered lives, and while it got easier somewhat for her siblings, she being the eldest had been held back the most. For some reason she couldn't fathom in later years, marriage seemed an escape.

She hadn't felt able to set herself free in the world, perhaps because it was hard to imagine the world when all that you knew lay around you. When even the backwater town down the road seemed appealing. Jack Mannion was older, and a regular around their house on farming business with her father. He might have been good looking enough, but he was too rough, too raw to carry it off, and he'd no charm to speak of. But she'd worked out that didn't count for much. Marriage, she'd gathered, was for procreation, duty, the stability of community and church. It was a respectable holy union that imparted status, and she thought, freedom. Love, even lust, didn't feature, certainly not by any example she knew.

By her early twenties Mary worked in the local shop and was still living at home. On finishing school she had taken an office skills course in the local tech, but those kind of jobs were thin on the ground unless you left and went to Dublin, or one of the big towns. She'd never had a boyfriend, which in those days marked her as lacking in something. Like it wasn't normal.

To her, Jack Mannion was the most eligible man to hand and her best chance for escape. She'd decided to do whatever it took to get him to marry her. One thing about Mary, she was very persuasive. Once she'd made her mind up about something it was as good as done. For his part, Jack enjoyed his bachelor lifestyle and had no intention of settling, and besides, she wasn't his type. His tastes ran more to dark haired women with green eyes like that Jaen Cleary. He'd been after her for years without success. Mary was just a plain country girl like a hundred others. Of course, he never saw himself.

She enjoyed the game at first, enjoyed flirting with him anytime he came around. It gave her something to think of other than piety, prayers and the mortification of her soul, not to mention the never ending housework and helping her mother with the children. Sex, she'd discovered years before, was a way to rebel against the boredom of her life. That boredom, the lack of life experience, of possibility, kept her mind on one thing. That soon she'd be Mrs Jack Mannion with all the respect afforded only to married women. She would have her own house since he lived alone in a beautiful old farmhouse on the edge of the town. It was a bit of a wreck, but she'd soon see to that. It was close enough for her to go to town anytime she felt like it, and he had a good farm of land. He could provide for her.

Every time he came over she became more daring, in her dress and in her actions, from the way she moved to the way she talked to him. She was careful about it, not wanting her parents to know, but her actions matched her intent, she wanted him and she was making it plain.

For his part he gave no thought to why this young woman would be interested in him all of a sudden when they'd never so much as talked before. He told himself he was a good catch, a fine looking man, a big man, with a good farm of land. Everything a woman could want. Still, he was slow to respond and after a time Mary realised her efforts were going nowhere, so making up an excuse one day, she went round to his place.

As she walked she'd warmed to her mission. The sun beat down on her head and her heart raced as she approached the house and knocked on the door. It had been a pretty house once, could be again, she thought.

But Seán wasn't in the house, he was in the barn stacking bales. He'd heard the dogs bark and looking out shouted 'come up' at her before turning back into the darkness. He didn't look up when she walked in, either.

'Well, Jack.'

'Mary,' he grunted without stopping his work. 'What takes you here? Your father looking for me, is he?'

'No,' she said.

He stopped then, wiped the sweat from his brow and looked at her.

'Oh?'

'Don't you want to see me, Jack?'

He shrugged.

Mary turned as if to go, but she stopped, closed the door and turned back to him. The sultry air, stiflingly close and sweet, was broken here and there with slivers of dusty light. In the distance a dog barked, a lone car trundled past on the road. She moved closer, close enough to hear his heart beat, to see his pale skin smooth and glistening. And without another word she pushed him back in the hay and climbed on top of him.

From then on they met often, at his house sometimes, that was her favourite, but if they were seen too often people might get suspicious. He had no intention of being in a relationship, no, this was purely sex. More often than not he brought her to the quiet places, like the woods, or the lake, or the river. She'd been surprised not to fall pregnant right away, they weren't using anything, and in her house you'd never think that could be a problem. It seemed no sooner one sibling was weaned than there was another on the way. The sex was nothing special, he was a selfish lover with no style and little imagination, but she was a woman on a mission. Love, tenderness; they weren't on her radar.

When finally she did fall pregnant, her mother told her in no uncertain terms that she had better marry the man, if he'd have her now, or take herself off somewhere, either way she was never to mention it again. She had, of course, already arranged all that with Jack. He'd been raging, but then he'd never wanted to use anything himself so what could he say? He was too settled and old to run off, and he had the farm to think about, what was left of it. He'd tried to convince her to have an abortion but she'd called religion and scandal on that one.

So they were married, and at first everything seemed fine, exciting even, but it wasn't long before Mary had cause to regret. The saying is 'marry in haste, repent at leisure.' While she'd known he was a heavy drinker she hadn't thought of him as an alcoholic, or abusive, before they got married. He was careless with money and the farm, was reported a number of times for animal rights and worse, for rape. He'd got off with that one.

Even her dreams of the house, of doing it up, came to nothing. If she could have had that at least it might have been something, but it never felt like a home and she was as much a slave as she had ever been. She worked cleaning jobs to make ends meet and did the best she could by keeping everything in the house scrupulously clean. Later, when the drink took greater hold of him and then after he disappeared, she was able to take over the books and keep the place, what he hadn't gambled or frittered away at that stage.

She had suggested she help in the early years but he wouldn't hear of it. He didn't want her near what he saw as his money, and then of course she'd experienced the worst of him, the violence. It didn't start until Seán was a baby but once it did it kept up. The slightest thing would set him off. She had no friends, no one to tell, and she'd have felt too ashamed anyway, so she turned back to the only place she knew, back to the church. She found her escape into the very thing she'd despised in her mother, into martyrdom, and it had gotten her through. The only choice was to accept, make the best of things.

Two things came to matter to Mary, her son, and her church. In these she invested every waking breath and thought. She disapproved of the Clearys with their open ways. There was no man in that house, but there were children. It was disgraceful, and then this healing business and all the other rumours, like witchcraft. It didn't help that Jack had a thing for that Jaen Cleary and made no bones about it either. For certain he wasn't much, but he was hers. She had her pride, her respectability in the town to think of.

She and the Clearys went back a long ways, they'd always been enemies. Of all the women in town he could have a *grá* for why did it have to be Jaen Cleary? Jaen already had her pick and choose of men, not that she seemed too interested. Hadn't stopped her having three children, though, the twins and Caer. Shocking. If it was anyone else they'd have been locked away, but those women were a law unto themselves and Mary was jealous, disappointed and tired of life.

The Cleary women lived a life that seemed to make a mockery of hers, a life she couldn't even comprehend, a life of self-determination, or so she thought. She had enough time on her hands to fixate on the women, to see them as something that must be pulled down so she could stand tall in herself.

The idea that her boy was friends with a Cleary, a child of Jaen Cleary, who everyone knew had gone mad, was not only shameful and infuriating, but was not part of her plan for his life. She was determined to stamp it out. Over the years she asked the different teachers to sit them apart and not put them together for any activities, but it didn't have the desired effect. The die was already cast, the players already set.

Chapter 14

Caer - Revenge is a dish best served Cold

In the Cleary house no one gave much thought to the boy who was Caer's friend. They'd just assumed it wouldn't last. But as time went by they learned he too was different. His life was not easy. He had seen things and had responsibilities no child should have, and over time he became like just another child of the house. It might not have been the best thing, but they hadn't foreseen. Besides, not one of them could resist a bird with a broken wing, and you can't stop love growing where it will.

For Seán, Caer was his good friend, his safe place from the dark of his life. The first time they met on the first day of school she was sitting in a circle of chalk. For protection she told him. That need was something he understood. Theirs was a soul connection. From day one they were inseparable.

And time would come they'd find themselves in other circles, love, danger, death. When it was no longer safe for them to be together.

Her main tormentor at school, aside from the Sisters of Mercy, was Aileen Boyle. She and her band of populars led the bullying in a long list of relentless ways. Making her feel her own existence too keenly, she became to herself a cage. But it was a strong cage, with a strong heart, and they couldn't break it.

They said her father was one of the Tuatha Dé Danann, Irelands mythical race. Others that he was an unsuspecting wanderer who'd come by the house looking for work. Whatever the truth, they had all seen for themselves the animals made better, the illnesses taken away, and none of the women worked, so how did they live? They were always there, always home. And they were connected to the Cailleach of the mountain, though no one knew how, exactly. When it came to the Clearys every possible theory about them had been explored. Or so they thought.

These were only stories, but stories have a basis in truth. The first time Seán witnessed Caer's dark powers they were about fourteen years old. They'd been walking from school into town when Caer stopped, suddenly transfixed. Looking ahead he saw Aileen and her gang, about to cross over the bridge. Was she anxious about having to pass them? He was just asking her again if she was feeling all right when the air grew warm and menacing. It weighed on the young people, either side of the bridge, so that they all stopped walking.

The sky grew dark and darker, then the wind rose loud and whistling. It routed down from the mountain, bending the tree tops, lifting still waters, until it became a struggle for Aileen and her friends to hold their ground or even cry out against the sheer force of nature, and they clung to the bridge, the road, and to each other in desperation. All the time Caer was perfectly still, with no sign of life or emotion. Seán had a feeling like being submerged in warm sea currents, and the screams that came to them rose and fell as if they too were under water. But they took on a new pitch of terror as Aileen was lifted clear off her feet and blown in front of an oncoming car. The car swerved, on account of her or the wind or both, almost hitting the bridge, its brakes screeching in protest. The wind died just as quickly as it had risen and everyone rushed to her side. School children and some of the townspeople who had heard the commotion came running.

'What happened? What happened? Someone, call the doctor.'

'It was the wind, the wind blew her out on the road.'

'A freak wind, it was only on the bridge, nowhere else!'

'It came from the mountain. We watched it come.'

Somewhere in the chaos Aileen found her tongue. 'My ankle, oh my ankle,' she cried.

'Aileen, it's okay, hold on, doctor's on his way, and your mum.'

She cried now at the pain in her ankle, the cut knees, hands and face, the shock too. It had been so scary, the wind had physically lifted and thrown her, just as a strong person might. She had felt it close around and take hold of her. She hadn't known wind could do that. Who had seen, she wondered, scanning the crowd. Everyone was huddled in groups, talking, giving their version and theory of what had happened. They looked grave, interested, concerned and sincere. All except one.

Caer Cleary stood apart from the rest, smiling at her. Aileen started to shake and couldn't stop shaking. By now the doctor had arrived and declared the ankle broken, and shock as the cause of her shaking. The driver of the car was unharmed. Seán was in shock too. Caer stood beside him, smiling, a uniquely cold blooded smile. Could she have been behind all this? Deep down he felt that she was, but that was crazy, wasn't it? How could she possibly be? In spite of what a bitch she was he did feel a little sorry for Aileen, the meanest girl in the school. But how cool it must be to have power like Caer, he thought. Between school and home he didn't have much control of his life so the thought held some appeal. They had never discussed her abilities, not even the stories of her and her family.

Someday, he vowed. *Someday when I'm an adult I'll have power, I'll be the strong one, for both of us.*

As for Caer, she didn't give a damn about the victim of the 'freak wind' as everyone called it. But wasn't it nice how everyone helped, Seán had said. A fact Caer was scornful of.

'Wait until something really serious happens. See then where the help goes.'

She laughed, every time she thought of it she laughed. It was the first time she had used her dark power with intent and it changed everything for the better. The 'freak wind' had broken more than Aileen's ankle, it had broken her power. She didn't bother Caer or anyone else again.

One time, just once more she taunted Caer.

'Who do you think you are anyway, Caer Cleary?'

'I showed you who I am. You need reminding?'

'No.'

'I'm ready any time you do.'

Caer's only worry now was the aunts. They wouldn't want her to use her power in this way. How many times had they warned her of how dangerous it was, of how dangerous she was? The dark register, she'd heard it often enough. But the idea seemed a silly one, how could she be dangerous? So she ignored the signs, from the new quickening she felt in her hands, to the knowledge it had taken all her strength not to let the girl die in the road.

The remaining school years passed quickly. Any time she or Seán were alone someone was bound to ask, where is Caer? Where is Seán? Where's your shadow today? But they rarely spent time in the town. Outside of school they were either at Caer's house, or out on the mountain. They'd be out there in all weather. The people thought it reckless, dangerous, why, anything could happen them out there. Anything.

...

'Friends forever.'

'Yes.'

'And we'll live here, on the mountain.'

'Yes, one day all the mountain will be ours.'

'How do you know?'

'Because it already is.'

'And the Cailleach? And your family?'

'Neighbours enough to keep others away?'

They'd laughed. It was one of their favourite things, to imagine one day they'd have their own lives and be free.

As it was they saw each other every day except Sundays, which for Seán were all about mass and his mother. As he was getting older he was becoming more involved with the church. It was another thing he and Caer didn't talk about. The list was growing. It now included his life at home, her family, her powers, his family, and religion. That might seem strange, that they could be so close all their lives and not speak of these things, but it didn't seem strange to them. They knew the heart and soul things, the things no one else knew.

The priest at the time, Fr. Sullivan, often quizzed him about her, and told him to pray for her.

'I will, Father,' said Seán. He couldn't help but wonder sometimes if he should be worried about her, but mostly he felt she was not governed by the same rules as everyone else. She had her own vocation, something to do with nature, healing, and the mountain, he thought. Fr. Sullivan, like his mother, wondered if he thought he might have a religious vocation. He didn't think so. When he imagined the future, it was only Caer he saw.

Chapter 15

Memoirs & Memories

We finished school in June of 1960 and he was going away for the summer to make money for college. The thought of being apart so long had not occurred to us before. We had just a few short weeks before he had to go, and they were some of the happiest weeks of my life. It was the innocent time, before I understood my fate, before he chose his, when we had hope still.

We had a spell of fire hot days, balmy nights, and lightning storms. Rising early, spending our days together, was all we knew or wanted to know. His leaving, our age, even the weather had brought a new charge to our relationship that seemed to crackle around us. We grew happy, and without knowing, we fell in love.

In the culmination of those short weeks, on what was to be our second to last night together, I'd been looking forward for once to going into town. We didn't do that very often but there was a festival on and we'd it all planned, so I was surprised when I heard the familiar tractor roar. It had to be, it couldn't be, Seán? But it was him all right, walking through the gates still dressed in his work clothes.

Coming towards me he called, 'Tell me, Caer, have you ever been on the bog?'

'I live on the mountain, so yes.'

'Well how's about you come with me again now? I'd say that's an offer you can't refuse?'

I shook my head. 'What the hell is wrong with you?'

'Caer, you have to make hay or in this case turf, while the sun shines. You, as a farmer, should know this. Nice dress, by the way.'

I folded my arms and he wrapped his around me, lifting and swinging me around. He'd grown stronger and taller lately.

'I'm sorry, Dad was going to do it but, you know, he can't. Has to be done now.'

'I don't believe this. Right, I suppose I'll go but you owe me.'

'Fair enough.'

'I'll go change.'

'I'll wait.'

A few minutes later I was back. 'I'm ready.'

'You're still wearing a dress.'

'Won't stop me bagging more turf than you.'

'Nothing would surprise me at this stage. Right, let's go.'

He jumped up on the tractor and held his hand out for mine. I took it and jumped up beside him. He'd made a kind of makeshift seat for me with coats and turf bags, and adjusted it now before physically sitting me down and tucking my dress round my legs.

'Can't have that flying up down the road, give old Con Ryan a heart attack.'

As we hurtled down country roads ablaze with dust and heat for a change, he asked was I 'okay' and said to be sure to 'hold on.' I mused on this change, he was treating me differently, with more care, more tenderness. It was not needed. I was strong, *for a slip of a girl* he'd tease in that mock old fashioned way of going on. Feeling small, in the way of one who's protected and cherished, was new. It was not in my nature or how I was reared. I liked it from him, let it happen. Like a different style of clothes you might try for a change. It was not going to be a feature of my life for long.

Like a queen, on a throne of heat, dust, and the immense green and joy that only early summer brings, I felt drunk. With youth, and with happiness. I admired Seán's strong arms and shoulders, the slim waist, how the muscles moved under his t-shirt and I had the strongest urge to kiss his warm neck right there and then.

'You okay?' he asked again, looking back with a smile.

'Yes, perfect.'

The ancient indifferent bog stretched as far as the eye could see. Ever open to the elements, rain soaked and windswept or like today, burning. To most who had lived here, now and before, it represented only hardship, and the hope of keeping warm in winter. Only the artist or the witch knew it beautiful. And the emigrant of course.

There's a lure to this work that goes deep in us. It's the work of saving something from the land. And this, bagging the turf to take home, was most satisfying. A small triumph for man. Even as I watched my hands become scratched and torn I cared little, about as little as the mountain did. I took pleasure in it. We worked fast and furious in comfortable silence until it was time to eat. The sun was high and merciless. I brushed droplets of sweat from my eyes and ran my hands down my dress. Seán threw down a few turf bags and brought out the feast that Mary had made. Like gods of the heather, we dined on sweet tea and rough sandwiches, while long legged spiders ran over us, on their way to other lands.

We ate and drank our fill and looked long, too long at each other, the way people in love do. The world faded away. It was just us two. And he reached out his hand to me, to free some heather that had wound itself into my hair, without success.

'Oh well, it suits you,' he said, fixing it instead.

Our eyes locked as his hand went slowly round my neck and pulled me to him, and we kissed.

'I've been wanting to do that,' he said.

We kissed again.

'Me too.'

'Why didn't we?'

'Maybe we were afraid it might change things.'

'I know but I'm glad now, only sorry we waited so long.'

'Your mother wouldn't like it.'

'And since when has my mother come between us?'

'That's true, but it's not for want of trying.'

We stayed in our embrace, burning inside and out, with the sun and desire, for as long as we could.

Eventually we went back to work. It was harder now, hotter, with not a breath of air.

'Caer, you sit this out.'

'Well, well, that's rich, now the work's done and I did the most of it.'

He laughed.

'And why exactly did you bring me here then?'

'For the company of course, what else?'

'Now you tell me! I could have been sunning myself the whole time.'

'Sun!' He scoffed. 'Clearly the sun has no interest in you.'

He was starting to heave the filled bags onto the trailer. 'Well, that's us done and I will say this, you're some worker, dress or no dress, Caer Cleary.'

'Why thank you.'

'So what will we do now,' he said. 'It's too late to go to town.'

'It's still hot and we're pretty dirty, how about we go swimming?'

'What, now?'

'Why not? You hardly want to go home?'

'No, I don't want to go home,' he said, pulling me into his arms. 'When do I ever want to go home when I could be with you, and yes we could go swimming, but we've never gone this late, or are you suggesting we go skinny dipping?'

'There's a full moon, I'd say anything could happen.'

We drove the short distance to the river, the noise of the tractor an assault to that beautiful night. And parking in a gap we wove our way through a shortcut of dew laden grass, with the scent of woodbine and the sound of falling water all around us. Shivering from the wet grass we made our way down the warm rock face as light and effortless as moths in moonlight.

I could feel the day's heat rising and I longed to dive in the deep, to lie on my back and be weightless, formless, and to gaze at the stars. To kiss and be kissed in his arms. I started working on the buttons of my dress. Seán had already gone in and was calling to me from the other darker side where rods of sally, willow, and whin formed a thick wall to the water's brim. He was barely visible but for the moon beaming down on his white hair. I was about to say I could see his halo but in that moment I thought I saw something, or more likely someone, move in the thick growth behind him. Feeling uneasy, after all I was naked, my white skin glowing like a beacon, I dived straight in from where I stood, touched the flag stone bottom and swooped back up again. As my head broke the surface and my flesh hit the air I looked for but couldn't see him.

'Seán? Seán?' No answer. 'Stop messing around... I swear I'll kill you if you give me a fright.'

Still nothing. I moved towards the centre of the pool, my eyes scanning the water and bank. It was very different here by night. I felt as if I was in a bowl, the sides of which were very high and dressed in rocks and trees. Damn him, wherever he was. I was braced for a fright and cried out when it came. I fancied the trees on the other side moved again, though I'd barely chance to register that when Seán grabbed me from under the water. The shock and fright, then excitement and pleasure as we wrapped our bodies together for the first time didn't stop me from watching the river bank.

'What is it?' he asked. 'What are you looking at?'

'It's probably nothing. I thought I saw something move over there.'

'We'll stay in the water, that way they won't see anything.'

We were kissing again then, kissing and touching and floating together, getting more and more lost in each other. I felt like I was spinning, then dissolving at every gorgeous sensation, from the silk of the water to the silk of him. I wrapped my legs around him, pulling him closer, and that was when I saw her, the Cailleach.

The shock was absolute, the symbolism, the crushing reality of her being here was not lost on me. I couldn't let him know or even suspect, most of all I couldn't let him see. I nodded at the Cailleach to show her that I saw and understood, but was not afraid. Bile rose in my throat as I wrenched my eyes away from hers and backed away from Seán slowly, back to the river bank, leading him, keeping my eyes locked with his. I was counting on when I climbed out that he would follow me. He did, mercifully. I told him then I was scared, that I was sure someone had been watching and wanted to go. But I was on edge the whole way and held his arm tight. I didn't dare look back again. He had no reason to doubt me and anyway it was true, I was frightened. I was a smart girl after all, a *Bean Feasa* of some power, and I knew this was bad.

That night in bed I tossed and turned, feverish with dreaming, and a shadow that filled me with such foreboding and dread. I was still asleep when she spoke to me.

'First love. You left it late, very late in the day.'

'We've lots of time yet,' I answered.

Next in the dream I was the river. Flowing fast and free over the rocks. That felt better, but then I became a girl again, in the water with Seán again. And this time the Cailleach didn't stay on the bank. She climbed into the water, slithered in like a snake and came out the other side, transformed into a beautiful young woman, but we didn't. She came out of the water but we were lost.

And I woke as if paralysed, a dead weight on my chest. I should have written all this at the time but I was too frightened of the word power, of what I could make true by writing. And of what I might learn of myself. But in time I did write it down. And though it's not the same as when the heat is in you, I tried to write the truth. And to make it what I wanted. For as long as I could. I tried.

...

Mary Mannion

Mary Mannion had been growing more uneasy about all the time Seán was spending with Caer. As far as she was concerned she couldn't get him away from here fast enough. She hoped while away he'd gain some perspective and forget all about the girl. His dad had sent him to the bog yesterday and for once she'd been grateful to him for something. He'd come back very late though and the clothes he'd been wearing were in the machine when she came down in the morning. She decided better of asking him, but what had he been up to now, she wondered. God, she hoped they weren't sleeping together.

When he came down she had a full breakfast waiting. She was determined he'd stay home today.

'Ah great Mam, thanks, I'm starving,' he said sitting down at the table.

'I thought it would be nice, what with it being your last day.'

'I'm only going to work for the summer, I'm not dying,' he said.

'I know, but still, I want to send you off well. I've your favourite dinner planned for later, 1:00 pm. Before then we need to go through all your stuff, make sure you have everything. And I want you to take a look at that paperwork for me too, remember.'

'That's grand, thanks, but will you just keep me some dinner for later? I have to go say goodbye to Caer.'

'Good lad,' said his dad, folding the paper. 'She as tasty as the rest of em? Bet she is eh?' He hit Seán with the rolled up paper before digging hungrily into his fry.

'That's my boy,' he said with a wink. Seán bristled.

Seeing his displeasure only encouraged Jack who went on jibing with his mouth full and open.

'Want me to take care of her for ya while yer away? Would be a pleasure.' He laughed salaciously, licking his knife.

He was so disgusting, thought Seán, balling his fists under the table. But he didn't want a fight with his dad now, with him gone it would only come back on his mother.

Mary ignored her husband as she often tried to do.

'Ah Seán, please stay. I've barely seen you at all lately.'

'I know Mam, I'm sorry, just for a while. I'll be back early.'

'Ah Seán, I...'

'For Jaysus sake will you shut up woman and leave him alone. Stop your whinin. The lad wants the ride before he goes, isn't that right, lad? Tell me now, what's she like? I've heard some stories about them women, mad for men I hear.'

'You're disgusting, you know that?'

'Jack, Seán, please,' Mary said.

Seán went on. 'Don't ever say her name to me again.'

Jack turned puce with rage. 'Don't you talk to me like that, boyo, if you know what's good for you.'

He went to give Seán a clip over the ear but Seán deflected the blow, causing his dad, who was already half cut, to fall awkwardly off the chair.

This only made him angrier and he picked up the poker and beckoned Seán. 'Come on, let's see what you're made of.'

Seán made a dive for the poker and Mary screamed as the pair crashed into the television and fell to the floor. Jack was struggling. He realised for the first time that his son had grown up, he'd had no idea he was this strong. He tried to take the first low blow he'd a chance to. He was about to bring the poker down on Seán when he felt a sharp blow to the back of his own head.

Stunned, he turned around to where Mary stood holding the frying pan. He pulled himself up to his full height and let Mary have an almighty punch that sent her flying across the room. He was laying more blows on his wife when he heard the trigger.

'Take your hands off her and leave this house now or I'll fucking shoot you, so help me.'

'You! You're not going to shoot me,' Jack sneered, squaring up to him.

Seán pointed the gun at the floor beside his father's feet and shot a hole in the floor before turning it back on him. Mary was weeping. Jack's eyes widened in shock, he would never have thought his son, a real Mammy's boy and a great disappointment to him would have anything like this in him at all, and where had he learned to shoot like that? He'd never had an interest in hunting like his father.

'All right, all right, no need to get all emotional,' he laughed, raising his hands in mock surrender.

'Right, I've had enough of the pair of ye, I'm off to the pub.' He walked out, slamming the door behind him.

...

Seán

Seán spent the next hour tending to his mother and pleading with her to leave Jack.

'What if he kills you? You know he's capable of it.'

Mary made no response, only stared off into space. He sighed, it was so frustrating, how often they had this conversation. He agreed to stay with her, but he was restless, thinking of Caer waiting, and kept looking out the window towards *Sliabh Earrach*. Mary could see this, of course, but pretended she didn't.

'I'm so glad you're here, Seán.'

'I'm here now, Mam, but how will you cope for the rest of the summer?'

'I'll stay out of his way, don't worry about me.'

'Mother, I have to go and say goodbye to Caer.' She started to speak but he beat her to it. 'Not for long. Dad will be at the pub for the rest of the day. I'll be back before you know it.' He planted a kiss on her forehead and left in a hurry.

Caer was waiting at the whitethorn. She took one look at the bruised face and knew what had kept him. Some things never changed. They had such little time before he had to leave.

'I don't want to say goodbye.'

'Then don't, don't say it, and I won't either.'

They both smiled, happy and sad at the same time.

'It's just one summer,' she said, as much to herself.

'Just a few weeks,' he corrected. 'It'll fly. Before you know it we'll be in college in Dublin.'

'Yes.'

'Okay, I really do have to go, do you want to walk with me a bit?'

'No, I'll wait here.'

'Until the end of August?'

'You never know. Anyway, I'll be here when you get back.'

'That seems right, this is where I'll imagine you. Here at our tree with wind in your hair and leaves swirling around you.'

...

Caer

We kissed one last time before parting. I stood rooted like the tree and watched him go. My heart was heavy but I smiled every time he looked back. I didn't know why it felt so severe, his leaving me.

We were very young that day but I had a knowing beyond my years. There was passion, young love and the drama of our lives, but it was mingled with a sorrow no young person feels. As if I knew we were dying, our time already spent. I was only nineteen and Seán eighteen, but we were already at the midpoint of our lives.

All that time Honor and Erin had thought it well for me, off gallivanting from morning to night. They thought it strange as well that the aunts let me off like that with all the work to be done at *Sliabh Earrach*. But our lives were about to dramatically change and they didn't feel that way for long.

For Ellen and Mae time was ticking. They had given me all they could give. The day after Seán left I learned of the curse and my fate as the dark one. I was called to the quest.

Chapter 16

Her Kind

June 1960

'Is there something troubling you, Seán? It's normal you know, not to be sure about a vocation, to have doubts.' So this was why Fr. Tom wanted to see him. He'd wondered at the invitation to tea and 'a chat.' Of course his mother had set it up. An 'old friend' she'd said. That was all. No agenda. Yeah, right.

'Is there a girl?'

Oh, there was a girl all right.

'You could say that.'

'I see. What's her name?'

'Caer. Caer Cleary.'

'Caer, what an unusual name. Well, there's no hurry, you're young, you don't have to make any final decision, on either side, for some time yet. But I'm sensing there's more to this than the obvious conflict, if you want to talk?' Fr. Tom put down his tea cup and leaned in expectantly.

Did he want to talk? Yes and no, it felt disloyal but maybe it would help. It might be better than talking to anyone at home about it. The only possibility there was his friend Joe. He'd thought about that a few times but something always stopped him. Joe was a mutual friend, and a bit too keen on Caer himself.

'She's... different.'

'Oh, different how?'

Seán stood and crossed the room to the window. The sun was out, the sky calm and blue, but some leaves had already started to turn. You could see mountains from here too. It was a larger mountain range than *Sliabh Earrach* and yet there was nothing dark about its presence. That had surprised him. The people weren't living under its influence either, like they did at home, something else he'd only realised since coming here.

'She's one of a long line of healers, *Bean Feasa*.'

'A *Bean Feasa!* Really! How fascinating. Is she practicing? What does she do?'

Seán told Fr. Tom about the Cleary family, their lives of service in the community. He was careful not to reveal anything too out there, and he didn't mention Caer's powers, or the Cailleach. This telling the story, and keeping parts of it secret, showed he knew more than he thought he did. It was latent knowledge, something in the blood, like the love of the land.

Tom was a good listener. And it felt good to talk. Only when Seán was finished did he start asking questions about the local priest and how he 'dealt' with these women. And he advised caution. Of course, his idea of caution was to avoid temptation and not get too deeply involved.

'You haven't had intercourse with this girl, have you?'

The memory of their last night took him back there. To her green eyes looking into his and her laughter. Her skin like moonlight, and the way she moved, over land, in the water, against him. Something had frightened her and he didn't know what it was. But he'd felt it too, the fear and the danger. He didn't like Fr. Tom's interest, or choice of words. And he was sorry now he'd told him anything.

'No Father, not even close,' he lied, thinking how close it had been and of how he'd thought of little else since. It was unspoken between them, the almost, the not quite, the new longing.

'I think I'll go for a walk.'

'Yes, good, good, you do that.'

'Thank you, Tom.'

'You're welcome lad, any time, my door's always open.'

He supposed he had gotten off lightly, another priest might have outright condemned her and any bond between them. Still, he felt troubled. As if he'd betrayed what they had.

'What do I know for sure?' he asked himself angrily. *I love her,* he thought. *I know that I love her. And I might have a vocation they say, is that real? Or is that just what my mother wants? What if I make the wrong decision? I can't lose Caer, but why do I feel if I choose Caer that I still lose Caer?*

Things are not right with her. She's in trouble beyond my power to help or understand. The townspeople would say it's because she's a dark one. Cursed. It seems ridiculous but there is something to it. Shivering, he stuck his hands deep in his pockets, bowed his head against the wind. Caer would have never done that, he thought. She was impervious to weather.

...

Inside, Fr. Tom was watching him as he picked up the receiver and dialled the telephone.

'Hell-O, Fr. Sullivan?'

'Yes!'

'This is Fr. Tom O'Rourke here. I have young Seán Mannion with me.'

'Oh yes, great young lad, how is he getting on?'

'He's just been telling me about these Cleary women.'

'Ah, I see.'

...

One thing for sure, he could do nothing for Caer as things stood, what could he do for her or for anyone, he thought bitterly. He'd never been able to help his own mother or even himself against Jack. His father had always told him how useless he was, what a disappointment he was as a son. Now, since coming here, he'd felt lighter. It was good to be away from home, away from worry for his mother, and growing worry for Caer. He felt guilty as usual, but he had to think about what to do, and soon.

Before summer had ended, Seán, with growing pressure from the authority figures in his life, had decided to go to Maynooth and study for the priesthood. After, all he was only eighteen, it was time to go to college now, not to be thinking of settling down or even of love. These were the words he told himself.

His mother, he knew, would be thrilled and he was glad she'd be happy for once. He didn't know how he was going to tell Caer. *But it's just college*, he reminded himself, *just a few years*. Who knows what will happen yet, and they could still share a house in Dublin, couldn't they?

Jesus, she's going to kill me. But she never stays mad with me for long. Yes, he was sure they could stay friends, but would that be enough? God, what was he thinking? He couldn't bear to think of her with someone else but he could hardly ask her to wait. Tom had said to give it time and space, if was meant to be it would find a way. He wasn't sure he believed that.

The truth was that deep down he knew they were meant to be together, that he wanted it and she wanted it, but he doubted himself. He didn't think he was enough, so he prepared to let her go.

Chapter 17

Called to the Quest

Seán wasn't the only one worried. Caer's aunts and sisters worried too. Honor had long foreseen dark things for her sister. But they all felt it. Her pulling away from them.

'Your sisters are all you've got in this world, all you can ever rely on from this day to your last. When everything else has faded away your sisters will still be there.' These were the words they'd been reared with. Honor asked Mae. 'Did you feel that about our mother?'

'Jaen was always one of us. She would have broken the curse, had she lived.'

'And Caer?'

'Of course.'

But her words lacked conviction. And earlier she'd overheard Ellen and Mae speaking.

'We should have stopped her when we had the chance. Before that day at the school.'

'That was not within our power.'

'Then we should have done more to protect her, to warn her.'

'The dark powers, and now love. You know what this means for her? What it could mean for all of us?'

She'd tried to hear more but they'd moved away deeper, into the house. When had Caer used her dark powers? She, Honor, hadn't seen that. And why did it matter that she was in love? Why shouldn't she have some happiness?

She wanted to talk to Caer about it, but how? It felt disloyal even to think about. Like all the things you can't say to the people you love.

Honor at sixteen had little thought for love, freedom was her only interest, and would become her obsession. To her, this place, where everything was mapped out according to tradition, or depended on Caer, was a prison. She'd felt it always, even before Caer was called to the quest. It didn't occur to her until years later that perhaps she should have been called instead. Mae had warned they mustn't try to help, but Honor had sworn she'd find a way. She believed Caer was strong enough to free them, even more so with her help. Erin, meanwhile, accepted their part, their given roles. Honor could not understand what she saw as Erin's blind acceptance of things, not to mention her crazy love of the house. Deep down Erin thought Honor disloyal in her desire for freedom. Freedom from the family? Their home and way of life? And even from her. It hurt.

But there were more revelations to come. Their mother Jaen had died young, they knew that much, a terrible accident in the woods they'd been told.

'That's not exactly true,' Mae now said.

Outside the air was full of light and life and summer. But inside the house had turned chill.

'How did she die?'

'The same way our mother died,' said Mae, 'and her mother before her.'

'The quest. The Cailleach.'

Mae nodded solemnly.

'She must have been close.'

'Yes, we believe so. The women of this family have been battling the curse a long time. It has consumed us all, one way or another.'

Ellen sighed darkly. 'Some more than others.'

Mae squeezed her shoulder.

'But not you, Caer, you will be the one to end it,' Mae continued more brightly.

'How can you be so sure?'

'Because it's in you, it's your destiny, and it's time. All things have their time. All you need is a trigger. That will come soon. The power of the dark ones has been growing with each generation. Our sister, your mother, our mother, and all who went before, even though they perished it was not in vain. Each contributed something that brought the quest closer to an ending. And in each one the powers grew stronger. Jaen was stronger than our mother and you are stronger than Jaen. So it goes.'

'And if I refuse?'

'If you don't try, the curse will destroy you and all that you love.'

'Yes, but it seems it will do that anyway. Why should I give up everything? Go willingly to an early grave?'

'The dark will consume you,' Ellen snapped, 'and the Cailleach welcome you with open arms, but maybe that's what you want? Is that what you want, Caer?'

'What do you mean?'

'Ssssh, ssssh now,' said Mae, walking over to Caer and taking her hand.

'We, your aunts, your sisters, we know the struggle you have. We know that sometimes the dark side wins. That sometimes you want it to win. Like that time at school. When you threw the girl in the road? We understand that, we do.'

So they'd known about that, of course, they knew bloody everything.

'You want to live, you want your sisters and any future children to live, to live freely, and you have the power for that. You do. Don't give up so easily, Caer. Don't give up so soon.'

'But how?'

'Fight. You must fight. As well as you're able, with all that's in you and for as long as you can.'

Caer felt her spirit stir to action. To fight, that was something she could do.

'And you must give up the boy,' Ellen warned.

'What? No!'

Mae sighed and shook her head at Ellen before going on, 'I know it is hard. If you didn't love him it wouldn't matter, but you do. It puts him, and all of us, in greater danger. I'm sorry, but Ellen is right, you have to give him up, or risk everything.'

Was there any end to this nightmare? Was there any way out? In the midst of it all Caer thought it strange to hear Mae say that she loved Seán, when they had never said it to each other.

'I don't think... I don't know if I can do that.'

Mae rose slowly and crossed the room.

'You know the women in this photograph, you've heard stories about them. At the front is Dea Cleary. She was some woman. Do you know what happened her?'

The girls shook their heads.

'She was the first to have the new power. She went herself to the otherworld to get it.'

They gasped. The idea of anyone going to the otherworld voluntarily, to steal a power, it was unimaginable. All power had to be gifted, passed on freely. A sacrifice would be demanded for such an act, a price would have to be paid, and that price was usually a life. So this was what the quest did. This was what they were dealing with.

'She must have been very brave,' ventured Honor, inspired.

'Brave? Yes, and selfless too. When you read her book, Caer, you will find she didn't tell her sisters. She was trying to protect them. She'd been on the quest a long time. But her sisters, Dana, and my mother, Rachel, they became distrustful of her quest. The sisters always know the quest will take the seeker to dark places. It's a journey that allows no room for other purpose. The sisters have always known this, and they knew it then. Their role is a shadow one. Sadly, these sisters, they forgot.'

'What happened?' asked Honor, impatient. She felt this story was being told for her benefit.

Mae paused before going on. It was hard to say what must be said. 'They started to believe that she'd been swept away.'

'A changeling!' cried Erin.

Mae nodded. 'What began as worry soon turned to distrust, and then fear. They came to believe she'd been taken over by the Cailleach and was no longer their sister. So they made a secret plan to test her, a ritual to try to drive the Cailleach out in the open, and they hoped, to free Dea. But it failed. And in the commotion, they smothered her.'

'She didn't die by her own sisters' hands?'

'I'm sad to say that yes, she did.'

How could this happen? They'd always been told, always known it was only their sisters they could trust, or could rely on. Aside from the house itself, it was the only constant sure thing in their lives and now this? This horror, this betrayal.

'Why are you telling us now?' Erin asked. 'You're not suggesting...'

'I'm not suggesting any of you would do such a thing, or could. Remember, this was long ago, and people, we, were different then. But it's important for you to know what you're up against, how serious all of this is. After Dea's death the sisters read her book and learned of the sacrifice she'd made. Naturally, they were devastated. She'd paid the blood price and by their hands. They figured the new power, which had a dark code, must have affected them all.

'As a result, Rachel wanted to give up the quest, not pass it on to the next generation, let the Cailleach win. With Dea's blood on their hands she felt it was what they deserved. But Dana felt that Dea's sacrifice should be honoured. She had stolen the power, paid the blood sacrifice and now that power would stay with the family, and was rightfully theirs. The quest must go on, she said. The powers would have to be watched, balanced, the good and the bad. No doubt that could prove difficult, but the chance of success would be greater than ever, certainly by the next generation.

'Unfortunately, it wasn't to be, as you know, we were the next generation.' She looked to Ellen who sat silently staring out the window, and wringing her hands. 'Our sister, your mother Jaen, perished too, and now the powers are darker still, the challenges greater. Now the quest falls to you.'

Of course, thought Honor, it made sense now. Dea had died here, had been murdered here. She, Erin, and

Caer, now saw in the house, for the first time, what they had always felt and taken for granted. That duality of light and dark.

'That explains a lot.'

'It's a dark history, but it's ours.'

'But if they'd read the book first it wouldn't have happened.'

'I think it's safe to say they weren't themselves by that stage but no, the books can only be read by the sisters of a seeker who is lost. To their minds they were trying to save her. The best way they knew how.

'We are allowed, therefore, to read Jaen's book, but not the others. They are for the next seeker, and besides, she is only one who can truly understand their contents, the one who is closest to the Cailleach, the most in tune to her ways.'

'Well that's a lot of help,' said Honor.

'I know it's frustrating, but Dea did find a way to help us. The law of no interference. The sisters must accept the journey of the seeker.

'So now you know the truth. The quest is all. The sisters must not get involved. There are many dangers along the way. In the end we buy time, then we win, or we lose.'

'But there must be something, how are we supposed to just sit back and do nothing?'

'Not nothing, Honor, not nothing,' said Mae. 'You keep the house.' Honor rolled her eyes. 'The land, the people, you stay the course. The sister on the quest needs you, needs all... this.' She gestured to the four walls. 'She'll never break the curse and we'll none of us ever be free without that support.'

The five women sat in silence. Only the house sighed. Only the light shining in moved like waves on the floor. Still, there was comfort in it. Their world was shifting, but the seasons wouldn't, nature wouldn't. Spring would always follow winter, and summer after that. So the house and their supporting role was central, not very exciting, not as active as Honor would like, but vital nonetheless. They had to *go the course* Mae had said. They had to keep things normal. How ironic, as if any of this were normal.

But still in her heart she believed that was more Erin's role. She would do all that was required of course, but there must be more, had to be. After all, Mae had said the powers were in constant flux and she knew herself that her power was greater than the aunts. No, this job of passive sister, much like that of the seeker, was evolving, had to be, it made sense. She just had to think of how to apply herself in ever more creative ways.

Erin's mind was on the smothering. She'd heard of such things but never dreamed it could happen in their family. Were they really that afraid of her? Was she that much of a horror? Or was it as Mae had said, a measure of the power they were up against?

The Cailleach was a landscape figure, could the landscape ever be beaten? And did they want that, really? Them, of all people, who loved the land and practiced healing. And if it was possible that Dea was a changeling, then it was possible one of the other sisters had been the real deal. Rachel perhaps, she was the one who wanted to give up on the quest. Perhaps she'd been the true changeling?

Looking at the photo of Dea and her sisters she imagined them watching and listening. Their eyes, piercing, intelligent, seemed almost alive, and she shivered in spite of herself. And she noticed, too, how much one of the sisters looked like Ellen, who looked cross and unhappy now, more than usual, Mae's hand still on her shoulder. Was she crying? Erin frowned, she'd never seen Ellen cry in her life. She presumed it was memories of their sister Jaen and all they'd been through. Could she ever hurt one of her sisters? Looking at them now she saw how tired Caer seemed and how distracted. Honor was no doubt inspired by Dea's daring, and dying to be away from them all so she could do her own plotting. The thought made her smile.

No, she believed she would never hurt or betray them no matter what they did, or what they might become. And Caer wasn't the only dark one. It was strange, but that was one thing the aunts had wrong, Honor. Should she have been called to the quest instead? Erin didn't know for sure, she could only know her own path. And she knew she was the one who would keep the house, the people, the land, and the sisters, under her watchful care. Honor would never be able to help her, it wasn't her nature. She vowed there and then to protect them all, and to do whatever was required. She might not be able to help Caer directly, but she believed in her, she believed in Honor, and she believed in herself. She, Erin, would deal with anyone or anything that stood in their path.

Caer wondered if she'd always known this was coming. And the answer came instantly, yes. In some ways she was glad to be chosen. She knew she had the power. Knew she had to believe it, too. The quest would require iron clad focus and single minded self belief. But so far, every Cleary woman on the quest had died tragically one way or another, and young. She didn't want to die. Surely they'd all been exceptional women? Yet they'd floundered. Why? Especially after Dea stole the power, victory should have been certain. So what had gone wrong? Something did. And why should she be any different to those incredible women?

But she mustn't think like that or she'd be beaten from the start. Time to get tough, that was all, to grow up. But what about her life? What about her and Seán? All their dreams and hopes. Give him up the aunts said. She could not do it, she would not do it.

How could he possibly come to harm? She would never hurt him and he would never go near that part of the mountain. But then she thought of that night they'd gone swimming, of her fear on seeing the Cailleach there. She'd never had to fear the Cailleach before, it had to be on account of Seán.

The answer was clear, stay off the mountain.

But the Cailleach was everywhere, this was her territory. And now it seemed she had no choice. And she thought, *If only they'd chosen Honor instead.*

After that she missed Seán more than ever. She'd been used to sharing everything with him, but she could never tell him this. He wasn't mired in darkness, well he was, but it was different. He'd been her hope of a different kind of life. It was a life she now knew was impossible. The aunts were right, she had to find the strength to let him go. But absence is to love what wind is to fire. She thought they were over, they weren't over. They hadn't even started yet.

...

Late August, 1960

As predicted, Seán's mother had been thrilled at his news. He didn't even have to tell her, Fr. O'Rourke had hinted to Fr. Sullivan, she said. And once home it took her no time at all to suggest that he stop seeing Caer.

'This already. I'm only in the door.'

Not that he shouldn't see any girls she pointed out hastily.

'You're young and not a priest yet, but, to be in a relationship with a known pagan and worse, a girl whose family openly practice rituals, and healings and even it seems deal in witchcraft, well, it's not right.'

'Listen, Mam, we need to talk.'

Mary revised quickly. 'All right Seán,' she conceded. 'I know she's your friend and the family's been good to you.' The words nearly choked her.

'Mam, Fr. Tom, he had no right. He shouldn't have said anything.'

'And I know that house has been an escape for you from...other horrors.' Seán felt miserable. This was awful. He placed his hand on his mother's.

She smiled, this was better.

'But look at it another way. You're going to be leaving soon, where is this relationship going? Do you think for one second she is ever really going to leave here?' Seán was a bit taken aback at this, but he said, 'We're going to Dublin. She wants to leave here as much...' he almost said as he did but caught himself.

Mary smiled, she could hardly blame him for that. *Don't go too fast,* she said to herself, taking time to put the kettle on.

'Seán, dear,' she said gently, 'none of that family has ever left here. Why, in all the years you've known her, even that time you all went to the seaside, remember? And to Dublin for shopping, or other trips, she, stayed, here.'

'She wanted to go, she was sick that day, I remember. She's never seen the sea.'

'Oh Seán, foolish boy, she's never going to.'

It was a blow, especially coming from Mary. Why hadn't he realised this? It wasn't true, was it?

Mary continued, 'This is your chance to make a clean break of it. I asked you where this relationship is going, well I'll tell you, nowhere. I'm sorry if that seems harsh but much kinder to let her go now than later. That girl, that family, they have...problems.'

'We all have problems.'

'Yes we do, all the more reason why you don't need this, you have enough on your own plate, your own demons. Two damaged people together.'

'Damaged!'

'Listen to reason, Seán, it would be a disaster. Plus, as I've already said it isn't fitting and, as she's never going to leave here what is it all for?'

'But...'

'I've said my piece, Seán, you can't have it all. You can't have her and have me to support you through college.' There, it was said.

The two stared at each other.

'Mam, I'm sorry to tell you but I'm not going to college, not to Maynooth anyway, or not anywhere now, it seems. Okay, grand, I'll make my own way. I'm afraid you just have to accept this. I don't want to be a priest.' He shuddered. 'Being away from here this summer I've had time to think about what I want from life, and it's not that. That's what you want.'

Mary didn't flinch. He thought she'd be upset at this news but he was wrong, she'd anticipated it. It was cold feet, that was all. And the effect of being back here. But she had one card still to play and she played it coldly now.

'Oh yes, you will go to Maynooth, yes you will. Life decisions can be made after that, when you're older, and wiser. You see, Fr. Sullivan's been to see me.'

'Oh?'

'Quite a few times, in fact. He's very concerned for you, and the parish of course, Caer too. He mentioned there are homes for girls like her.'

'What?'

'He said Fr. O'Rourke offered help to arrange it. He wants to meet her privately, O'Rourke that is, as soon as possible. Though, I'm not sure that's the best idea. He has a terrible reputation with young women. Perhaps you've heard of it? Anyway, poor Fr. Sullivan was in a right state. Said he'd heard of other girls being sent away, after O'Rourke's seen them. Maybe, and it's just a thought. But maybe if you stop seeing her, and go to Maynooth, it will all just, blow over.'

She sat back and sipped her tea like all of this was normal, was nothing.

'You would do such an evil thing?'

'Oh don't look at me like that. It's time to grow up, Seán. You can throw your future away on that girl or you can go and get an education, up to you. And what would you do anyway, at your age, and for the rest of your life? Work in some dead end job? Live in sin with that girl? Who would even rent a young single couple a place? Even in Dublin? A girl who won't ever work a day, mind. Who most likely won't ever leave here. What if she gets pregnant?'

'This is the sixties, not the dark ages.'

Mary laughed. 'Make no mistake, child, it's still dark ages in Ireland once women, sex, and babies outside marriage is concerned and it will be for a long, long time. You want to end up like me? Be realistic, Seán. You're only eighteen.' She laughed her fake empty laugh again and he hated her for it.

'Not everyone is like you and Dad.'

'True, but at your age you don't know that, you could be more like us than you think, more if you stay here, after all, you are our son. Listen to sense. Go to college, it's just a few years. You can do what you want after that.'

The swollen lip and black eyes pleaded with him. She'd done an excellent cover job as usual but he could still see. The weight of her life played out in this place weighed as heavy as it always did. Being away for the summer he'd dreamed of freedom, but now Caer was in danger, because of him. He knew about the homes. Girls and women were sent there, for being pregnant, and

Cailleach~Witch

sometimes just for being pretty, or different. And they never came back. Had they the power to do that to her? He didn't know but he knew his mother and the power of the priests.

'And if I go to Maynooth, you'll leave her alone?'

'Yes.'

'You swear, because if I hear...'

'I've no issue with Caer once you're away from her. The priest would like to get his hands on her, but I can handle him.'

'You know I'm never going to be a priest.'

'Maybe you will and maybe you won't. We don't need to think about that today. Seán? Where are you going? Seán?'

'Where do you think I'm going? I'm going to see Caer. And then I'll be leaving.'

'Yes, go and say your goodbyes.'

'The only goodbye I'm saying, is to you.'

Chapter 18

Jaen and the Cailleach

Before the growing season, when all of nature's sleeping still, this too is a quiet time for me, and when that great bursting forth of new life begins I hold it back a while because I am not ready.

There was a time the women needed me, but for generations they have tried to free themselves. And they are growing stronger, while I follow the same cycle year on year, from maiden to hag and back again, always back again, forever.

The trouble started with Dea, not a woman to be messed with. She went to the otherworld to steal a power, build their strength, and speed their so called victory. Letting her return home, that was my first mistake, but she had taken me by surprise. And she paid the ultimate price, her life, and the life of her unborn child. It was a shame the child she carried was lost but sacrifices must be made. From then on I became more vigilant.

Jaen was next, a bold creature, different again to those before. In her was all the best of evolution plus the new power. I watched with interest her progress on the quest to free them. I was quite in love with her, the twists and turns of her mercurial mind. I waited to see if she would solve the quest, and what her choice would be. And I listened, as she plotted my demise. I had to stop her, and fast. I had no power in the house and she had almost reached it. It was then my next problem revealed itself, Ellen.

Ellen, who had slowed their path and helped me, without intent, without their knowing, now sensed my hand and didn't like it. She was in the garden, she could warn and help Jaen. I was livid. How had it come to this? I sleep, I turn my back, and they grow stronger. It should bring us closer, this new strength, not drive us apart, but the relationship is a complex one. Time was the sisters were watchers, guardians, now what had they become?

Ellen was moving fast. Jaen was moving quickly too, but not paying much attention to her path. How to stop her, how...? It was Ellen herself gave the answer, for when she got to the gate she froze. And she didn't take another step.

The ways in which humans will limit themselves never fail to surprise me. Years of being tied to that house had crippled Ellen with fear. She wouldn't help Jaen. She tried. She screamed. A scream that would rival the banshee, that would wake the dead. 'Jaaaaaaen.' It might have worked, but the wind, the beautiful wind, caught Ellen's words, and carried them away.

Jaen sensed the change, and she wasn't alone. A great cloud of birds burst forth from the tree tops, crying and screaming, forsaking the forest. And in that moment, she too looked up. She looked up and as she did she stepped into my trap, a real trap I assure you, made of iron. Its rusted jaws snapped shut, crushing her ankle. She cried out, in pain and shock and knowledge. Knowing this was my hand.

But she wasn't finished yet. While Ellen collapsed on the spot at the death sounds, Jaen, whose foot was already part severed, determined to free herself. She started to twist and pull at it. I watched in admiration and I knew, I knew she would do it. She would free herself and crawl on that forest floor, she would reach the house and write my secret in her book. And then, she'd be coming after me.

I saw that strength, that determination in her. That was the power of her will. I was never going to allow it and because I liked her so much I ended it, quickly. A sudden storm and bolt of lightning brought the tree down, and that was the end of Jaen.

After that I wasn't taking any chances. I kept a close eye on all the sisters. Ellen was clearly no threat but some use, maybe? Mae was a handler, but too wrapped in concerns of this world to be any real trouble for me. Erin was just like Mae, tough, intuitive, but up to her eyes in the troubles of humans, and in her beloved house. Caer I didn't worry about, she was mine, my dark one, the closest I had ever been to any of the women. I had high hopes, such high hopes for her, for our future. But Honor... for sure she was a dark one too. But she wasn't theirs and she wasn't mine. I'd have to watch her.

Chapter 19

Journal of Devin Cleary - September 1995

I was the one who wanted to come back here. To practice my skills and become a great healer, like Erin, but I'm still surprised at my depth of feeling for the place. I've never known peace like this. As much as dark days lie ahead I see my life here. Strange to say, I don't believe I'm ever going to leave again.

Those first days back I walked the land, deep mapping the familiar, but with a woman's eyes now. I revelled in it all, the old house with its ghosts, the cosy kitchen and fire that never goes out, my own room with its cosy nooks and views of the valley. Most of all the stillroom. Here the herbs from the garden and mountain are infused, distilled, hung and dried for use in cooking and medicines. I feel like I'm in heaven.

This morning, like every morning since we arrived, I went outside to watch the great show, a play of water, cloud, and light, across the valley. Breezing back into the kitchen, the first person I met was Dara, and she wasn't long about putting me out.

'What are you doing now?'

'I was just in the garden.'

'In your bare feet?'

'Yes... to make connection with the energy of the place.'

'I see, is that wise?'

'I'm just being myself.'

'Aren't you lucky, that being yourself is a good thing to be.'

It bothered me, and I told her, 'It won't always be this way you know, it will change.'

'Will it?'

'Yes,' I said confidently.

'Where do you see yourself in ten years? In twenty?'

'I hope we'll all be here, free of the curse, but here, together and happy.'

She looked at me like I was the village idiot, someone beyond reason or help.

'I'm allowed hope, aren't I?'

Drew came in then. 'What's going on. What are you fighting about?'

'Nothing, we're not fighting, Dara just wanted to know where I saw myself in years to come.'

'And?'

'I said I hoped we'd all be here, free of the curse, happy.'

'I see.'

'Do you?' Dara asked coldly, glaring at our sister. I was just glad her attention was gone from me. Besides, Drew could handle her better.

'Do I what?'

'See. Have you seen the future? Our future?'

'You know I can't answer that.'

'Why not? You're the one with the gift of sight.'

'It doesn't work on command, besides, would you really want to know?'

'Yes, why not? Besides, I have a fair idea already.'

'Well I don't believe in destiny,' said Drew. 'I don't know about you guys but I'll make my own.'

'That's fighting talk in this family, some might say betrayal.'

Drew rolled her eyes. 'You're so dark and twisted.'

'I know what future I want,' I continued. 'And I was thinking, it's time we went to town, Dara. Dara?' She was ignoring me now, her nose in a book.

'Yes, we should,' she replied finally, without looking up, 'but not yet.'

Here's the thing. Dara hasn't left the house since Mae's funeral. That evening she went out for a few hours and came back in a black mood that hasn't lifted since then. It's how she gets when things get thick around her. She's quiet but it can't last, like the calm before the storm. She will explode. The storm is coming.

Just yesterday I tried to bring this up with Erin. We'd been out on the mountain gathering wild greens and herbs. I've been spending every minute I can with her and I'm not sure what has surprised me more, her scale of knowledge and skill as a healer or her popularity with the people. They are curious about me and sometimes ask too many questions, but they're friendly which is more than I expected.

Erin is supremely open, warm, generous about her work, but is hard to know. She's enjoying our shared bond and interest, the whole teacher, student, and aunt with grown up niece thing. But she's closed on all matters of self, and it seems, on all matters of Dara.

It worries me. I know Dara is set on revenge but I also know that that's wrong. Revenge can't be her path. I'm afraid of where it might lead her, lead all of us.

Even though I'm the middle child I've always felt like the eldest. Drew, the youngest, has always been independent, does her own thing, without chains of identity. All my life I've looked out for Dara who is somewhat... incendiary. Truly our sister is not of this world, a bit like Aunt Honor, I think.

I tried to broach all this with Erin, but to little avail. Finally she said, 'You mustn't worry, Devin, your sister is conflicted but she will work this out, soon. Just focus on your own path. That's the best thing you can do.'

I was disappointed, so hoping she'd support me. At the end of the day I believe my sister's fixation on revenge is affecting her ability to *work things out* as Erin put it. I don't have the gift of sight but I know we need to talk more in this family. Something terrible is about to happen.

Chapter 20

Ellen Cleary

Erin did understand, and did want to help. But she wasn't about to interfere in Dara's path. It would be better, as she'd said, if Devin would just focus on her own path. But it was difficult to influence that when the girls hadn't been called to the quest and given clear boundaries. Boundaries that would have stifled and hurt them in ways, yes, but would have been protection too. She hoped they, the family, had made the right decision. One day, hopefully a long time from now, Devin would take her place as caretaker of this community, the family, and the house. In the meantime, it would be best if she didn't get too close to the energies of the otherworld. That was Dara's path.

On the night Caer died, Honor had stopped her, Erin, from making a new curse, and instead they had made a promise to end this thing. Since then each in her own way had set about bringing that ending. It must come with this generation. They would sacrifice themselves if need be, but not the girls. And would do everything in their power to keep them from harm.

Mae had helped by sending the girls away when she did. If she hadn't, Dara would have been called soon after. She and Ellen had been too strict with Dara. After what happened to their own sister Jaen and then to Caer they'd been overprotective of the young girls, and what that had achieved? The incident on the mountain that led to the death of that boy from the town. And all the trouble thereafter. By setting Dara free in the world, by letting her feel the call in her own time, and trusting it would happen, they had taken a risk. Another bold move in the quest.

But they had to be careful now. They had hoped the girls would be older, wiser, and stronger when the time came, and mercifully they were. But whatever about Dara it would be best for Devin, Drew too, not to get too close to anything to do with the quest. So far Drew seemed detached from it all. She was spending her days swimming, writing, and day-dreaming it seemed, but Devin was a worry.

They had discussed it, she and Honor, and decided to continue as they were, at least for now. To offer only subliminal guidance. Drew could be left to her own devices, and she, Erin, would keep Devin busy with healing work, and away from Dara as much as she could.

Long nights they'd spent, going over the happenings so far. And Honor pored over the books, all the books, even the forbidden ones, for the common threads and moves their fore-sisters had taken to disaster, always to disaster. It was not only forbidden, it was slow, painstaking work.

Mae, and even Ellen had agreed with their plans, what they'd told them at least. But with Ellen especially, that had surprised them. From when she'd heard the girls were coming back she had changed, there was almost a lightness to her.

The thing about Ellen was she was not who people thought she was. She was not Mae and Jaen's sister, she was their aunt. One of the women in the old photo that hung on the wall, and her real name was Dana.

Years before, when Jaen and Mae were little girls, their aunt Dea was smothered by her sisters, Dana, and Rachel, Jaen and Mae's mother, because they believed she was a changeling. At the time she'd been pregnant with a little girl she'd already named, Ellen.

Dana was one who had long foreseen her own death, the particulars of which were so colourful, so gruesome, and so very precise, that she was able to avoid them. She had told Rachel she thought she might be able to avoid it forever, though of course she couldn't remain here as *Dana*, she'd have to assume a different persona and become one of the children as it were, and so she assumed the identity of her niece, the never born *Ellen*.

To do this she hid herself away for years, never leaving *Sliabh Earrach*. Meanwhile, the orphaned Jaen and Mae were reared by Rachel and Dana, or *Ellen,* as she was now known. They were told to call *Ellen* their 'sister' growing up and eventually began to think of her as such. Supernaturally beautiful, she seemed to grow not older but younger to meet them, and she never really changed, not at first.

This explained Ellen's strangeness. She was from a different time. But her deeds became a curse all their own. Years of long life and confinement to the house meant that by the time she might have left she couldn't. This too explained, at least in part, why the curse had not been broken yet, for while the individual women were growing stronger, the power of three had been broken.

On the day the Cailleach killed Jaen, Ellen working in the garden saw what was going to happen. She wanted to go to her adopted sister, her niece in fact, to help her, but she couldn't do it. She couldn't cross the threshold from their garden to the outside world. It devastated her. She would never have believed this of herself. That she, who had been so bright and beautiful, so gifted with powers, would stand by as Jaen met her end.

By the time Caer took Jaen's place on the quest, Ellen had already helped kill her own sister, taken the identity of that sister's unborn baby, masqueraded as sister to her nieces Mae and Jaen, and found herself powerless to help Jaen in her last moments, instead watching her die that most terrible death. She had seen Caer walk to disaster, though she had tried to warn her about that boy, to stay away from him, to no avail. And then she watched her do the thing that she could never do, that none of them had ever been able to do, leave. And that had in some way renewed her, for a time.

It was possible after all, because Caer had done it. She had new hope, and it stayed with her, even after Caer's death. She'd long thought it a curse to be immortal, to have to see each generation play the same game over and again, and to have played a major part in that repeating doom. She felt certain the children of Caer would be the ones to break the curse forever. And she sometimes pondered the question, if Caer had not fallen in love with Seán would she have been the one to break the curse? Would she have lived? Or was it she, Ellen, who had long ruined any chance they had? If that were true, then her own part was yet to be revealed. For it couldn't end like this. She was ready, she decided, to do whatever must be done. She had buried too many sisters.

Chapter 21

Gifts

Something else played on Ellen's mind. A snatched conversation, when she'd heard Caer ask of Mae, 'What is Ellen's power?'

Mae had been surprised. 'Don't you know?'

Caer had shaken her head.

'Why the sight, and great beauty of course.'

'Ellen was beautiful?'

Ellen was shocked at Caer's reaction, and the use of past tense in describing her beauty. Her hand darted to her face and as they talked she went to an old mirror that hung nearby.

'Oh yes, the most beautiful.'

'But I thought that was Dana, and beauty's not a real power is it?'

'Yes,' said Mae slowly, 'she is very like our aunt Dana. And of course beauty is a real power, if sometimes a curse. I swear, you young girls!'

'But Ellen! I'm sorry, it's just hard to believe, she's just, so strange.'

'I don't see what that has to do with it.'

Ellen looked in the mirror and for the first time in years really saw herself. It was not what she'd expected. None of us ever really see ourselves but in that moment she did. Her beauty was gone and not because of age, she had avoided that, but because of life not lived. And she'd had two chances, had thrown both away.

Hiding, that was all she'd done. She'd been vain once. Afraid of aging and dying, but now, after all these years, perhaps it was time? No one wants to die and the desire to hold on to life is strong, but she'd already lived two lifetimes and now she didn't even recognise herself. Who was she? What had she done? Nothing.

She walked into the kitchen, always enough to stop conversation, and went over to where baby Dara was playing. She lifted the child up to eye level and looked at her closely.

'What are you doing, Ellen? You'll scare the child,' chided Mae, wiping her hands on her clothes and coming over quickly in a bid to take the baby, but Ellen was faster, she darted away, whispering something to Dara that no one else heard.

It really wasn't like Ellen to take interest in children.

'What did you say to her?' Caer asked.

Ellen smiled a rare smile and it took Caer's breath away, seeing that side of Ellen for the first time.

'I just made her a promise,' she replied, pleased. It would be a long time before she'd have a chance to deliver on that promise. A lot would have changed by the time came for Ellen to die.

...

The young generation, they were citizens of the world, not slaves of a dead end backwater. Powerful in the old ways, even if they didn't know it yet, and worldly wise, a different species to that which went before. It was a potent combination, that old and new, the best of past, present and future. It had been an expensive gift, given first by their mother Caer when she left, taking Dara with her. Then by the aunts, who sent them away as teenagers, and finally by Ellen herself. They didn't know, but she was the reason they didn't have to come back for so long, until the call grew so loud in their hearts that they had to. None of their line had known freedom like it before. It would give Dara an edge when at last she took up the quest, the aunts were sure of it.

...

'But what if she won't go through with it?' Erin had asked Honor, whom she considered expert. Not only from all her study, but from her own courage and sacrifices.

'Oh, she's going through with it.'

'But how do you know?' Erin was surprised at her own fervour on the subject, after all she didn't really want things to change too much. But for the memory of Caer and the others, and the protection of the young people, she wanted rid of the curse. They could all get on with their lives, here, or out there. They could choose for themselves, that was the point, that was the freedom she wanted, for all of them.

As she'd gotten older it affected her more. She was happy in her life, was living her purpose. And she could be out here with the wind in her hair, on her face, and feel a happiness so great, a perfect joy, but her sister couldn't. Her nieces couldn't, and sure as hell Caer and Seán couldn't. They never could. And they'd been gone for so long. Not one of her family had what she had. It was time for Erin to stand up.

Now her twin, Honor, was in danger for her meddling in otherworld energies. She remembered the day Honor had shared her discoveries, what she planned to do, and how the only problem was time. It was typical of Honor not to think that putting herself in danger was a problem, to think only of the bigger picture.

Time, Honor had explained, was against them, in ways both practical and mysterious. The girls had to come at the right time, not too late, not too soon. The danger then being too soon. They might have been far away, but the aunts knew the force of the call that was in them.

'We have to keep them away a while longer.'

'How?'

There would be no easy answer. To keep them away meant to make silent the call. To achieve it would take more sacrifice. They had precious little left by that stage – their lives? They were needed yet. But a voice had come from the shadows.

'I know of a way.' It was Ellen.

Honor's voice cut across her remembering.

'Deep down Dara knows, in her soul of souls, she has already taken the quest. It's true that hate stands in her way but she'll get to a point she can use that.'

Relieved, Erin felt she now understood a bit better. Her niece was in the same place Caer had been in the weeks after she learned of the quest. Before the Cailleach hunted her and Seán on the mountain. Not until after that terrible night had Caer fully accepted her fate. What would it take for Dara to do the same? To find healing? Free of hate, free to live.

It was no surprise that in order to manage the quest great sacrifices had to be made. These dark women, Honor, Caer, Jaen, Dea, even Ellen, had courage. They weren't a part of this world like she was. And so they didn't have as much to lose. But Erin's day was coming and she would meet it just as bravely as any of them.

Chapter 22

Ellen - Part 2

Ellen knew what the problem was, why the curse had yet to be broken. It was her. She was the one to blame. She had cheated death, assuming the life of the never born Ellen, living with her nieces, not as aunt but as sister, and killed the real Ellen's mother, her sister. That had been her idea, not Rachel's. She had believed their sister was a changeling and that they could get the real Dea back, had convinced Rachel too. Were it not for their actions, Rachel might have had a third child. But she was too traumatised by Dea's death, and she never fully recovered. She, Ellen, had broken the power of three, she had deepened the curse.

She wanted to put things right. It would take all her strength, but she had promised Dara all those years ago and she was determined to see it through. It would be the ultimate sacrifice for her, her life.

And in return the call in the girls would go silent. That, at least, would keep them away for longer. Long enough for Honor to learn more that would help them, long enough for them to grow stronger.

She knew what she must do. It had to happen in the way she'd avoided to now, her death vision.

On the first day of rain after a dry spell, wearing a black dress and carrying a bunch of fuchsia, she would walk up the steps to the house with one of the family walking behind her. On reaching the top a bird would fly too close, startling and causing her to fall. She would manage to hold on until the other one present reached over to help. And then she would fall to her death.

All these years Ellen had easily avoided the wet days that followed a dry spell, and wearing black. As for the fuchsias, that explained why she'd spent years chopping them down. And still they covered the mountain. It didn't help that it was Dea, the sister she'd killed, who planted them in the first place. They didn't belong here, she'd always said. Now it was her didn't belong. Hadn't belonged for a long time.

She was ready, she said. And as Mae, who had lived with this person as sister, all her life, couldn't bear to be the one, it fell to me, Erin. Honor had enough to do, and besides, I was the healer, the protector, the one who did the practical things that had to be done.

On the appointed day Ellen and I set out to walk those fateful steps together, Ellen leading the way, a dead woman walking. For me every step was a dagger. When we reached the top she paused and looked at me briefly. She was, I'd say, eerily calm. One minute she was filling the space against a darkening sky. Next, a large hawk, or crow, appeared, as if out of nowhere, startling us both. And she was gone. Just like that. I lurched forward on my hands and knees, my heart threatening to fly from my rib cage. Peering over the edge I didn't know what to expect. It had all happened so fast, she hadn't even made a sound. So it was a further shock to see her there, below me, hanging tightly to an old tree root, jutting out from the rock face.

We had locked eyes for only a moment before I heard myself say, 'Don't do it, Ellen. We'll find another way, it's not too late, I can help you.'

I'd seen more than my share of deaths untimely but never the death of a family member, not like this. Maybe it was that, or my loyalty, my vow of protection working against me, but this shook me in a way I never imagined.

'Hold out your hand, Erin,' Ellen commanded. So she didn't mean to be saved but to fulfil her death vision.

'ERIN!' she hissed. 'I can't, hold, much longer. If you don't hold out your hand to me, I'm still going to fall, but it will be for *nothing*.'

There wasn't a moment to lose, I had to act. Quickly I lay on the flat of my belly, on the wet slab that made our front door step. I reached out my hand to her and she to mine, to fulfil the prophesy, and braced myself for the fall. Only that isn't what happened.

I held out my hand and she held out hers, but she didn't miss it or fall, she grabbed on to it, hard. The shock of that, the sudden force, nearly cost me my hold on the ledge. She was holding on tight, and she was starting to climb.

Now I was the one struggling, I was the one going to fall. We were practically head to head and she was moving slowly but determinedly upwards. The realisation, too late, the betrayal, hit me hard. Not only had Ellen decided not to die but she was going to kill me. Did she mean to kill me? Take my identity next? Had that been her plan all along? It all flashed through my mind, the smothering of her sister, the not helping Jaen when she was so close, she could have helped her. Was she in league with the Cailleach?

For the first time in my life I was truly afraid. She had used my loyalty to gain the advantage and in another moment I'd have nothing left to hold on to. It was raining now and I could see the sharp rocks and thick trees of the forest below rising up to me. I was going to die. How could that be? How had Honor not known this? How could she let this happen? And where was she? Were they all with the Cailleach, was that it?

But Honor did know and the next thing I felt was someone grabbing my legs before something whooshed and fell past me. It was Ellen falling to her death and Honor, holding me tight. Between Honor and Mae they pulled me back on the ledge. I sat there shaking, battered and sore.

'What the fuck just happened?' I said finally, gasping for air.

'We're sorry,' Honor shrugged, 'we had to do it, it was hell though.' She lay down dramatically, holding her chest, her pale face turned to the mizzly rain.

'Tell me,' I demanded.

Mae had been staring down the ravine but now she sat, heavily, pale beside us.

'The dark register, we think it had taken her over, think it happened a long time ago.'

'But what did she mean to do, kill me? Why?'

'In league with the Cailleach most likely, a deal for continued immortality perhaps, she wants the girls back.'

'And you *knew,* you saw. How could my own sister, my twin, do this to me?'

'I know, I didn't like it either, but she was dangerous. I couldn't just confront her, I had to let her think she'd fooled us, let her think we believed her plan, and her motives.'

'So much for her promise to Dara and making things right. So how...?'

'She hadn't banked on my powers being stronger, that I would know her mind. Or on my will to end the quest either.'

'Took you long enough to get here,' I said sulkily.

'I had to wait until all the elements of her death vision had been met. If I'd stepped in too soon she'd have known I was on to her. If we'd survived that we'd have had to find another way to stop the girls from coming back too soon. As it was, one of you had to walk with her, hold out your hand and all of that. I've learned how to hide my mind but if you'd known she'd have known, she'd have seen it.'

'You cold creature,' I said, impressed. 'Still, big chance to take.'

'I know,' said Honor, tipping her shoulder to mine, 'but I knew you'd be fine. You'll outlive all of us.'

'Okay, is that just a line or an actual prophecy? No, wait. Don't tell me. I've had enough. For the rest of today at least let's not think about the future or the quest.'

Honor jumped up and pulled me up. I turned to Mae and held out my hand. She looked tired and no wonder.

'Mae, what do you say? Tea?'

'Something stronger I think.'

'Good idea.'

And so that was the end of Dana, or Ellen as she'd been to us. The next day Mae reported the accident, her sister had lost her footing she said, had slipped and fallen into the ravine. The guards came and a search was organised but they wouldn't find anything. It was suggested, not for the first time, that we fence the perimeter. We agreed, we just didn't do it. After all, the ledge had done more to help us than most people had. It was deterrent and protection, even weapon when we needed it.

...

And this was why the girls didn't hear Ellen had died. They had been dreaming so much of home lately, but it stopped now for a while. And besides, there was no funeral.

The Cailleach was furious with them all. She needed Dara here, needed a clear ally. But that had been seen to with Ellen's death. Damn that Ellen to eternal damnation. Curse and damn these mortal women, their ways, and her need of them. So Honor was plotting against her, that was in the open now. The time had come to deal with her finally.

Chapter 23

The Stranger

Journal of Honor Cleary - 1994

I had stepped into the shadowy space between Caer and Dara, but the light of hope still burned in me. I knew I would pay a price, it just wouldn't stop me. I had one desire and one desire only, freedom. Even if once won that freedom could never be mine.

There were no lengths I wouldn't go to, and the price when it did come was high. The more I read the books the harder it was to see. I brought them into the light, and when that didn't work, I brought them into the dark. And I doubled my work load. Erin and Mae took charge of everything else. This was my life now and it suited me. Besides, I had to be ready when Dara came back. I didn't tell Erin or Mae I was going blind. How much time had I left, I wondered? A year? Less? Would it be enough? It had to be.

A knock on the door brought me back. Looking up from the books I winced in surprise and pain of stiffness. Rubbing my neck and shoulders I called for Erin, but no answer came. Slowly I made my way to the door. I was always doing this, getting myself in a set. Even when I felt myself in pain I wouldn't take time to change my position, as if part of me liked it. Work took me away from my life, the pain at least said I still had one.

I'm not sure what I expected to find when I opened the door, but it wasn't him. Someone in need, seeking a cure or a charm, someone in trouble, or bringing news of trouble. Any number of things it might have been, but not the stranger who stood before me. The attraction was instant, and the suspicion.

'Yes? What is it you need?'

'What I need? Why, nothing. I'm just... a new neighbour, making a social call.'

When I didn't respond he went on, and held out his hand to me. 'Dealan is my name.'

I looked at the long slender hand, and I knew if I took it in mine I would somehow be changed, and everything would be different. I reached for it. I let those long cool fingers close around mine, and then he pulled me, ever so lightly but powerfully closer, and we stood like that, our eyes locked, each one trying to read the other. He was cold to the touch, and his eyes, clear as they were, betrayed nothing. I couldn't read him, but to my pleasure I saw he couldn't read me either. And I smiled, pleased. And he smiled, I think for the same reason.

'I'm a writer,' he said. 'I just moved in to the old cottage up on the brae.'

'I see,' I said coolly. 'You're not superstitious then?'

'You mean, because of the Cailleach?'

He was still holding my hand, still too close, still watching me.

'I've heard the stories but no, I don't mind. I'm... Scottish, we have plenty of ghosts ourselves. I kind of like that it will keep people away, though I hope, not all people.'

I took my hand back. 'No doubt you've heard of us too then.'

'The Cleary sisters? Oh yes, famous in these parts.'

He was sorely mistaken if he thought he could charm me, but he was a beautiful creature and I enjoyed looking at him. Was enjoying our play too.

'I'll leave you alone, but if you ever find you have need of anything...'

'Thank you, but I'd say that's unlikely.'

'Never say never. It's been a pleasure to meet you, Honor, truly.'

He had started to leave, which I suddenly, badly, did not want him to. I didn't want to go back inside, back to the work and the monotony of my life. I wanted to say to him, 'stay.' And so, stepping out of the house I said, 'What are you writing?'

He came back. Only this time we were both on the ledge with its treacherous drop. He placed his hand on my waist, to protect or to harm me I didn't know, but it was an oddly familiar thing to do to someone you'd just met, especially when that someone was me.

The rain still fell and the wind still blew like it always did, but no one had ever touched me like this before, with such effect. I didn't know what to think, but I felt more alive than I'd ever felt.

'It's a book about ancient wisdoms,' he said.

What was his game, I wondered, why had he come here? Had he meant to throw me off? Did he still? I didn't really think he meant to kill me, not today at least, but perhaps I was being naive, or was under a spell. Because he was here for me, of that I had no doubt. I searched his face, and then I saw. I knew what he was, and he saw that I knew. He drew his hand back.

'Dangerous drop here,' he said, unperturbed.

'Yes, but I'm not afraid.'

'But I'm afraid for you, especially now.'

'Why now?'

'With all this unexpected rain.'

'Don't they have rain like this in Scotland?'

He shook his head slowly.

'HONOR...' It was Erin calling from inside. 'Why is the door open?'

'I'll be seeing you soon, Honor.'

'I look forward to it.'

He nodded. 'And I.'

'Who were you talking to?'

The spell broken I came inside, closed and then leaned on the door.

'Who was here?'

'He said his name was Dealan.'

'Dealan who?'

'I didn't catch a surname... he's a writer.'

'Well? What did he want? And why are you standing here with that strange look on your face, you're soaked.'

'He's rented the cottage up on the brae,' I said shivering.

'What? Seriously?' She couldn't believe it. No one had lived there for a hundred years easy, how was it possible? And without any work going on. If there had been we'd know.

'Well that's just great, as if we didn't have enough on our plates. Something is bound to happen him and then we'll get blamed.'

'I think this one can take care of himself.'

'Oh really, how is that now?'

'Just a feeling.'

She frowned. 'You haven't said what he wanted? Honor?'

'Just to introduce himself, see if we needed any help, or work doing around the place.'

'Well that's new, he must not have heard about us yet. What's his story do you think?'

'I don't know, just... different I think.'

'Different indeed, until he needs our help and then he'll bleed like the rest of them.'

I made the excuse of my wet things and left my twin still giving out. I wanted to be alone with my thoughts. With the memory of those eyes and the touch of that hand, the long fingers in mine, on my waist. And to ponder the danger. The sweet, sweet danger. Impatiently I pulled off my wet things, put a match to the fire, and curled up beside it. How often in my almost fifty years had I sat here, dreaming always of the day I'd take the road. Now I found myself thinking of other, unexpected things. Of a cottage on our mountain, and a man. No ordinary man, but one of the fae, an otherworld stranger. And he'd come here, in flesh and blood, just for me. Not only that but he knew me, we had met before. Though not like this.

It had to be the work of the Cailleach. So this was good, very good. I must be close to the truth. She sent him to keep me busy, no doubt. Distract me, make me fall in love? Hah. And yet, here I was, thinking of him, feeling things I hadn't felt in a long time, or ever felt perhaps. Was her plan already working? And where did he fit into it all? Did he have any say or thoughts his own? Or was he just a lap dog for the Cailleach?

For some reason I didn't think so, I felt he had agency, his own power, but then why had he come? Because he could? Because it would be easy? I bristled. We'd see about that. Not one to be fearful I could say this event had inspired me. But I knew too it was not something to be taken lightly. I had more to do, more to think of than just myself. The Cailleach meant to take me out one way or another. And I thought, *She thinks she knows me, she doesn't know me.*

Chapter 24

Erin

Erin had never loved a man. To her was entrusted the land, the people, the house, and her sisters. Her love was cast wide. Death was a part of it, the losses while difficult could be borne. But the premature and violent deaths, the personal losses, they were different. For a healer they were catastrophic. Her mother Jaen, her sister Caer, Seán, the babies, her babies. Three in all, two miscarriages, and one stillbirth. Mae had said it was because they were boys, though they only knew that for sure about the one she'd carried five months, Aodhan, and Aaron, the one she'd carried nine.

It might have been true, as midwife she'd seen it herself, the women who could only carry one or the other. Or it might have been the curse, they didn't know. And what difference now anyway? She would have liked to be a mother. When Caer died and the children came to live with them first, it was just after she'd lost Aaran. There had been no sign, no warning. He'd been alive that morning, she'd felt his kicks, his strength, he'd been ready to be born. But something went wrong during the birth, and he didn't make it. Having her nieces around, in some ways it helped, in others it made the pain harder.

Sometimes late at night when despair came upon her, she would start to think it was something else, no mystery or quirk of nature, no otherworld geís but a punishment. For things she'd done, the things that haunted her. She was a healer, a protector. A creature, not of fire or air like her sisters, but of the earth, and that is to suffer.

She saw and felt things that they in their passions simply didn't. And she had found other, less visible perhaps, but very necessary ways in which to help things, and survive.

In this game of life there were still some certainties, these were what she clung to. Like her love for the house and her sisters. And when the weight of things became too much she would retreat into her house and work, and when that wasn't enough there were men. Just because she didn't love or want to marry them didn't mean she didn't want to be with them.

Her easy beauty, natural sensuality and intoxicating scent drew people to her. What the scent was or where it came from no one knew. An otherworld gift perhaps, or pleasant side effect of her work with natural plants and herbs, though that might have been too simplistic. Along with her earthly charms there was something else different about her, a potency of the feral.

Erin was the kind of woman people told dark secrets to. They knew she wouldn't be shocked, or judge them. And she inhabited her body like no one else, assumed you would too. Because of this, affairs of the flesh were easy for her.

Men, women, no one could resist her, and she'd always had her choice of lovers. It was never serious, that was not for her. It was they who always wanted more than she could ever give them. They wanted her. Her power. To possess her, reduce her, and they wanted her to need them. But she was not part of the world that had made them like that, and it was never going to happen.

Pleasure, fairness, kindness, was that not enough? For years now, she'd had only one lover, the detective, Shane Cogan. He'd been in love with her since the first day they'd met, the day he came to question her and the aunts, and to search the house after Seán's disappearance. She'd never stayed with one man this long but it was easy with him because he wasn't like the others. He was strong in himself and he loved her just as she was. It had been years before he'd got the courage to ask her out, now he wanted to marry her he said. She'd laughed at that.

'Just when I think you understand me you start this talk of marrying.'

'I love you Erin... I want to be with you always, take care of you.'

'We wouldn't need marriage for that, and anyway, I can take care of myself.'

'Just because you can doesn't mean you have to.'

'I like to, it's worked for the past fifty years.'

She pulled away from him. Why did they all have to do this? Why did he have to do this?

'You know this is a lot for me, Shane. Time was I'd have left you for saying that, god knows I've killed men for less.'

He laughed, he'd become used to her dramatic turn of phrase.

'It's okay, don't stress about it. I never expected to find this kind of happiness. You know, I'm happier than I've ever been and I believe you are too. If I have to settle for that I will, and count us lucky. I just can't promise I won't ask you again.'

It was true what he said. They were happy. It wasn't right of her to push him away, to deny what they had was special. So marriage wasn't for her, but he was. If only she'd learned it in time. If only she'd known what would happen.

Chapter 25

Drew – October 1995

Each morning Dúlta helped his brother with the farm before driving to work. He'd only been in the job a few days when he'd met Drew Cleary in the graveyard. Since then he couldn't get her out of his mind. Had their meeting been the start of something or was it was only on his side? He'd never felt like this. Was it normal after seeing someone only once, he wondered? Like love at first sight or something? *God, listen to yourself lad.*

Arriving in the sleepy town he parked the car and crossed the main street to the shop. It was quiet as usual, a few workmen and staff, a few parents after the morning school run.

The female staff looked forward to his coming in, it was a nice change to have some new blood in town, someone good looking too. Dúlta, oblivious to the attention, gathered his things and crossed back to the library. He was thinking how before that fateful day he'd

215

listened to Joe wax lyrical about the Cleary family, their long running and strange history, their charms, cures, and healing powers. The terrible things people said about them, the disappearances, even murder mystery, that surrounded them. It all sounded mad, and he'd wondered if Joe had had something with one of the women, the way he talked about her it seemed likely. What had been her name again? Caer. Died young enough. What had happened to her?

He'd teased him about it once, meant it good naturedly. 'I'm thinking you must have had something with this Caer Cleary?' He cringed now, remembering the awkwardness that followed. Joe hadn't taken the tease very well. Normally easy going and laid back, he'd gone quiet, his face had flushed, and even his hands trembled. Not wanting to embarrass either of them any further, Dúlta pretended absorption in a sheaf of papers. He supposed Joe at least fancied this woman, possibly more than that, and maybe didn't like to remember, or for people to know. After all, he'd said himself, they weren't just that accepted in town, and in small places that meant something.

He'd been busy with something else when Joe finally said, 'We were friends, Caer and I, just friends. Well, more truthfully Seán Mannion and I were friends. We all went to school together. I always liked her, but she only had eyes for Seán.'

Seán, Seán Mannion, where had he heard that name before?

'Seán is the one who disappeared. Everyone knows that story. They never found him.'

'What do you think happened to him?'

'Ask anyone hereabouts, they'll say she killed him.'

'And you don't think...'

'God no, she was crazy about him, and heartbroken after. I spent a lot of time with her then. You should have seen her in those days, beautiful she was. She was troubled, that didn't make her a murderer.'

Dúlta didn't want to probe further but he vowed to look into it just as soon as he got a minute to himself. All that was forgotten when Drew walked in. She'd hitched a lift into town with the post woman who was far from keen but didn't feel she could refuse. It had been a tense ride for Bridget, though Drew seemed normal and friendly enough. But you never knew, did you? Drew hopped out on Main Street, thanked Bridget, and headed straight for the library. Bridget had sighed with relief and then laughed at herself for being so superstitious. *Comes to us all*, she thought.

Drew surveyed the quiet street with its neat rows of houses, a sharp contrast to the wilderness that surrounded it. It used to be a busy market town, but that was before her time. As far as Drew could tell the only fast moving thing now was the river that flowed from the mountain.

She'd come today because Devin had asked her. Since Mae's funeral Devin had been trying to figure how best to broach the subject of the library talks Joe had proposed, but after seeing Erin's reaction in the graveyard it wasn't easy to get up the courage. And as both she and Erin were always so busy, always on some mission or working in the garden, stillroom, or with a patient, it was hard for her to get away herself.

Meanwhile, she, Drew, could have walked right into the Cailleach's cave and not one of her aunts or sisters would have noticed, and maybe not even the Cailleach herself. They were all too wrapped up in Dara or their work to see anything she did, and that was fine by her. Since her arrival all she'd done was explore the mountain, go swimming, write in her journal, sleep, and dream. She loved wild nature, and had felt her connection grow stronger, day on day since coming here.

Devin had told Drew that even though Erin was keeping her busy she hadn't forgotten the proposed library talk or given up her dream of a more peaceful existence between town and *Bean Feasa*. Drew didn't know why she felt that way, or how she thought this would help, but each to their own. She was happy to do it.

Before coming back she'd fancied herself as being one of those Clearys who were more, what was that expression? Of the people. Like Devin, Erin, and Mae. But the more time she spent here the more she knew it wasn't true.

From the magpie at her window that first night to the wolf in the street, and other things, all trying to reach her somehow, make her see, but what? And every night now she had the same dream. She was outside the church, and there was music playing, beautiful music that drew her inside. But when she went in she saw the people transfixed and obviously frightened. And the priest, a very young, fair, and handsome priest, and a dark-haired young woman, standing in the middle aisle. The woman was Caer Cleary, her mother. And the priest was Seán Mannion.

Every night the dream ended with Caer pulling away, and Seán trying to stop her. He'd shout for someone to bolt the door, which they did, every night. But every night the doors blew open so you could see clear across town to the mountain. And then the church filled up with crows, turning everything to black, and Caer was gone.

Lately she'd been trying with some success to get closer to them. And she tried to add her voice to the others. Calling for the doors to be closed, and to be kept closed. Helping them do it. And then, calling her mother. But though she formed the words, no sound came.

Increasingly, she found that she could move around within the dream, so that she was circling the pair, among the crowd, by the door, or above them, but she was still voiceless. That was until two nights ago, when she heard herself say, 'Mammy.'

No one else seemed to hear but she knew it had worked, she had spoken in the dream. A word she hadn't spoken in a lifetime and had no memory of speaking. All the next day she felt sad and depleted. This vision of the past, of her mother and Seán, what was its purpose? Why did she have to visit the past? She didn't want to. But what was going on that night? And what happened next? She had to find out. She knew it was important.

She thought about telling her sisters, but how could she tell Dara she'd been seeing her father and their mother every night. She wasn't sure how she'd take it, but not well seemed reasonable. No, she'd tell her when she'd figured it out better herself. When she could, hopefully, answer the inevitable questions. She thought about telling Devin too, but she felt it would devastate her, being so opposite to her hopes and dreams. She wanted peace, but this was a great plunging into the darkest depths of their history, and their power. Besides, she wasn't sure she was ready to tell, or that they were ready to hear, that their little sister wasn't just a rebel without a cause, and a seer. She was a shapeshifter. And a powerful one at that.

She was beginning to wonder where she fit with the family, or if she fit at all. And she couldn't deny a growing feeling that she was closer to the Cailleach than to any sister or aunt. Should that have felt wrong? Because it didn't. How could she tell them that?

For now, she would bide her time. She would trust, no matter how lonely, the forces growing inside. She would let everything come and go, she would not resist anything. The others were far too distracted to notice. They saw only her brightness, depended on it perhaps. And that was how it should be. She wasn't lonely, really. She had fallen for the mountain. She was happy. The landscape her companion.

Entering the library she saw Dúlta coming towards her. To her surprise she felt butterflies. This was a new and welcome distraction.

He rushed up so quickly he almost collided with her, again. *Invasion of personal space*, he thought, *not the best start.*

'Drew, hi, you came.' He remembered hearing or reading somewhere that staring for six seconds or longer at someone meant you either wanted to sleep with or murder them. No prizes for guessing which, he thought.

Drew spoke first. 'I came for Devin, I mean, she asked me to come.'

'Oh?'

'To hear more of what you and Joe have in mind for the talk?'

'Oh sure, great, let's sit down.'

For the next hour Dúlta and Drew talked of a different world. A new series, going to be very interesting. All about local communities and how to make them better, keep them alive for future generations. It was right up Devin's alley, Drew thought. Joe had said the Clearys had a lot to offer and the talk could cover any number of things from herbal remedies, *Bean Feasa*, the oral tradition, as well as growing your own food. Drew said Devin would stick with growing for now, best practice in wild places, for the best results kind of thing.

'Do you think people will come?' she'd asked him.

'Why wouldn't they?'

'There's not many people growing their own food these days and well, it's us.'

'Why would that matter?'

'I don't know. I'm new here, in a way. But in another way, I've always been here.'

'I'm new too,' said Dúlta. 'So maybe it's a crowd we'll have, curiosity might prove a draw.'

'Curious… yes, but from a distance.'

He was intrigued. And he was totally charming she thought, charming and fun. It felt good to be with him.

'So how is next Thursday for you guys?'

'To give the talk?'

She looked a bit disconcerted, he thought.

'Too soon?'

She was surprised to feel uneasy, especially considering the extent and depth of what she was dealing with in her personal life. Out in the world or on the mountain, she could be herself. But here? Here she would forever be a Cleary, and whatever that meant in the town. Forever marked by the past, labelled and defined, by people, many of whom didn't know who they were themselves. And who wouldn't have the courage if they did. That was what Devin was about with these talks, being true to herself, working to write a new story. It would be a difficult path, and different to hers, but it was important too, she saw that now. But she, Drew, she wasn't from here, and didn't want their stories. She didn't even feel herself to be a Cleary. And maybe none of them were.

'I'll ask her when she thinks is best and get back to you,' she said. It was time to go.

'Great. And I was wondering, if maybe we could go for a drink sometime?'

Her heart said yes but her mind had already left and was grappling for something, for the sap in the trees, the gleam of water, and something dark, for the mountain, and the aunts' words came unbidden, *Don't get too close to the people, don't fall in love, and don't get involved in the town.*

'Yes,' she heard herself say, 'sometime.'

That night Dúlta dreamed of her green eyes that wandered away from him, to places he couldn't follow, but wanted to. Drew dreamed too. First she dreamed she was in Devin's room, and they weren't alone. There was a presence, one of ill-omen. Drew came around by Devin's head, and seeing she was deep in sleep and seemed unharmed, she rounded on the spirit fiercely, and ordered it away.

The adrenaline rush was so great she had woken violently, ready to pounce, and thinking it happening in real time she raced to Devin's side. But finding her sister slept peacefully she went back to bed. And it wasn't long before she was dreaming again. This time she was back in the church, back with Seán and her mother. This time she got close enough to see their faces. And this time she said Caer, not Mammy, not Mother. And Caer heard her.

Chapter 26

Honor and Dealan – October 1994

On through the long darkening nights Honor worked, and dreamed no more of freedom, but of Dealan. Sometimes she dreamed of disappearing, though that may have been the same thing. It troubled her, but she'd given up trying to help it. Besides, she still worked for that freedom. Still wanted it. She was sometimes lonely, and often times filled with despair, so to think of him was pleasant fiction, nothing more.

It wouldn't keep her from what she must do. Remind her of her life un-lived perhaps, but so what, she'd made her choices. The end must be coming soon and her legacy would be that she had helped free them all. Their time with the quest, hers and Erin's, was coming to an end. They were still strong but winter was bearing down on them.

Outside her window the night seemed to whisper her name. It was late and she was tired. She'd been reading the same words again and again and she imagined it was him calling. Such fancy, she thought. Such foolishness. Meanwhile, the clock ticked, meanwhile, the fire crackled and shone. And the night came down, black and restless as her heart.

She hadn't seen him since that day when he called to her door, but she'd felt his shadowy presence, menacing, arousing too. Living life as she did, she was alert as any wild creature, to every change in the atmosphere, and she quickly got used to the darkening, pleasurable feeling, when he was around. Erin had heard the talk. A stranger, living up there, in that old place, a hippie, an artist. Strange fellow, quiet. Kept to himself. And she'd seen the change in her sister. A different kind of restlessness, a new longing, and a new peace. But she didn't put these things together.

Honor went to the window, opened it wide as was her habit, whenever the walls closed in. And leaning out into the pitch black she listened. The night was rich and ticking with life that nourished and maddened her. But there it was! Her name again, clearer now. She left the house. Now the wind sang a different tune, turn back, it seemed to say, before it's too late. But she wouldn't. She was the haunter now, the hunter, like the moon above her. And this was her terrain.

The old cottage looked two breaths from being claimed by the landscape. Only someone who was out here day and night could have found it in the first place. It had started to rain and it slanted down, warm and sultry. She wanted to knock on the door, and she knew in a moment she would. The mystery of Dealan, her attraction to him was a powerful force she hadn't known possible. Something had happened between them that day they first met, and it had changed her, had changed everything.

Taking the last few steps to the door she could hear her own heart beating and she knocked, softly at first and then as the rain came down, harder. The step and lintel and at least half the walls were of the black stone, and covered in moss. The local stone from the river bed was ever wet and no good for building, but it was all the people could get here years ago. There was no sense of being lived in at all about the place, and no answer, but the door creaked open just enough to show a faint sliver of light within.

'Dealan, are you there?'

She watched her own hand, white and glowing against the time sodden house, reach out and push the door in. And stepping in after, she waited for her eyes to adjust, for her heart to stop racing, to see him again. If she could just see him, she thought. It was colder inside than out. The only lights were a low burning fire and the pale moonlight that spilled over the floor, and stopped where she stood.

But she was not alone, and a movement at her shoulder as the door snapped shut behind her, revealed him at last.

'You came,' he said. 'Why did you come?'

'You called me.'

'Did I? I suppose I did, I'm sorry.'

'I wanted to come.'

Outside the rain poured down, it ricocheted off the windows and the tin roof, while inside a silence grew.

Her voice broke it finally. 'Should I go?'

'Yes,' he said, coming to stand before her, 'but don't.'

He looked at her, with eyes clear and blue, and deep as a mountain spring. That didn't deny what lay between them. And she led him to the fire that was burning brighter now. With every passing second she felt more aware of the shifting tension, the danger that seemed, not to come from him, but to surround them. And the shadows of the room were like the branches of a dark wood they'd traversed, and now stood in the centre of. A wave of heat crashed through her, fierce and crimson, consuming as fire. He was not human, but he was more real, more vital to her now, than anything in the world.

She raised her hand to touch his face. He grabbed it and held it tight in his.

'You would never hurt me.'

'Don't you see, that's why I've stayed away. Why I'm trying to resist you now.'

'Don't resist me.'

'But the darkness.'

'The darkness and I are old friends.'

His arms closed tight around her as they kissed, with wolf-like intensity. She could feel herself growing in passion and power, then dissolving inside the fierceness of their desire. Soon there was no more thinking, no quest, no curse, no family. He was her and she was him. She never wanted to return. They each had something the other needed, like a part of themselves they had lost and hungered for a long time. Some essential, awful, necessary part. And they'd found it at last.

She woke early to sunlight glittering in green stained windows and doors, and her first thought was that he hadn't spirited her away. But was that not what the fairy folk did? She sighed with a transcendent joy that eased her disappointment. How often had she dreamed of disappearing? Now she had, if only for one night. It had been a long time since she'd been with any man, and it had never been like this.

'Good morning,' said Dealan. 'Did you sleep?'

'Like a cat. Your place looks different in the morning light.'

'It looks better with you,' he said, pulling her to him again.

It was the most alive she had ever felt, being with him. He made breakfast of foraged foods and the clearest coldest spring water. And by late morning they still lay entwined in his bed. She was thinking how awful it was, to have go back.

'How do you spend your days?' he asked.

'It's a full time job to run the farm, the house, and then there's the healing work.'

'I see. You, your sisters, and aunts.'

'Yes. I don't have children, or a partner. That never interested me. My sister and nieces, they're my family. And I never knew my father. Saw him once, with my mother, when I was very young. At a dance. No one said it was him, I just knew.'

'You didn't find that strange?'

'Who finds strange what they know? My mother, she's been dead a long time. Her name was Jaen Cleary. The Cailleach killed her. Of course, you know this.'

'I'm sorry,' was all he said.

'It's not your fault.'

'Do you ever think of leaving?'

'Leaving,' she sighed, staring off to the distance. From here you could see clear for miles, you could imagine Dublin, the port, ships at sea, and all the places beyond.

'I think about leaving all the time. What about you? What do you do all day?'

'Writing, walking the mountain. And I think about you.'

'I see, and you don't find *that* strange? A young man, here, in this place, in this damp, crumbling cottage, you don't find that lonely? The townsfolk are calling you a hippie you know?'

'I don't know this feeling, loneliness, and I'm not so young. Is the cottage damp?'

She laughed. She didn't mind what he was, in many ways it was more right for her, but it was getting late and sadly time for her to leave.

'I have to see you again,' he said.

'When?'

'Tomorrow.'

'I can't tomorrow, I have, things I have to do.'

'Must you?'

'Yes, it's important.'

'Soon then, that's if you want to see me?'

She hesitated.

'I do want to see you,' she said. She wasn't about to tell him how much, how even with the life or death work she had to do, that he had come to prevent her from doing, she didn't want to leave him now, she had to. They made a plan to meet again two days hence.

She paused in the doorway, looked back to him.

'Why didn't you take me away?'

'Because you're not ready to go.'

It was what she had needed to hear. He wanted to take her away, was supposed to, but he hadn't. She wanted that too, but he was right, she wasn't ready, it wasn't time for her to leave yet. And now all that was known and not spoken between them, mattered less. He was trying to do the right thing. If anyone met her in this moment and saw her like this, all lit up and smiling, what would they have thought? Touch has a memory, and she'd had to stop as the tremor surged through her, wave after wave, had to cry out. And she wondered afterwards if she had closed her eyes, or even fainted? If that was when it had happened? Or had distraction caused her to get lost somehow? Or was it what the old people said? That she'd stepped on a stray sod? She'd heard about such things often enough, but they happened to other people, not to her, not on her mountain, and not this close to the house.

She'd walked into a field she knew, had known since a child, had passed through countless times, even on moonless nights. But when she got to the place where the gap should be, there was no gap. She made her way back in the direction she'd come, but that gap had gone too. Shocked and angry she walked the perimeter, but it was no use. There was no way in, and there was no way out. Was this the work of the Cailleach, or was it, could it be him? Did they have some grisly plan for her?

By now Erin would be worried, would be lured away from the house into danger, to search for her. She was livid at the thought, at her stupidity. To have trusted him. It was one thing to take a chance herself, but to put the family in danger. This was what the Cailleach really knew, she thought, the way to get to her.

In passion of rage she picked up a stick and attacked the ditch. She'd retraced her steps so many times and had got in such a state she no longer had any idea what part of the field she was in. She didn't care either. She hit and kicked and cursed it before finally giving in. Think, Honor, think, what do you know? She remembered then that with stray sod stories the enchantment didn't last, so this would have to pass too.

It was raining again. Rain was real, was a friend. So she stood, arms outstretched like a tree, her face turned to the endless sky, letting the water rush over her, and turned her thoughts to Erin. Erin was always her calm place, she thought, her port in a storm, her best friend, her only friend. But as much as she tried it was Dealan she saw. And her tears mingled with the rain, as she turned from warm to cold, again.

Honor didn't see the enchantment end, one minute she was under its spell and the next, as was the way with a stray sod, all was back to normal. She could see the gap plainly, wide open and flanked in sweet woodbine. Wiping her eyes she walked towards it and through it, poised for attack. But all was quiet with the strange world. She arrived home just in time to explain somehow to Erin, who was not pleased. This was all she needed, she said, for Honor, of all people, to get tangled up with a man. She would never have thought her capable of such irresponsible behaviour. But no sooner had she said it than they had both laughed. The idea of Erin to think this way was too ridiculous for either of them. Erin apologised for attempting to keep Honor in a box of work, and duty. After all he was only a man, where was the harm.

If she'd known then the truth of what he was, that might have been different, but Honor didn't tell her. And if she had remembered that not all people thought in the easy way she did about love, that might have been different also. But Honor was strong, stronger than even she knew.

She was furious with Dealan, and with herself. The stray sod incident had shaken her. This was what came of taking someone into your world instead of staying independent. She felt hurt, betrayed, suspicious of someone she had feelings for, strong feelings she wasn't sure she wanted. She didn't go to see him two days later as they'd planned. To stay away, it was harder than she hoped. But she had to take back control. She vowed never to see him again.

Chapter 27

Going to Town

It was one of those mornings when country life takes its blood price. When it's been raining too long and the cold has crept into your soul. You can't remember the last time you saw sun, or blue skies, or felt heat in your bones. From air to clay, the world is dark, depressed, frozen. And you, like a creature caught, are forced to stay in the monotonous stream, the din and steam, of a house.

'I'm going to town,' announced Dara.

The pronouncement, welcome and unexpected, was met with silence at first.

'I'll come with you,' said Honor.

Dara nodded, pleased. She was going with the sole intention of seeing her old adversary Una McGovern and setting wheels in motion for the anniversary day. It would help her mission to have Honor by her side. Erin, standing by the range, slowly stirring a large pot and humming, stole a look at her sister. *Don't worry, I've got this,*

Honor's eyes said, at least she hoped that was what they said.

'I'll come too,' said Devin moving quickly, before anyone might suggest otherwise.

'Me too.' Drew followed her.

'Great,' said Honor.

There was a hectic quality to her lately, a glow that seemed almost feverish. Erin didn't know if it was some kind of sickness, or just the thrill of moments like this, the power surge of being with the nieces. And now Dara taking action. Enough to make up for not having the man? Honor hadn't said what happened but it seemed she had given him up. Erin was glad. She felt bad about it, but they needed her now.

Today Honor would walk through the streets of town with her nieces, three sisters by her side. She would feel herself grow, in stature, in courage, in purpose. It had been a long time since she, and Erin too had felt this.

'I wish I could have gone with them,' Erin mused, to the now quiet house. But she was grateful too, to just be at home, and not have to deal with or care for anyone. That was freedom, was it not? To live life as you wanted to live it. The problem was no one person could be truly free when those around them weren't.

...

It had taken some wrangling to get the old car moving but they worked it eventually. Then the sisters had waited while Honor pulled a long black coat around her thin shoulders, and a wide brim hat down to her cheekbones. All that was visible now was the red hair streaked with silver, that lay in folds down her back, and her eyes, should she raise them. A while later, as they walked up the main street, she was taken aback at the girls' easy aura and confidence, while she herself was hiding. Had been hiding a long time she realised. All these years they'd thought Caer had been the one to run. But they had run too. Not in the physical sense, perhaps. But somewhere along the way they'd become smaller, less than what they were. Especially her.

It wasn't entirely her fault. She'd had to build her armour for the life here. One had to think of protection. While Erin dealt in comfort, house, and garden, to the growing and tending of things, she, Honor, cultivated detachment, coldness, solitude. She had never fully known this until now. How life here would shrink her.

Sleep descends where nothing changes, she thought. A waking sleep that doesn't lend itself to living free. First Dealan, then Mae's death and the return of the girls had stirred her, and now she was feeling it deeply, the loss of youth and life and all that might have been. And she found herself wondering if she'd ever get it back again. Not the years, the years were gone. It was herself she wanted, and lightness.

As they strode into the shop that dark grey morning the people whispered and stared. Aileen Boyle was standing, eyes wide, mouth open.

'Aileen,' said Honor.

Aileen snapped her mouth shut. She was older than Honor Cleary and she wasn't afraid of her... not really. But how did she look so good? Sure the face was thinner, and showing signs of a life in the wind and rain. But the bones and the eyes were sharper, and the look was just the same.

She, on the other hand, had sunk into middle age. As her own mother would say, she was letting the water in. That was the way of it here, everything happened sooner, marriage, children, old age, and everyone's favourite, death.

She followed Honor, her desire for news greater than envy or fear.

Through the shop the women scattered, spreading tension and interest. It was a lift from the grey at least. Dara started filling a trolley with an array of seemingly random things. Almonds, kilner jars, notebooks, elastic bands. Devin was reading gardening magazines, no harm to see how things were developing in Ireland she thought, though most of these were English titles. She'd buy a few, for inspirational purposes, though she'd want to hide them from Erin. She'd only say they knew everything they needed to know already, and she'd have more than a point. After all, there was no better farm, or garden, in the country. They grew all their own vegetables, herbs, and fruit, as well as keeping chickens, a few horses and cows. They even made their own wine. She didn't want to upset her aunt. Hurriedly she selected a few, sticking them under her coat before making her way to the fish counter. Erin had said to bring something fresh, but what to go for, trout? Salmon? Had they almonds, she wondered? She found herself suddenly longing for the house.

Honor was choosing wine. To bolster their stocks.

'Take a drink, do you, Honor?' said Aileen.

Honor ignored her.

'We don't see much of you in town anymore? The girls are back anyway? Shocking weather we're having. This cold, and so many power cuts.'

Dara passing, filled her basket with candles, matches, firelighters, batteries. She had just taken wine glasses from the shelf when around the aisle came Una, and the two came face to face for the first time in ten years.

Seeing Una was a shock, and for a moment she was a young girl again, the day they'd lured her to the Cailleach's cave. At the memory the glasses went to pieces in her hands, a fact she barely seemed to notice. Una froze. Then the lights in the store started flickering. The shock of coming face to face with Dara was bad enough without all this. A store manager came racing over.

'It's those women,' someone hissed, as Aileen Boyle rushed from the shop, wailing and blessing herself. Memories of her own dealings with Caer Cleary haunted her mind.

'Are you okay, Una? And you, Dara? Your hands are bleeding, we'd better get you some help.'

Drew and then Honor came and stood by her side. Their presence soothed and emboldened her. But what she needed to say to Una she needed to say alone.

'Go ahead,' she told them. 'I'll join you in a minute.'

The women walked away slowly, made their way to the check-out. Looking back they could see Dara talking to Una. About the anniversary no doubt. Honor sighed. It was a worry, she was a worry. The lights had stopped flickering and Devin was waiting for them.

'Where did Drew go?' remarked Honor. 'She was here a moment ago.'

'She's over there, talking to that lad from the library.'

'Oh! Right, well let's go before things get any worse.'

'Home?' asked Devin hopefully.

'How about a drink first?' said Drew rejoining them. 'Hot whiskies?'

'I could do with a drink,' agreed Dara, back with them again and plucking glass from her hand.

'But your hands,' Devin protested.

Dara held up her hands, marked in blood but free of glass now.

'These hands of mine have never been better,' she said.

The staff didn't know what to think but it was the strangest checkout they'd ever experienced.

Una had known it would be only a matter of time before she came face to face with Dara again. She'd known it, but that didn't make it any easier to see her after all these years, especially knowing what lay ahead. There were times she said she wouldn't do it, she wouldn't go back there, they couldn't make her go. But there was also a part of her that just wanted to get it over with. It had been hanging over her for ten years, a shadow over every happiness. In the early years she'd thought it all nonsense, but the dreams now told her otherwise. Terrible dreams, about that day and maybe the day that was coming. It was real, all right, and like a lot of things in life the only way was through. At least she wasn't the only one. John and the others, they shared the same fate. It had created a kind of bond between them, not that they ever spoke of it.

Looking back, she was ashamed of what she, what they had done. The way they'd bullied and lured Dara like that, what were they thinking? Talk about playing with fire. They should have known better. At least it would be over soon. A few more months and that would be the end of it she thought, one way or another. Surely no one would get hurt or killed this time? They just had to do what she told them.

After work she went home, lifted the telephone.

'John?'

'Yes.'

'It's Una.'

There was a pause.

'I met Dara Cleary today. The plans have changed.'

'Oh?'

A new meeting place for the anniversary.

Chapter 28

Hot Whiskey – November 1995

Dúlta had gone ahead to the pub as Drew suggested. He ordered a hot whiskey and sat up at the bar rubbing his hands against the chill winter air and nodding to the other customers, two old men, who nodded back before going on with their conversation.

'Such a place for a house.'

'Aye.'

'Who in their right mind woulda built a house there, even without the old Cailleach breathing down their neck.'

'To be sure.'

'Think of winter, that high.'

'A shocking wild spot.'

'That's how they know every whit of weather that's coming down on us, though some says it's them that sends it.'

'But look-it now, you don't believe that?'

'I do. I do believe it, mad as it sounds. And another thing. That land should be worthless, pure daub. Nothin' will grow past Con's, except Cleary land. Best land in the country. Holds winter longer than the rest of the country mind, but summer too.'

'Aye, tis great land. However they do it.'

'I'll tell ya how...'

'Have either of you been there?' Dúlta interrupted.

'No lad, no. Seen it from the road many's the time, when I was a gossun like you. Never had reason to call on them, thanks be to god.' The old man blessed himself. 'People only goes there if they need help they can't get from the doctor or priest.'

'So people do go to the house? For cures?'

'Oh sure, sure, but they'll rarely admit it. It's not easy to go on any account, and then there's a savage drop right at the door. Fall there and you'll never be seen or heard of again. Not a dram of shelter about the place either, only cold that'll cut to the bone. You'll not go knockin' for nothing, not if you've the sense God gave ya.'

'Sure isn't that what I'm trying to tell ya, *Bean Feasa* be damned, them women is witches.'

Of course it was in that moment the door swung open and in walked the witches themselves, bringing the shelterless cold and rain with them. The old men, dumbstruck, stared at first, but as the women came nearer feigned greater interest in their pints. Dúlta smiled to see Drew, happy she'd come. And now he'd meet some of the others again. He didn't know what to think with all he was hearing about these women, not that it made much difference to him.

'What can I get you ladies?' asked the proprietor.

Hot whiskies ordered, the women relaxed, enjoying the vibe between Dúlta and Drew. The attraction there was undeniable. Honor wanted to ask Dara about what passed between her and Una in the shop. She wanted to, but of course, she didn't.

Looking about her, she noted the pub was shabby and worn but it was warm at least, and the change of scene was welcome. She hadn't been here in years and the decor hadn't changed much since the seventies. Twenty odd years, had it really been that long? A few more people had come in and were lining the bar. There was plenty of whispering and sidelong glances. The bar woman turned up the volume on the jukebox, and shushed the ones getting loud.

'Another one,' said Drew getting up.

'I don't think so,' Honor said, 'we should be getting back.'

'Why?'

'It's getting dark.'

'And?'

'All right, I suppose I can still get us home on two drinks.'

'Honor, you could get us home blindfolded.'

Honor sat back, drained her glass. Why shouldn't they stay? They had as much right as anyone. The door had opened again. Travellers. Probably the only people the town was more against than the Clearys.

Reluctantly the bar woman served them. 'Just the one,' she cautioned.

Honor frowned at the injustice.

Drew was still at the bar waiting for drinks when one of the girls spoke to her.

'Pretty, aren't you?'

'Thank you,' said Drew. 'So are you.'

The girl smiled. 'Your sisters too, and your Mam is it?'

'Thanks. She's my aunt.'

'But you're the least pretty one, aren't you?'

'I'm sure you're right.'

Drew ignored her, but the girl wasn't finished yet.

'Shame you're all going to die.'

Drew turned back to her now. 'What did you say?'

'I said shame you're all going to die.'

'Everyone dies.'

'Yes, but some sooner than others.'

'Where's this coming from? Why are you saying this?'

The girl went to leave but Drew grabbed her arm. She tried to free herself, to lash out, but found she couldn't. Drew's grip was too strong. In a moment her people were by her side, while Honor, Dara, and Devin, were by Drew's.

'What's this about?' asked Honor.

'This one here says we're all going to die soon, the family. I just want her to tell what she means by that.'

The girl's friends were poised to attack but Drew warned, 'One more move and I break her arm.'

The girl, Kate was her name, winced in pain and fury. Everyone else was so shocked by the scene they just stared open mouthed.

'Well?' commanded Honor, standing up to the girl, searching her face. 'Have you the sight, is that it?'

The girl shook her head.

'No, I didn't think so. So a curse then? A joke? Or a mistake?' She narrowed her eyes at the girl. 'Which is it?'

Kate didn't answer, only struggled and scowled at them.

'Listen girl, we mean you no harm but I have to warn you, there are worse things than broken bones, so mind your words.'

'I didn't mean anything by it, just trying to take miss high and mighty down a bit.'

'That went well, didn't it,' said Drew, letting her go.

The girl glowered at her, red faced and nursing her arm, before leaving.

'Jesus, Drew. Where did that strength come from?'

She shrugged. 'Damned if I know.'

The door opened again and a woman's voice called out, 'I'm looking for the *Bean Feasa*,' to no one in particular.

Honor and the girls turned to face her.

The old woman walked towards them.

'Honor,' she said, 'long time no see.'

'Yes,' smiled Honor, 'too long, Sally.'

The two women moved away from the others and chatted a while like old friends before embracing and parting again. Meanwhile the bar woman approached the girls and Dúlta.

'Listen girls, I have no problem with you being here but there's shocking things being said at the bar, they're drunk and rowdy and I don't like how it's looking. If they get out of hand I'll put them out. I'm just letting ye know, watch your backs.'

'What are they saying?'

'Talking about that lad that was killed, on the mountain that day.'

'We're going anyway,' said Devin, 'just waiting for our aunt, and here she is, thanks.'

The girls were waiting for an explanation from Honor, but 'old friends,' was all they got. It was time to go. As they were leaving there was a rush of applause and insults hurled at their backs.

'Murderin' witches.'

'Good riddance.'

Drew and Honor pretended not to hear, but Dara was furious, and Devin felt it heavier now, the oppression of the place. Not for the first time today she thought she'd be glad to get home. And she felt even more discouraged in her mission for peace between them all.

Waiting for the young couple to say their goodbyes Honor mused on Drew's sudden change, the strength that seemed to come from nowhere. Her whole demeanour had been so fierce and out of character. She would have to speak to Erin about this.

'This takes me back,' she said, nodding towards the young couple.

'Oh yes?' They loved to hear stories of their mother and the aunts when they were young, and so seldom did.

'To days spent waiting for your mother.'

'She took a long time to say goodbye too, did she?' asked Dara.

'To your dad, oh yes, she could never say goodbye to him. It caused a lot of trouble.' She sighed.

Back at home Erin was waiting to hear all the news. She'd been stretched out by the fire with a good book and a big glass of wine and she poured one for Honor now, too.

'You went to the pub!!! Jesus Christ, why?'

'Why not?' Honor shrugged.

'Because WE don't go there. Trouble that's all it is, trouble. But okay, what happened?'

'What makes you think anything happened?'

'You can't fool me, Honor Cleary.'

'All right.' She kicked her shoes off and curled up beside her sister. 'I was going to tell you anyway. It's Drew.'

'Drew?' That was the last thing she expected. 'What about Drew?'

'She's a dark one. Possibly more so than Dara.'

'Jesus. You're sure?'

'Yes.' Honor drained her wine.

'Like you.'

'No, not like me, I'm afraid.'

'Jesus Christ.'

'We'll just have to make the best of it.'

'We have to be careful,' said Erin, 'that's what we have to be.'

'Can't we do both? Another glass?'

'Yes.'

'Good, cause there's more to tell. I was talking with old Sally tonight.'

'Tell me.'

Honor, shuddering, poured the wine.

'You okay?'

'Yes, someone dancing on my grave is all. Being back there, the people, it hasn't changed.'

'Let me guess, evil witches, killers?'

'Close enough.'

'Well you're home now, where you belong,' she emphasised teasingly.

'So tell me, what did Sally say?'

'She said the girl threatening Drew was only part wrong.'

'Oh?'

'Death coming. A lot of death, and a split in the family. And Drew already knows.'

Chapter 29

A Murder

Journal of Caer Cleary - August 1960

In just a few days Seán would return. I'd had time to think things over and for the first time in a long time felt a sort of happiness again. I supposed it was naive of me, with all I'd learned, but I couldn't help it. The aunts had been right, I was in love with him. And I didn't hear the car until it pulled in. And Jack Mannion offered me a lift.

'No, thank you, Mr Mannion, I'll be grand.' He'd pulled in so tight the verge between car and ditch were virtually non-existent. When I tried to walk on, he grabbed my hand.

'Hold on there now lassie, oh such cold hands,' he said.

'You're my son's, friend, aren't you? Caer, strange name that.'

I tried to pull my hand back but the bastard tightened his grip, all the time smiling, confident of his position, and watching me, his swarthy face glistening with sweat.

'Oh. You're very pretty aren't you, and all grown up too. I have to give Seán credit for something eh? I'm sure I can give you my blessing, you know his mother doesn't.'

I snapped at him, 'Can I have my hand back, Mr Mannion?'

'Oh sure, sure girl.' He let it go but at the same time, got out of the car.

'Tell me now, have you and Seán been together yet? Of course you have, healthy youngsters such as yourselves. How would you like to be with a real man for a change, instead of a boy, eh?'

The niceties dispensed with, I knew that once I moved he was going to make his.

We couldn't have been in a worse place. The chances of another car coming along was unlikely. He was big enough, and fairly strong. He might catch me, if I stayed on the road. The forest was my best chance. I knew the forest at least, he didn't. It would give me the advantage, and places to hide.

I was fast, and I didn't panic. I made a bid for the ditch, almost cleared it too. But in that moment he was faster. Caught me by the ankle. I kicked as hard as I could, my fingers clawing for purchase on the other side.

'That's it,' he panted, and 'good girl,' making me want to vomit. He laughed breathlessly as he half lifted, half shoved me over into the field, before roughly straddling my body with his legs so even my arms were pinned by my side.

And then I was scared, for a minute. He slapped me, hard, across the face. The staccato sound rang out across my mountain, and along with it, the fear. With fire in my brain, the rumble of storm clouds overhead, and the warm sweet earth, damp and humming beneath me, I knew it would be my last vulnerable moment for a long, long time.

'Now, let's see what you can do for me,' he panted.

The fear and stress that had left with the slap had been replaced by a new sense of calm and control. Even as he pulled at my clothes I felt nothing but pure raw adrenaline coursing my veins. The burning in my hands, an irritation I'd always known, now intensified like never before, making me claw the ground, which only seemed to charge them all the more. And then I heard myself speak, in a voice, and language unknown to me.

'What did you say?' He stopped suddenly.

'Let me up and I'll show you instead.'

'You'll do just fine as you are,' he grunted.

'If that's what you want, but you could at least kiss me?' I opened my mouth and arched towards him, as much as I could with his dead weight bearing down.

His breath was laboured as he bent to kiss me with his stinking mouth. He released my arms, which I promptly wrapped tightly around him.

Across the lonely bog, a low rising scream rang out in the gloaming, a man's scream. It was Jack Mannion in my embrace. He couldn't see but it felt as if something had scalded his back. I laughed and rose to my feet as he cowered in pain.

'My back, it's burning,' he cried.

I shrugged. 'Ants?'

I saw that he looked at me differently now, what was it he saw? No longer the girl he had seen in the lane? Someone vulnerable, he'd thought, and that meant for the taking? Fuck him. But what was it had changed me? And what part had he played in that change? Was I older now? And not so pleasing to his gaze? Or was it my eyes? And the stories being told there? It was something he hadn't reckoned on, for he swallowed slow, his sagging mouth a quiver. His own eyes, wide with blood and terror, darted about, like an animal in a trap. He was lost.

'We, we should be getting back.'

'I thought you wanted to play?'

'Look here girl, I didn't mean anything by it. You shouldn't be out here on your own.'

'So it's my fault.'

'I didn't say that, don't be twisting my words.' He was looking frantically for the ditch, thinking he'd had enough of this bitch. Thinking he'd get me again, another time, show me what was what.

'I don't think so, Jack.'

'I didn't mean any harm.'

'This is no place to be alone. Follow me.' I started to move away. He didn't want to follow but he didn't have much choice.

'Come on, Jack, that's it, good boy.'

'I can't see you,' he cried.

'Just follow my voice... just a little farther... just a little more.'

That night I slept better, deeper, than I had for a long time, and I dreamed. I dreamed of rain and mist and the rocks of the earth. I dreamed I was the Cailleach.

...

Dawn the next day, two lone figures were abroad on the mountain. There was the car all right, but it was just as she'd said, there was no sign of him.

'Bastard,' said Erin. 'Wouldn't you love to have happened along.'

'I'd say she handled him well enough on her own,' said Mae.

By the time Caer arrived home from her ordeal the family were sick with worry. They might not have been normally only she'd been so troubled of late. Now here she was, soaking wet, dirty, clothes torn, walking over the grass like she hadn't a care in the world. Walked right passed them, humming quietly to herself. The aunts looked at each other then back to her.

'Caer?'

'Yes?'

'Where are your shoes?' asked Mae.

Caer looked at her feet and went on humming.

'Well don't just stand there, come in, come in, where have you been? What's happened?'

'Jack Mannion,' she said at last.

'Seán's father?'

'Yes.'

'What about him? Did he hurt you?'

'He would have.'

'Would have?'

'He's dead. I killed him. I think I'll have a bath now.' She padded past them, headed for the stairwell.

They'd need to work out what to do, thought Erin, it would only be a matter of time before the car was found, the body too.

'You don't doubt it then?' Caer said back over her shoulder.

'Oh, we'd never doubt you,' said Ellen.

'Good. And don't worry, they'll never find him.'

'How so?'

'I buried him deep.'

...

'There'll be hell to pay if this gets out. We'll be suspected, but they won't prove anything. Even if they did, what's to prove? A known violent man, a drunk, chases and attacks a young girl then disappears.'

'Ah, but not any young girl, is it?'

'No, but who'll miss him anyway? Not his wife.'

'It will never get that far. More pressing is that we know Caer couldn't have done this until recently, it's the change. It's happened so soon.'

'How will Seán take it, I wonder?'

'She'll hardly tell him.'

'I suppose not.'

'We'd better be getting back before someone else comes along.'

By the time they got back to the house Jack Mannion's car had been found and the search to find him was on. All day the sounds of men and dogs could be heard on the mountain. But it turned out as Caer said, they never did find him. His long suffering wife, Mary, was free of him at last, and secretly grateful for whatever had happened to him.

Chapter 30

Revelations

Joe hadn't been to the house in over twenty years. Not since those last days with Caer, when Dara was a baby, before she'd left with Marius. It had killed him when she'd left. He didn't think anyone knew that. To Caer he'd been a friend, nothing more. But to him she'd been everything. Too late, he knew it.

Bolstered by his evening's mission he took a deep breath and began the steep ascent. From here there was no sign of life to the place at all, not even a light in a window to guide you. Good thing he'd thought of a torch. Reaching the top he was met with the crumbling ledge over the forest on one side, and a weather worn door, with a knocker shaped like a hand on the other. He was saved from having to touch it by Dara herself, who opened the door without warning.

'Ah, Dara,' Joe said, relieved. She wasn't a friendly face exactly, but he felt something like fatherly towards these girls. And that gave him strength, a sense of greater purpose.

'It was you I wanted to see. I won't keep you, and I won't beat around the bush. Dara, this is difficult, and possibly unwelcome, but as someone who considers himself a family friend,' he cleared his throat, 'certainly a supporter at least, I've come to ask that you call off the anniversary plans.'

There, he'd got it said.

'Won't you come in, Joe?'

She didn't seem surprised to see him, or to hear what he'd had to say. He followed her down a long winding passage of shadows, eerily quiet and dark. But up ahead the soft orange glow of the kitchen was a welcome sight in the general gloom.

'Of course, I'm not claiming to know what went on, only those who were there can know for sure. You could tell me, I might be able to help. You want people to know that you weren't responsible, don't you? So you can all get on with your lives. You, and the town kids who were there that day too.'

'I don't care about those people, Joe. And besides, how do you know I wasn't responsible? Everyone else says I was.'

'But you weren't. That's what I believe, anyhow.'

Dara smiled at his loyalty.

'You loved my mother, Joe.' It wasn't a question. 'Why didn't you ask her to stay? To choose you, instead of Marius.'

He stared at her, shocked into silence. This was the last thing he'd expected.

She went on before he could even try to answer. 'Maybe you didn't know, at the time. Do you know what killed her?'

'Yes,' he said softly, 'a car accident, may she rest in peace.'

'No, it was this place that killed her. She had tried to free us, free herself. She couldn't do it. The conflict was too great.'

'Free you? From what? What conflict?'

'From the curse.'

He took the glass she offered and sank into a comfortable armchair. He'd known this was part of their ancient lore but hadn't realised it was still relevant today. He didn't think Caer had ever mentioned it.

Dara continued, her face half in darkness, half bathed in firelight, her voice calm and low. 'She didn't want me to have the same fate, but I do, I do.'

'What fate is that?'

'It's a game, you see. I have no choice but to listen and the mountain has ways with me. I have power, only it's not all mine, not all from the family. These powers have been growing with each generation, growing, changing. If I can find a way, then perhaps...' she trailed off.

'You can be free of the curse?' offered Joe.

'Kill the Cailleach.'

'That sounds very dangerous. Are you sure that's the answer? What about the others?'

'What others?'

'Your family, and the townspeople.'

'Oh, them. There are still things I need to work out.'

'I see.' Joe looked at his glass, wondered what he was drinking.

'Leaving here wasn't the only rule my mother broke, you know.'

'Oh?'

'She let it in, the dark. Embraced it, loved it too.'

'But you won't? Family first and all of that.' He was watching her, she had the strangest look on her face.

'You know Joe, rest in peace is a phrase I don't favour much. People like my mother don't rest in peace.'

'Yes, I don't suppose anyone does, if they weren't ready. If they went before their time.'

He could have sworn he saw someone in the corner of the room watching them. 'I suppose there are ghosts here, Dara?'

'Only people, and memories.'

'I see. What of your sisters and aunts? Where do they fit in to all this?'

'They would say it's my quest of revenge I'm about.'

'And it's not?'

'At first it was all I cared about, but being back here has changed me in ways I hadn't expected. I'm closer to the soul of this place than I knew. I watch the landscape and it watches me. Sometimes I feel as if I am the landscape. That makes things more difficult.

'I had a dream a few weeks ago. There was a tree root growing in my head. It was gnarled and wet, growing inwards, twisting its way through my body. I tried to break a few pieces of root embedded right here, in my forehead, and it hurt so bad, I couldn't break any piece of it. I realised the tree was not dead but sleeping. And it was this place, and it was me.'

'Haunted.'

'Yes, I am a haunted house, more haunted than these walls could ever be.'

'And what of the anniversary, what will you do?'

'I will try to find the answers, to solve the quest, and I must go ahead with the anniversary plans.'

He was about to protest but she stopped him.

'Don't you see, Joe? There's no choice here, the wheels are already in motion. The anniversary of the incident may be the opportunity I've been looking for.'

'For what?'

'To invoke my powers, to find out how I kill a monster without becoming one myself.'

'So the Cailleach, she will come?'

'Oh yes, she must.'

'But, what will happen? What of the danger? You have to tell someone, get help.'

Dara shook her head and stood to show that it was time for him to leave.

'All right, what can I do to help?'

'Nothing, I'm afraid, but thank you for coming. I have to walk this path alone. Come, I'll see you out.'

Honor's heart was beating so hard she was sure they must hear it. It would be terrible if Dara discovered her now. Good fortune it was that the shadows were always so active here. So Dara was not only deep in the quest but had come to such understanding. It was all Honor had hoped for, more.

All this time she'd let them think she'd been busy with plans for revenge on the town folk and avoiding the quest. But this boded very well indeed. A surge of love and then just as suddenly fear for her niece gripped her. She understood what had happened to her mother and felt the same struggle herself. But she was resisting, and they were close, so close to a resolution. As always, the shadows ran the gamut of feeling with her, and she was grateful for them.

'She has come far,' they seemed to whisper. 'She is strong, powerful, she can make it, she can break the curse.'

'She can make it,' said Honor. But now something else had revealed itself. Why hadn't she seen it before. Joe and Caer. And Joe was Devin's father! It seemed so obvious now. It would have hastened her leaving, perhaps? They'd never know now.

Back home, Joe poured himself a whiskey and going to his library took down the book. The book was a collection of stories from the area that had been passed down over centuries by word of mouth. Here the Clearys had been written about for the first time. Written by him. It was different this time because this time he knew it was real. Dara's words and all he'd learned played over again in his head. If only he'd known then what he knew now, if only she could have told him more, told him anything, he might have been able to save them. But it was a different world then, people didn't talk, didn't speak of these things the way he and Dara had done tonight. It was good that had changed, that times had changed, but maybe, not enough.

He'd been in love with her. How did Dara know that? He'd barely known himself. Or had he just been afraid? They'd spent that short time together, after Seán disappeared. Before Marius came on the scene and stole her away. But that wasn't fair. They'd grown closer, even slept together that one time. He could have tried harder, could have fought for her. He wished he had. Instead, he'd let her go.

Chapter 31

Parting is Such Sweet Sorrow – 1960

Late summer, when everything is sweet and heavy, and apt to rot. Seán had left his mother's house to tell Caer he was going to Maynooth to study for the priesthood. What he hadn't banked on was that she had news too. She told him hers first. She wasn't going to college after all, she said. She was staying here. It was just like his mother had said.

'It will never be over between us,' he said.

'It would be better for us if it was.'

He was going off to college, to a life, and she to the quest. It was for the best she thought, especially now. If he knew what had happened with his dad, well it wasn't as if she could tell him. Since the aunts had revealed the extent of her duty they'd been waiting and watching her every move.

'Days are getting short,' Mae had said.

'Not yet,' she'd told her aunt.

'I know,' Mae stroked her hair, 'but soon.'

Mae understood she needed time, to say goodbye to all she'd hoped for her life.

She didn't know yet how to handle the quest, what she was supposed to do exactly? The books, that was all Mae had said, would be her starting point. She'd been finding it harder to resist or even pass them by. Just yesterday she'd run her fingertips along their brittle spines again. They seemed to come alive under her touch. She told them the same thing she'd told Mae, 'Not yet.'

'Then when?' the shadows seemed to ask her.

'Summer's end.'

'Caer? Caer are you listening to me? You're miles away.'

'Sorry, Seán! You have tears in your eyes? Why? It's not like you're going off to war.' *Like I am,* she thought. 'You'll be home weekends, it's me should be lonesome. I'm the one being left behind, not swanning off to Dublin to live the high life. Oh, I'm sorry, is this about your dad?'

'Hardly. At least with him gone I won't have to worry about Mum. Though there's always the chance he could come back, I suppose. Between you and me I'm hoping he won't. I still can't believe you're not leaving here. Might you change your mind?'

'Maybe, but I suppose this is where I belong.'

He groaned, he hated when she said things like that. 'Caer, I have something to tell you, too.'

'You found another girl?'

'Ya right, it's about college.'

'What about it? You're going, aren't you?'

'Yes, but, not to Dublin.'

'Then where?'

Seán swallowed and said the word she already knew was coming, 'Maynooth.' He was saying more but she couldn't listen. Sickened, she rose and walked away from him.

He should have let her go, but instead he followed her. 'Caer, wait. Caer, let me explain, will you?'

'Explain what, Seán? That you've decided to give your life for something your mother wants?'

'That's not fair, slow down, will you? For god's sake, Caer. I'm only going to college, it doesn't mean I'm going to be a priest! But I can hardly ask you to wait for me, can I? That wouldn't be fair, or right.'

'What is wrong with you? The Seán I knew, have known all my life, is not more sure of the priesthood than he is of *me*, of *us*.'

'That's true, and I'm not, but you're not even going to college now, you're staying here. That wasn't our plan. Maybe it's you isn't sure about us.'

'It's not that, it's just, I have things I have to do now.'

'What things? What's been going on with you, and don't tell me it's nothing.'

'All right, it's not nothing, but I can't tell you, I'm sorry. The thought of you going to college, moving on with your life while I stay here, that was bad enough, but now this.'

He had caught up to her finally.

'Caer, you look like a wild thing.' He leaned in to kiss her.

'Seán, are you serious? No, and we can't stop here.'

'Just for a minute.'

'No, not even for a minute, besides I don't want to kiss you. We have to go, *now.*'

They had come very close to the Cailleach's cave, closer than most would dare, even the women themselves.

'The Cailleach's cave, the mouth to the underworld. I've never been here before,' Seán said with interest. 'Maybe we should take a closer look, after all, I'm safe with you, right?'

'Maybe,' she replied, folding her arms. 'Maybe not.' What the hell had she been thinking, leading him here, coming this way herself. And how typical, the way they'd fallen back into their old and easy ways, as if nothing had changed between them.

The temperature had dropped, and nothing stirred, no sound. Only a mist that seemed to rise from the ground caused her to shiver. So like that night they went swimming. Too late she realised it.

'Seán, wait, don't go any closer, I mean it.'

She started to walk back down the way they'd just climbed. It was steep and slippery with wet stones and moss. She was hoping he'd quit fooling around and follow her like he had last time.

'You would leave me here,' he called, 'in a fairy mist? At the mercy of the Cailleach? I don't believe it.'

'Ssssh,' she hissed, 'don't joke about things you don't understand.'

'Okay, wait, I can't even see you now.'

An eerie cry rang out through the forest, ancient and menacing. She scanned the ghostly silhouettes, the trees, black and gnarled against the pale grey mist, and shivered.

'Seán,' she called, 'are you okay?' Before at the river had been a warning but this was the real thing, was what the aunts had meant. And she herself had led him here. What had she done?

'Hold on, Seán, I'm coming.'

Mae's words came back to her. *'You're putting him in very real danger, Caer, you don't want that, do you?'* She would never.

'Ah, you came back for me,' he said playfully.

She sighed with relief. He was fine.

'I should have left you here.' She took hold of his hand, tried to pull him away, but he wouldn't budge.

'Seán?'

'You don't belong to any of this.' He gestured towards the gaping black hole, still visible through the mist.

'All right, anything you say, so long as we leave here now.'

'I mean it, Caer. You and I, we belong together.'

This time it was her who gave pause. 'After all you said?'

'Yes.'

'What do you want from me, Seán? To wait for you, is that it?'

'Caer, I... it's complicated. My mother...'

She rolled her eyes and walked on, pulling him as she went.

'Don't say any more, Seán, I shouldn't even be trying to stop you.'

'Are you, though? Trying to stop me?'

'No, you should definitely go.' *If you stay here you'll hate me,* she thought sadly.

'Then come with me.' He had stopped walking again.

'What? You're serious?'

'Never been more serious.'

'That's impossible.'

'Why? Why is that impossible?'

'They'd never allow it.'

'Then we won't tell them. We can just leave here, and never come back. I don't have to go to college. We could live and work in Dublin, decide what we want to do, just the two of us, be free of all this.'

It was the most perfect, most wonderful idea she'd ever heard. It was everything she wanted, and it filled her with such pain, and unbearable sadness. For put to her now, by the person she loved most in this world, she knew her answer was no.

Chapter 32

Journal of Caer Cleary – August 1960

I knew that Seán meant what he said now. Despite everything he'd said earlier, spoon fed him by Mary no doubt, still he was prepared to throw it away for love.

He had delivered those lines with little more than a flushed face, devoid of any visible feeling or emotion. And I had let him, though it angered me, though I wanted to scream and shout at him. I had let him say all those things because I knew, I had to let him go. His excuses, the mask he'd been wearing, would just make it easier for me to do. But here he was now, the real Seán, and I didn't know if it was love or the effect of being this close to the otherworld, but here, of all places, he was being real and honest with me, and I wanted to do the same.

Even though it was hopeless I wanted to have this moment, and I heard myself say, 'You really love me then.'

'Yes, I love you, always have, always will, and you love me too.'

'Yes,' I said. I did love him, but it was too late. I had long taken winter into myself and the Cailleach was with us. We stood, suspended in the moment, our hands joined, like a bridge between two worlds. It burned, but we held on tight. My duality was our only chance now.

'Whatever happens, don't let go of my hand.'

He nodded slowly, as if in a trance, and we ran. We ran over the mountainside, we hurtled through trees, branches tearing our clothes and our bodies, we leaped over streams, and we little knew what we were running from.

At last we could run no more. The landscape seemed to close in on us. All around the woods cast out sounds, enough to strike terror in the strongest of hearts. I knew the mountain, but knowing it and being hunted on it were very different things. And we were being hunted, slowly, stealthily, by one who was sure of her prey. I felt my own blood course in my veins, my senses heighten, and with every step I grew more afraid, as the Cailleach came closer and closer. Would we get caught in a trap next as Aunt Jaen had? Would she bring a tree down on our heads? Or had she other plans. Anger gave strength, every step fear and relief. We walked on. I know this place, I said to the darkness, I am this place. These woods will never harm me. I was ready to fight for his life, for mine too. I was a dark one, bound to the Cailleach and the Cailleach to me, but I would take him safely off this mountain tonight, or my name wasn't Caer Cleary.

'Feeling brave, Caer?' the Cailleach whispered, but I was. For we had reached our tree. And we fell against it in a wild, delirious joy. We were as good as home! I could see the lights, not only of town but of the house. And I felt great joy, to be back in that world. So when he kissed me I responded passionately, our hearts pounding together like drums.

'Brave and fair is your boy, but how brave I wonder?'

'Jealous, are you?' I taunted.

'Be careful my pretty, very careful, you belong to me remember, only to me.'

'Yes, only to you,' I lied, drunk in my power. I belonged to myself.

By now our passion was too great to be contained, and my flesh burned enough to consume us both.

'And you to me,' I cried, as we fell to the ground, exploded beneath the stars.

As we lay together for the first time, under the arms of the whitethorn, we slept a while.

I spoke to her again. 'You know you have nothing to fear with me. And he's leaving, he's going away.'

'Yes, he is,' she replied.

Something, a bird, swooped too close to the earth, and passing again caught my hair. I tried to free it, but it screeched and pecked me viciously. Seán, startled awake, tried to help, and in that moment a dog leapt at him from the shadows, red eyed and snarling. Then just as suddenly as they had appeared the creatures vanished again and the Cailleach appeared in their place. She strode towards us and gripped my face with her long bony fingers.

'You know the truth of things and what you are. Remember it was you brought him. It was you did this, and you'll do it again. I'll leave you alone, for now. Enjoy your time together, what's left of it.'

With that she was gone. Only then did I feel the pain. I ran to where Seán lay bleeding, fearing the worst, but he was breathing. Quickly I did the cure to stem the flow of blood, and wondered how long it would be before we'd be found. I couldn't leave him, but if someone didn't come soon, the cold might carry us both off.

The Cailleach didn't want me to die, she needed me. Lying close to Seán, feeling how cold he was, caressing him, seeing the marks on his poor face, I thought of our friendship. He had always been there for me, was it so wrong he had wanted to leave here? Was it his fault that I couldn't leave? I thought too of what the Cailleach had said. That I had done this, and would do it again.

'Hold on, Seán, hold on,' I whispered. I summoned my aunts and sisters.

...

Honor and Erin gathered blankets and medicines. 'We'd better let the aunts know.'

'We know,' said Mae, appearing in the doorway. She was dressed and ready, a hammock in her arms. 'Ellen says we're going to need something to carry him.'

'Erin, call Joe, if he's as badly injured as I think he is it will be hell to get him back here.'

The party of four headed out as soon as Joe arrived. No strangers to bloodshed they were still shocked at the sight of Caer and Seán stretched out, bloodied and torn on the ground. They lost no time checking for injuries and getting them warm.

'Bitemarks,' said Erin.

'Bitemarks!' repeated Joe, shocked.

'He's very weak, let's get him into this hammock, gently now.'

Joe couldn't believe what he was seeing. He'd been surprised to get the call and had wanted to bring more help but Erin had been most firm on that one. No one else must know, she'd said. They had simply gotten lost on the mountain, been chased by a wild dog, and been injured in a fall. She was banking on Joe being loyal to Caer and Seán.

Joe and Erin lifted Seán onto the hammock.

'It's going to be a rough ride,' said Mae.

Mae linked Caer, half lifting her to her feet. 'Everyone ready?'

They all nodded. Honor, Mae and Caer led the way slowly with Seán, Erin and Joe behind. They were just coming up to a clearing when they saw the pair of bright eyes in the trees again.

'What the hell is that?' said Joe. Could this night get any stranger?

They all stared and then Honor motioned for them to be still, before walking towards the animal, who licked her outstretched hand. She was saying something they couldn't hear. They watched, stunned, as a large white dog that looked more like a wolf, though there hadn't been wolves in Ireland for hundreds of years, stepped into the light. Honor knelt beside the creature, touched, then kissed his blood stained face, tenderly. She watched as he walked away, stopping just once to look back at her. 'He won't bother us again,' said Honor, still watching the space where he'd stood.

Back at *Sliabh Earrach* Joe rang Seán's mother to say he was with him, while Mae tended Caer.

'I told her it was dangerous to be with him now,' Ellen complained.

'I suppose she couldn't help it,' said Honor.

'Is that a vision or an opinion?' Ellen asked her.

'A little of both perhaps, though maybe you're one we should ask, it was you knew Seán would need to be carried.'

'Good point,' said Mae with interest.

Ellen bristled. 'That's not the point at all. The point is she's supposed to be focused on the quest now. Only the quest. And you, Honor, have your powers extended to something new?'

'What do you mean?'

'I mean, are you in communion with the otherworld now, or just a dog charmer?'

'I think we all know that was no dog,' replied Honor, and then more brightly, 'I don't know, Aunt, I can't explain it, I just felt a connection. I knew he would listen to me. I suppose my powers, too, are growing stronger.'

Mae was watching her closely. 'Be careful there, dear. You know how it is if you get too close to these things, and then where will your sister be?'

'You don't have to worry about me, Mae. The family, my sisters, our freedom from the curse is what matters most to me on this earth. Nothing could ever change that.'

'Indeed, I do know that about you. I wonder now,' said Mae, 'if Caer feels the same.'

...

Mae went to check on Caer early. The room was empty, the bed cold. She expected she was with Seán but no, she was in the library. And so engrossed in the books that lay scattered about her, she barely looked up at first. Mae watched as her niece met her gaze and then picked up a new book and wrote the words, *Book of Caer*.

'I'll have to go back, try to remember what's already happened.'

'That's good, dear, you do that.'

'But from where should I start?'

'Start at the beginning, start from first you knew.'

Meanwhile, on the other side of the house, Erin was sitting with Seán, who had yet to wake up. She'd been caring for his physical wounds but not feeling overly disposed towards him.

'It's your fault,' she hissed. 'Your own stupid fault that you're like this, and my sister is injured. You could have gotten her killed. Shame you weren't killed yourself. Love,' she sneered. 'If she fails the quest it will be on you.' Looking at him closely, the fine features all peaceful now, she thought how she could hasten a separation by seducing him herself. But would he take her up on it? Probably not, she thought furiously, wringing the cloth and then tossing it back in the bowl. For all her charms, she'd never seen two people look at each other like Seán and Caer did, and besides, Caer might not forgive her, quest or no quest.

Just then Honor rushed in all flushed and lit up.

'What is it?' Erin said.

'It's Caer, she's in the library, Mae found her. She's reading the books.'

'What did it finally, do you think?'

'Oh, time, and him of course.' Honor nodded towards Seán.

'Him, why him?'

'You know, the aunts told her his life would be in danger if she stayed with him, because she loves him and the Cailleach would never allow it. Now she's seen it for herself and not only that but...' Honor looked at the sleeping lad and moving closer to Erin she whispered, 'Because of Caer he's come in touch with the otherworld, you know that makes him a mortal enemy of the Cailleach.'

'And?'

'And I don't understand it fully either but she's a different person now, and he can't have any part in it. Plus, she has to keep him away from here, as far away as possible.'

'She's giving him up? I can't believe it, never would have thought she'd do that. How strange.'

'Not strange, sister, love.'

Chapter 33

This is Goodbye

It was noon before Seán opened his eyes. He raised his hand to his face, someone had bandaged it.

'It's okay, Seán, you're safe now,' said Honor, who'd been sitting with him for the past hour.

'Caer?'

'She's grand, not a bother, up and about hours ago. I'll go get her.'

Sitting up slowly — he'd a fearful pain in his head — he went over the events of the night. Jesus, he'd been half scared to death. He felt fine now, aside from a few cuts and bruises and the throb in his face where that mad dog had bit him. They'd have to report it, you couldn't have a creature like that roaming wild. How had they gotten back here? Last thing he remembered was being attacked by the dog, he must have passed out. More important though was all that had passed between him and Caer before that. There was no question of Maynooth now. But they'd have to leave, and soon.

The door opened, it was her. He rushed to her side, was she hurt? Was she sure? What the hell was that dog about? He took her hand and led her to the bed, hugging and kissing her, passion he soon saw she didn't return. And looking in her eyes he didn't like what he found.

'Why are you looking like that? What's wrong? What's happened?'

She pulled her hand away. She wasn't about to be cowardly, not now.

'I'm glad you're okay. You'll have a scar I'm afraid, but it will fade in time. When do you leave?'

'I thought I'd go home now, gather my things and come back here...'

'I mean, when do you leave for Maynooth.'

'Maynooth? You know I'm not.... after yesterday, all we talked about, and then, at the whitethorn.'

'Oh that.' She stood up, walked to the window and opening it wide breathed deeply the clear mountain air that said summer was over.

'That? What do you mean, that?' Seán said, coming to stand behind her.

'Oh, come on Seán, you didn't really mean for us to leave here? To run away?'

'Yes I meant it, of course I meant it, and listen Caer, don't get like this with me. I know you and this isn't you, what are you playing at?'

'No, you listen Seán, I'm not playing. It's like you said yourself, we're young, too young to decide things like this, and it's only college, it's nothing, your mother is right.'

'My mother! Since when are you agreeing with her?'

'You might have a vocation.'

He smiled at that despite his rising fear, it sounded so outlandish coming from her mouth.

'Caer,' he said firmly, 'we're meant to be together you and I... we're a family.'

'I can't do that, I can't ever...'

'Okay Caer, look, don't say any more. You're in some strange mood, we don't have to talk about this now. I know you and we already said what we needed to say on the mountain, we left any doubts there too. You can't make me believe anything else because that's the truth.'

'You're wrong, Seán, you don't know me or what I'm capable of, you don't know me at all.'

He wanted to tell her he loved her, remind her that she loved him. He wanted to hold her and not stand like this, like strangers. He wanted to, but he couldn't. Besides, she already knew that. It was as if more than one night and a few hours of sleep had passed between them.

There was something else, something she'd been keeping from him. And he knew, with horrible certainty, that the gulf was about to go deeper.

'There's something I have to tell you, Seán. When you hear it, you're going to feel different about me.'

'I don't believe that anything you tell me is going to make me, or you, feel different than we do.'

'It's about your father...'

'What about him?'

'You'd better sit down.'

A short time later Honor and Erin watched Seán leave *Sliabh Earrach*. The door slammed behind him and he didn't look back.

'Where's he off to in such a hurry?' said Erin.

Caer appeared at their sides.

'That's him gone,' she said.

'What do you mean, gone? You'll see him before he has to leave for college?'

'He's not coming back, ever.'

'What? No way! Why? What happened?'

'I told him.'

'Not about the quest?'

'No, about his dad.'

'And he minded that?' said Honor.

'Of course he *minded,*' she snapped. 'He was still his father, and besides, it's about me too, what I am, what I'm capable of.'

...

Seán didn't know what to think, the shock was immense, or was it? Murder, for fucks sake, his own father, and he'd been going to rape her. He knew that was the truth, anyway. Thought he'd be sick before she got the whole story told. At the end of the day it was much better that she'd killed him than he'd raped her. But how had she? Jesus, he didn't know what to think, he'd seen some things with Caer over the years but this. No, stay calm now, he told himself, everything would be fine. He just had to get away, think, but where? Not home, not to his darling mother, not to the mountain that was for sure, and not back to *Sliabh Earrach*, or Caer.

He stopped and looked back at where the house was just visible through the trees. It pained him to see it. He felt sad, hurt, betrayed. For the first time in his life he was an outsider here. He supposed that was what he'd always been. The physical pain was small by comparison, and whatever they'd given him was wearing off. He hitched into town and rang the guards from the public telephone to report the wild dog. Knowing Caer and the others they'd never report it. He thought of going to the doctor for a tetanus injection but it was too late, he'd go tomorrow. He crossed the street and went for a pint instead.

Caer had been right, he didn't come to the house again and a few days later he was gone. He didn't come home at weekends either, but after a while he did write a few letters. She burned them unread. Finally he got the courage to ring, nothing had changed really he told himself, they were still the same people, weren't they? His heart pounded each time but she was never home, or at least that's what the others said. He had resolved to try one more time.

'Hello.' It was her.

'Caer, it's me, Seán.'

'Hello, Seán.' She sounded tired.

'You're a hard woman to get hold of do you know that?' he said more lightly than he felt.

There was a long pause before she said, 'Seán, go on with your life, forget about me,' and hung up the phone.

Chapter 34

Journal of Dara Cleary – April 1995

Seeing the house, and the aunts, after so many years, there could be no denying the new feeling of power, and yet, old traumas persist. I can't stay here, don't belong here. For who belongs in the past? The dead. The ghosts. Let them have it.

At first, though much was hidden and unknown to us, there was some measure of comfort and peace. But the strongest point of connection for me has come not from the aunts, but the Cailleach.

They were all, the aunts, the Cailleach too, watching me, waiting for me to save them. Filling my mind with their stories, duty, history, family, loyalty, survival. Was this how it had been for my mother? No wonder she'd left. But as much as I'd love to leave here, I know that will not be my answer to the quest. I will finish this, regardless of any connection, whatever the cost.

I decided finally to speak to Honor and I asked her straight, 'Why am I here, Honor? What do you want from me? What is it I'm supposed to do?'

'I thought you'd never ask.'

I listened as Honor stripped away years of silence and mystery, telling me all she knew, the family history, the deal made by the ancestors, how it had turned into a curse that became a quest, how it, and they, had changed in recent generations. She spoke of her parents and my parents, about Dana, Rachel and Dea. It was what she'd longed to do she said, to tell me all this. But it had to come from me first, that was what they'd agreed.

'So now you know everything.'

'Not everything.'

'How do you mean?'

'You haven't told me what happened my father.'

'I don't know what happened to him.' She frowned. 'If I knew I would tell you, especially now.'

'Why now?'

'Because it's your right.'

'But what do you think happened to him?'

'I think she killed him, of course.'

'My mother?'

'What? No! My god, what would make you think such a thing. I meant the Cailleach. You don't, you don't really believe it was your mother, do you?' She was looking at me now as if she'd never seen me before.

'I think it's what she always believed.'

'That she killed him?'

'Yes.'

'I suppose, I can see how she might have felt that way. I'm sorry she, and you, had to live with that. But you'll only be wasting time if you stick with these thoughts of revenge you've been having.'

Ah, the cool Honor I knew and loved had come back.

Looking at my aunt, her eyes, keen and sharp, and deep as the ocean, looked sad and bemused, for she was thinking of how young I was, and didn't yet understand what would happen. She was right, of course, I have many faults, like anger, distrust, and suspicion. I am wise in ways but I still have a lot to learn.

'You think I don't understand you,' she said, 'that I haven't known suffering or loss like you have. But I lost a mother too, and a sister. And all this time you've been out in the world instead of here, tied to the quest, how do you think that was done?'

I shook my head.

'It was me, Dara, I took it on until such time as you could be ready, properly ready that is.'

'But how? I thought it was one sister each generation, that none of the other sisters could... oh.' Honor had done something, had paid some terrible price. I didn't think I wanted to hear it.

'Look at me, Dara. What do you see?'

'I see my cool Aunt Honor, who used to scare us a little when we were children, though not as much as she scared the locals. A great and strange beauty, with a faraway look in her eyes. But it was always her strength we felt, more than anything. And she hasn't changed.'

Honor took up the description. 'Still here, never left this place, in all her fifty years, though she wanted to, more than anything. Fatally restless, but still has hope.

'Freedom is everything, Dara, you have to know that. After all, you don't want to be here either, and it's up to you Dara, it has to be you, you're our last chance. We've pushed things so far now, it can't be sustained. So ask yourself, are you willing to let this go on? Let another generation be destroyed?'

'No, I am not. And you? Would you help me still? Even though it's forbidden?'

'Of course. I can tell you what I've learned, beyond that there's not a lot I can do I'm afraid. It's going to come down to you, and your sisters. And she will know what we're up to. It won't be safe for you.'

'Will it be safe for you?'

'I've already paid for my — deviations. All she can take now is my life, but it doesn't seem to interest her, she knows she can hurt me more just by keeping me here, or hurting some of you.'

'But she can't come in the house?'

'She's not close enough to any one of us for that at the moment, but, she has her ways. She may hear our words, our thoughts, come to us in our dreams, or in animal form, and she can control the elements. It's a thin line between her and us, between in here, and out there. Make no mistake, once I tell you what I know, your life, your sisters too, will be in serious danger. Yours especially.'

'Why is that?'

'Because if she thinks you've turned away from her, perhaps even plan to kill her, she'll be after you.'

'Honor, you don't know how it helps me to hear this. I suppose it should be bad news but I've been worried, and all I feel now is relief, and hope. I came for revenge, you know that, only to find myself strangely drawn to the Cailleach. This is hard for me to say to you but there have been times I feel I am the Cailleach. Am I going mad?'

'Oh Dara, no. It was the same for your mother. And in the end, I think, it was too much for her. She was much

closer to the Cailleach than you are now. We should just
try to keep it that way. Don't fear the feelings, they are
part of you. Just, don't let them in.'

'I'll try. So what's the plan? What do we need to do?'

'We're close, I can feel it. It's hard to explain, only I
seem to find new things every day now. It must be the
influence of you girls. I don't know how significant they
are yet. You go ahead with your original plans for now but
stay close to the house and don't go to the mountain
again. I won't tell you anymore until I have to. We don't
want her to know. It will be hard for you to keep things
from her.

'And keep reading the books, see what you come up
with, they're quite amazing as you know, not all
decipherable but what is will give you strength. If we put
our heads together... Dara, you know, I've been here for
such a long time now... Thank you.'

It was good to see Honor happy, this was progress,
actual forward motion. Hard to come by around here. Not
to mention company for the path. Things had not changed
for a long time, and she was working herself to the bone
for it. I knew that.

She had turned back to the table, picked up some
papers and peered over them now, her eyes darting about

the page, looking very much like a bird, I thought. I felt an unexpected rush of love for her.

Look at all I'd learned tonight. Okay, nothing new about my father but I should bide my time there. Secrets, the house was riddled with them, but I was more conscious, and more able than she knew. Coming back had ignited latent strength in me, and this was just the beginning, I was sure.

I crossed the room and poured us both a drink. Handing one to my aunt I said, 'You don't need to do this by yourself any longer. Tell me everything you know, tell me now.'

Our eyes met. 'To freedom,' I said.

...

As I opened the first book, gazed on words written by hands that were no more, the words and the women themselves came alive on the pages. From full accounts to snippets of everyday life, the seasons, dark things, and light. So many dreams, theories, worries, happenings, tragedies, risings of the moon, secret ways and secret paths. I immersed myself in the worlds, so different to mine, and felt deep affinity with them all. What a gift that was. I thought from now on, whatever happened, I'd never feel lonely.

Honor, thrilled to see this, didn't tell me, barely dared admit to herself that she feared there was no real meaning to any of it, beyond records of lives once lived. Still, she'd kept up the search, and she believed my input would bring a final solution. One way or another.

I was determined that would be the case too.

I still wanted my revenge, but more than that I wanted our freedom. And I made my decision. I would kill the Cailleach. My mother had been too close to her. That could have been my fate too, were it not for the aunts' help, my years away, and perhaps everything that happened me too, all the events of my life. But I had to be smart. As Honor had said, the Cailleach would know.

I thought it strange the Cailleach should know of our quest, the desire to sever our link and yet remain as tolerant as she seemed. True, she had killed Jaen and possibly my father, though I wasn't yet convinced of that, but then why not kill us all? She could take human or animal form, converse with us face to face, so why had she never confronted the aunts about their disloyalty, their betrayal of her?

'She needs us,' Honor said.

We'd taken to the spending our evenings by the fire in the library, pots of tea, and cups of gin, and paper and pens scattered everywhere.

'And also I've noticed a pattern, see, most of the sightings of her, most of the deaths, happened in May.'

'Interesting. What of the Cailleach's power? Ours is growing stronger you say, what of hers?'

'Hers is cyclical, in the space of a year. The problem isn't so much that she does this, the problem is when? The most likely dates are February first, the spring equinox in late March, or May Day. By her activity through the years I feel certain now it's May Day. Has to be. This is when she turns from hag to maiden again. So now the question for us is, how does she do it? And how do we stop her?'

Chapter 35

The Lovers

Journal of Fr. Seán Mannion, February 1968

It's been years, but the changes in town are still shocking to me. Businesses closed, houses empty, the whole place is depressed. Walking the streets in those first few days back, I was struck by the air of decay. And it's not just the buildings, it's the people too. Work is scarce, and the farmers not faring much better. Animals dying, no hay or turf won last year. They don't say it to my face but I hear the whispers, I know it's Caer they blame, Caer and the Cailleach.

I should go see her, and the aunts. It's the right thing to do. I know that, but I suppose I'm wary after everything that happened between us. How will I feel when I see her again? Not for one minute do I think she's 'gone mad' as they say, or to blame for the way things are gone here. And I'm not sure what my motivation is in wanting to see her. I think maybe I need to make peace, get some kind of closure on us, if I can, and see for myself she's okay. Yes, that's most likely it. If I can just see her, speak with her, it might give me peace of mind.

Journal of Caer Cleary, February 1968

We were the soul of that place once. Eight years have passed, eight years without him. And now he's come back. As a priest this time. It was a small place and inevitable that we would meet. I thought I'd be able to handle it. I was wrong. And I thought it would be on the road or the streets of town, that might have been better. But in the end he came to me, to the whitethorn. It was a whirling February day, black, cold, and threatening.

'You're here,' he said, sounding pleased and surprised.

My heart betrayed me immediately. I was nineteen again. 'Hello, Seán.'

'You look great, you haven't changed.' It wasn't true, but maybe he couldn't see. It was strange to see him like this, all grown up. He looked, beautiful, I thought.

'Black becomes you.'

'Thank you, it's been good to me.'

'I'm glad.'

'How have you been?'

'I've been, I've been fine.' A freezing cold wind whistled round us.

'Why are you here?' I asked him.

'I wanted to see you.'

'What about?'

'I was worried. There's a lot of talk in town.'

'Talk in town, is there? Well that's one I haven't heard before.' He had a nerve speaking to me this way. 'I haven't seen you in eight years, now you're worried?'

'I just want to help, if I can.'

He said this tenderly, his face turned to one side in that endearing way of his, his eyes bright and warm, threatening to erase the space between us. No way could I let that happen.

'I'm sorry, but I can't see that it's any business of yours.'

'That's not strictly true. I'm the priest here now, what goes on in the community is my business.'

I flushed with anger, my eyes went to the collar then back to meet his, challenging, laughing at him.

'I'm no part of this or any community as you well know,' I said coldly.

Even now I was the stronger one, and here he was, trying to exert some kind of man-made authority. Pretending this was about anything other than us two.

'You could get hurt,' he said, 'like your mother.'

'She didn't get hurt, she died.'

'Yes, of course, I'm sorry, Caer. I shouldn't have come. I see that now.' He started to leave, but suddenly stopped, and coming back he said, 'It's not true either, what I said. I didn't come here out of duty.'

My heart started beating so fast I feared he would hear it. I wished he would just go away, not say another word.

'I'm here because I wanted to see you, because *I care* about you.'

'Well, now you've seen me, now you can go.'

'You don't want to talk? About anything?'

Talk about anything? Yes, I wanted that, and a whole lot more. Most of all I didn't really want him to go, and the knowledge only added to my fury.

'No, I don't want to talk to you.'

'You've changed, Caer.' Why did he keep saying my name like that? 'They said you had.' It was not said unkindly, it was true.

'Yes, I've changed,' I agreed. 'What did you expect? That my whole life would be for you?'

'No, but we were friends once, more than friends.'

'That was a different time.'

'It was better.'

'You made your choice.'

'You sent me away, ignored my letters, my calls.'

'Right, well, I've heard enough. If you're not going to leave I will.'

He reached out then, grabbed my hand. 'I'm sorry, Caer. I don't want to upset you, but I have to be honest.'

'No really, you don't.'

It had started to snow. It swirled in the biting wind, it clung to us and the frozen ground. I wished my heart would freeze along with it, I wished my memories would fall as silent. Instead, I remembered the last time. The earth had thrummed with heat and life that night, eight years ago. I'd felt powerful then, limitless, invincible.

'All these years, I've never stopped thinking about you, Caer. Never a day goes by I don't think of you. And seeing you now I... Do you remember, the last time we were here?'

'I remember, Seán.' It was the first time I'd said his name out loud in years, it tasted strange.

'I remember I said you should forget me, go on with your life. It wasn't safe for you then, it's still not safe.'

'I know you're in some kind of trouble, Caer. Couldn't you at least say that if you need help, you'll come to me? You know I'd do anything for you. You have to know that.'

I turned away from him, but he pulled me back again. For a minute I didn't know if he planned to kiss me or shake me. He was taller than I remembered, stronger too, no longer a boy, and his grip was strong.

'Forget you? Tell me how. I'd as well try to forget this place, the wind and rain, the mountain.'

Years of longing and guilt weighed heavy on him, he wanted to make me look at him, punish me for the turn our lives had taken, for how he loved me and had made the wrong decision. He thought we should have left when we had the chance. Maybe he was right. But now it was too late.

He held me tight to his chest and for a minute I gave up the fight, because it felt like home, his holding me.

'Caer,' he said, kissing the top of my head, the same way he'd always done. And brushing the hair from my face he looked into my eyes, to the truth. And we kissed, the witch and the priest. In the same place we'd played and dreamed as kids. The same place we'd made love, our first and last time together. We might have been any two people in love, who haven't seen each other in a long, long, time. But then, just as suddenly, he pulled away from me.

I was stunned but vindicated too. He'd let me go.

'I'm so sorry, Caer. I, I shouldn't have, I don't know what came over me, I...'

'No Seán, it's okay,' I said calmly.

'Please don't look at me that way Caer. This isn't a game for me.'

'Was I smiling? I suppose I was! This time how about you stay here and I'll be the one to leave.'

He watched me walk away, the start of tears in my eyes, not knowing what it took or how much I wanted to turn back. I wanted to, but I wouldn't. At least I knew that he loved me, for his eyes had told the truth too. But at the end of the day there was a big difference between us. He'd made the wrong choice for him. He should never have joined the priesthood. It was different for me, my choices were limited, but I at least knew who I was.

I was still naive enough to imagine this reunion marked the end for us. I suppose you could put that down to the quest. I was deathly consumed by it. But I hadn't counted on love, and it hadn't done with us yet. No one had to know, I thought, not the family, and not the Cailleach. We were apart, just like they all wanted. So what did it matter that when I got back I cried bitterly, or that the whole house bowed under the weight of my sadness. Why did he have to come back here, I cried, when we could never be together? He a priest, and I tied to the house and the quest, it was hopeless. So what if he loved me? What did it matter now? If only I didn't love him, but I did, I did.

After that I wanted to see him more than ever. I did everything to avoid it. We had days of snow that made anything but the most basic trips outside impossible. But the thaw and the day came, I did meet him. In the shop in town. I felt happy in spite of myself, smiled before I could help it. Only this time he didn't return the smile, only spoke coolly, making me angry.

'You've changed your tune again Seán, no surprise there I suppose.'

He snapped back at me, 'Never in all my days have I changed my tune, it was always you I wanted but I knew I couldn't help you or have you.'

'Ssssh.' I looked around. 'Are you mad?' Luckily it was quiet. What the hell had come over him.

'This thing about helping me again,' I hissed. 'Why are you saying that?'

'How can you not know? All the years growing up here, the way you were bullied in school, in the town, how do you think that made me feel?'

'How it made *you* feel? Forgive me if I wasn't thinking of you at the time.'

'I don't mean it like that, but I couldn't stop it, could I? Just like at home, I could never stop *him* either.'

'I didn't know you felt that way...' I whispered, looking around again. 'But it wasn't your job to stop it, you were a child too, and yet, still always there for me.'

'I wanted to protect you, protect my mam, but I couldn't. Then as we got older, and grew closer, I started to feel more certain with every day that I was losing you. I know it was wrong, but I couldn't trust the idea of *us*, I felt I wasn't good or strong enough. Nothing seemed certain or solid to me.'

'I didn't know any of this.'

'I know, it took me a while to work it out myself, but seeing you the other day, and then all this snow. Let's just say I've had time to think. There are things I have to tell you Caer, somehow...' He struggled to find the right words.

'Seán, I, you don't have to...'

'When it came to you it was like there was some greater power at work. It wasn't you was the problem, or our age, it was other things. My mother yes, her influence with me. It's shameful to me now, but there was something else as well, something I could never define.'

'How do you mean?'

'Oh hello Fr. Seán, hello Caer.'

'Hello Mrs Martin,' he said.

'Mrs Martin.' I nodded.

'Sssh, go on.'

'When I came back you had changed, something more than my dad happened while I was away, didn't it? But we got it back that night on the mountain, got us back. We might have been okay then, we might even have left, if we hadn't been chased by that dog creature. And don't think I've forgotten or don't have questions about that. That was what changed everything finally, wasn't it? Or it could have been Dad, but you know I don't blame you, could never blame you for that.'

It was a long speech, especially considering where we were, and we felt the eyes and listening ears on us.

'Come on, come outside.' He took me by the elbow as if to lead me out but I shook him off.

'For god's sake, Seán.' As if there wasn't already enough gossip. 'This will hurt you more than it will hurt me you know. They can't do a lot with me anymore.'

'I don't care.'

'How can you say that? You're a priest.'

'Not for much longer.'

We stopped down the pavement a bit. It was icy, bitter cold. No sign of spring at all.

'You remember, Caer, you told me about Dad, and you ended us, and that was what I'd felt all along, I knew deep down you would finish with me. And that's it, Caer, isn't it, that's the truth. I never had you and I never could have had you, because of *you*, and this bloody place.'

'Let's say you're right.'

'Oh, I'm right all right.'

'Can I speak?'

'Yes, sorry, go on.'

'You're only part right by the way, but you're the one wearing the collar so all this is in the past, why does it matter now?'

'Because I love you, dammit.'

There, it was said, and loud enough for the world and the crows to hear. The street's windows glared at us in silent shock. I stood transfixed for a moment myself before turning and walking away from him.

'Where are you going?' he called.

'Home.'

'So that's it, you won't face this even now, will you?' he called from across the road.

And they said I was the one gone mad. I ignored him, increased my pace.

He caught up quick, spun me round. 'I love you, always have. And you love me too, will you deny it still?'

I pulled away from him again and I didn't look back. He was telling the truth. I couldn't believe it, this made things even more difficult. I was grateful to the road, to the mountain before me. To the familiar fields, and trees, still brown and leafless. I never felt right in the town. I needed to be out here, to think, to be myself again. But before I'd reached Con Ryan's he pulled up ahead of me, stopped, and threw open the door.

I walked past, my sights firmly fixed on the turn for *Sliabh Earrach*, and I heard him get out of the car.

'Caer, I'm sorry I pulled away from you the other day, sorrier still that eight years ago I left here without you. I should have fought for us, but I was young and foolish. If you can forgive me, if you love me, I swear I'll never let you go again. But if you can't forgive me, and if you don't love me, then I'll leave you alone. I'll leave here. And I won't ever come back.'

That was it, he had told me everything. Everything he'd wanted to tell me for years. Whatever happened now he felt lighter, he was glad he'd done it. He thought it was hopeless, but as I came to the turn I hesitated. Above me the tall trees swayed musically, teasing. 'You're alive,' they seemed to say, 'still alive... Caer Cleary.'

I should have let him go then. Like I was supposed to. Like I'd been trying to do the whole time. If I had he might still be alive. But I turned and walked back to him. I was thinking I'd never reach the car, that the Cailleach would drop a tree on our heads, but I did reach it. Seán said nothing more. The collar was gone too, I noticed. I slipped into the seat beside him, afraid of what might happen next. He drove off slowly. I knew these roads, but soon I wouldn't.

'I thought a drive,' he said at last. As if this was the most natural thing in the world, and we a normal couple in it.

'Is there anywhere you'd like to go?'

I thought my head might explode.

'Caer? Where would you like to go?'

'I don't know.'

'It's okay, don't worry,' he said, squeezing my hand. 'I'm not kidnapping you, much as I'd like to. I promise I'll bring you back.'

I nodded, I knew that, of course. It was just that I'd never left home before.

'How about the sea? I've never seen the sea.'

'The sea it is so.'

'I probably shouldn't.'

'Why not?'

'She'll be angry.'

'Who'll be angry? Not the aunts?'

'No, not the aunts exactly.'

He was careful here, at any moment I might change my mind and this was important. He didn't know why exactly or what the problem was, but this was huge for me, that much he knew.

'It's okay so far, isn't it? And we can go back any time, just say the word.'

'Okay, let's do that. How long will it take?'

'We can be by the sea in under an hour, spend a little time there, walk, talk if you like, and be back before anyone knows a thing about it.'

I doubted that. Still, my mind was made up.

I was right to doubt it, but stepping out of the car, faced with the limitless sea, I was reminded there was a world out there, a great big world, and we so small in it. And I thought how we, the family, had become like the waters inland, the lakes and canals. Still, stagnant, and deadlier than the sea by far. We'd forgotten that we too had life, we could move, we could roar. And I thought, if I ever have children I want them to know this, and to never forget.

We were together again, Seán and I. It was easy. Like nothing bad had ever happened, or ever could. It had always been this way between us, that had been part of the danger. I told him I didn't care about the consequences, not for me, and certainly not for his vows. It was what was between us that mattered, had always mattered more to me than anything, and that was the truth. We walked and talked and watched the sun go down, and then we booked into a little hotel on the pier, and alone at last we took each other again, and again.

Traveling back in the early morning we were happier than we'd ever been. But coming closer to home he grew quiet, worried that once back he would lose me again. I couldn't blame him for that after everything that had happened, but something had changed in me that day. A shadow had left me, like a parting veil of mist. I could see more clearly now, and I assured him everything would be different.

'I'll see you tonight,' he said doubtfully.

'Don't be late,' I replied happily. I really did feel we would make it then, that our love was invincible, a greater force than any around us. And I'd made another decision while I was away. About the quest, and the Cailleach.

It was a hard cold morning as I walked the last hundred yards home, and the trees, no longer teasing or playful sang a mournful, anxious song. Looking up to the house I could see the front door was wide open and walking in I found Honor sitting ashen faced at the kitchen table.

'Honor? What's wrong? Why is the door open? What's happened, tell me?'

'You're alive,' she said finally. 'I thought you must be dead.'

'Why would you think that?' Then looking around me. 'Where are the others?'

'The Cailleach.'

'The Cailleach?' My heart stopped.

'She was here.'

'In the house?' I sat down, heavy with shock. 'How?'

Honor gave me the strangest look then and said, 'She was you.'

The whole house started to spin. I could see Honor at the centre, hear her voice, but it seemed far away.

'While you were gone, the house was left empty.'

'How can that be?'

'I don't know. I was coming here when I met Erin and Mae, we talked, they said you were home, and we went our separate ways. Then on the land I met Ellen and she too said you were home. So when I walked in I shouldn't have thought it anything strange to see you sitting at the table. Only I knew right away it wasn't you.'

'What did you do?'

'She spoke first. She said something like, "Oh very good Honor, you're not so easily fooled, are you?"

'I thought you must be dead, or her prisoner maybe, so I asked her, "How did you get in here? Why are you pretending to be my sister?"

'And she said, "She let me in, what makes you think I'm pretending?"

'I asked her what she had done and she said she'd done nothing, that you'd done it all yourself. So then I asked her what she wanted. And she stood up, came to stand right in front of me, right where you are now, and looking in my eyes she said, "WE haven't fully decided yet."'

'Oh no.'

'What is it? Do you know what she meant?'

'I think it's to do with the deal our ancestors struck. About how someone has to be at the house, always,' I lied. But the Cailleach was right about Honor, she wasn't so easily fooled.

'That doesn't answer the "WE haven't fully decided yet" part, though, does it?'

'No, but it might answer how she came to be here. I let her in by not being here, or something like that. Did she say anything else?'

'No, she just touched my cheek and left.'

'She touched you? That's not good.'

'So you're wondering if I've been compromised, damaged... turned, is that it?'

'Yes.'

'Or it might be something else.'

'Like what?'

She was glaring at me now, the shocked look of before gone, she was angry.

'Like where were you? Why weren't you here? Why was she was talking as if you were the same person? And why did she say WE? She was you Caer, you. How can she take your form unless...'

'Go on.'

'No, I don't think I will.'

'No, go on, I have nothing to hide.'

'Don't you?'

'No. You know me better than that, and besides, I was with Seán. You'll be shocked but he's leaving the priesthood, he's already written to the bishop. We're in love.'

She rolled her eyes. 'Yes, in all of this that's the shock.'

'Look, I'm sorry. I know she's managed to use this somehow, to come between us. I know I'm to blame but I am not her, and I am not in league with her, I swear it to you.' I got up and put the kettle on, though I could feel her

Jane Gilheaney Barry

eyes on me still, and my hands trembled. Did she believe me? Doubtful enough.

'And the quest?'

I turned to face her but leaned against the press to steady myself.

'It's not over yet.'

'And Seán? Where does he fit in?'

'I don't know, I'll find a way to keep him safe. I really do love him.'

'I know that.'

'We slept together.'

'High time.'

'Our second time.'

'You were kids the first time, doesn't count.'

The mood had lightened a little, but my body still shook and the house felt so cold.

She got up, took down two mugs, and shoving me aside she took over making the tea.

'How was it?'

'Amazing, he was lucky to get out alive.'

'You bitch. I hope the passion is worth the punishment, when it comes.'

'Passion always comes first with me, whatever the punishment. I'm sorry, Honor, truly. This won't happen again. You do trust me, don't you?'

'I'm not a big truster. You need to be careful, Caer. I mean it.'

'I will, and you too.'

I felt awful, lying to her, but I couldn't tell her the truth, not yet. That it was me and my decision about the quest had brought the Cailleach into our home, close enough to assume my appearance, and to let me know exactly what she thought of my plan.

Honor and I, we agreed not to tell Mae or Ellen about the Cailleach, though we told Erin of course. She was mostly livid at the idea of the Cailleach being in the house. She did sage burnings and chants to clear bad energy and even though she knew it wouldn't help anything she lit every fire and changed all the locks.

The aunts were worried, but at my age, after all my years on the quest, there wasn't a lot they could do. If things had been different they'd have been happy to have Seán back again, not Ellen perhaps, but we paid her no mind.

Even so, our happiness was infectious, and gave good energy for a while. We spent our days working together in the house and on the farm and our nights by the fire, making plans, making love. Love had made me strong again, strong enough to resist the curse. But love made us careless too. Because the Cailleach was quiet, and because I was strong and happy, I didn't feel her a threat now. The urgency of the quest, and awareness of the danger, seemed to fade. Maybe we were safe here, after all? Maybe we could find a new way? *Bean Feasa* and Cailleach, to live in peace? I felt safe, and I shouldn't have felt safe.

In the end, Honor came to me. She told me we couldn't go on like this, he was in danger she said, I needed to wake up, she said. So I warned him, he had to stay away from the mountain, and even from the house. Not for one second did he believe that. He didn't know the danger was real.

Honor came to me again, it wasn't enough she said. I had to find a way to make him leave town, now, before it was too late. It angered me and in my sorrow I accused her of being in league with the Cailleach, and this all being part of her plan. I even accused her of jealousy, because I had someone and she didn't. And that was when she told me that she was supposed to banish him, send him away forever. The aunts had decreed it.

'You would do that, to me?'

'I don't want to, that's why I'm telling you, so you can send him away yourself.'

'I can't,' I sighed.

'Why not? It's for his own good, for your own good too.'

'I can't because I'm pregnant, Honor.'

'Oh Christ.'

'I don't suppose we should be happy about it, but we are, I can't help it.'

'So that's it then. Be happy anytime you can I'd say.'

Idyllic days and nightmare filled nights followed. Winter had lingered long into spring, much longer than ever before.

'I tried to warn you about what would happen, we all did, but you wouldn't listen, would you?' Ellen said.

It was April now, white frost every morning, no growing. We were, all of us, troubled. I was protected somewhat by the baby. My focus had begun to turn inwards, even further away from the quest and *Sliabh Earrach*. The Cailleach was angry too. She knew my plan, and she had failed to make me change it. She began threatening me. She would kill them all she said, my aunts, my sisters, Seán, and me too, but she would keep the child. She would cut it from my belly herself she said, raise it as a child of her own. That was the last straw. I figured I had two choices. Kill her, or leave. But I couldn't kill her. That was my guilty secret. The one I couldn't tell my aunts, my sisters. Could barely admit to myself. I felt bad for the family but they would survive, not how they wanted but I couldn't see any other way. No one had ever left *Sliabh Earrach* before, but I believed that I could. And I thought we could survive it. I was wrong.

Chapter 36

Origins

In the time before there were three sisters, who came to the mountain fleeing persecution in their own land. They had heard tell of a green place at the edge of the world, so wild, so rich with forest, that no invader dared venture far beyond its shores. A place where women like them were accepted, even feared, not persecuted as in other lands. It had once been home to the Tuatha Dé Danann, a magical race who lived there for thousands of years. When the Tuatha were finally defeated in battle by the Milesians, they absorbed themselves into the landscape, tree, river, rock, forever. Landscape beings, eternal shape shifters, with supernatural power, they could take animal, even human form. We call them, the Fae.

These fair folk have been known to fall in love with humans and to spirit them away, sometimes leaving a changeling in their place. The people fear this very much. The fairies are sometimes jealous of humans, but even when they mean us no harm it hurts us to be near them. It's a rare person indeed, can handle the touch of the otherworld.

The sisters were the last survivors of a brutal cleanse of women and children in their homeland. They came here seeking freedom, and protection of the kind only an otherworld goddess could give them. A creature not unlike them in ways, a Cailleach, a landscape witch, from a place to the west, called *Sliabh Earrach,* in Ireland.

Disguised as men they bought passage on a trader's ship. Healing was the profession that they gave. As they watched the green rock emerge in the mist they knew they'd chosen well. When the ship docked they wasted no time in setting out westwards, to the very birthplace of the Tuatha, as far as it was possible to go.

At last they came to the forge on the green river, they gave the name they'd taken, Cleary, paid the toll and crossed over. The mountain that was their destination lay in their sights. They had fought man, beast, and elements to be here, and now they were ready to meet the all powerful Cailleach.

To achieve this they did what no mortal had done or would do, they entered the Cailleach's cave, a gateway to the otherworld. Their proposition was this; if she would gift them the land to build a house and farm and keep them under her protection, one of them would pledge themselves to her. At first the Cailleach mocked the sisters, why would she agree to this? Her power was greater than theirs combined, greater.

'That is true,' the dark sister said, 'but beware the thing that is coming. Your people came here a long time ago, a magical race, you brought darkness over the sun for three days and three nights. We know your power is very great but the world is changing fast. We've seen it. How long before you lose your hold in this place? I can tell you, not long. People are coming, more people than you can imagine. They will trample over your mountain and valleys, they will take and plunder until all the rivers run dry, until they destroy you. Someone who is not quite like you, and not quite like them, could strengthen, even protect your position over time. It could mean the difference between keeping a foothold in this world you love, or moving forever to the other one. You, the great Cailleach, spirit of winter, are protector of this land. We can be protectors too.'

The Cailleach narrowed her eyes at them. No one had ever come here like this before. But these women had no fear, not even when she'd shown herself to them. Had they more power than she knew? Or had they seen greater horrors? From what she knew of men it was possible. She considered then, that they might be of some use, if not now then perhaps as this dark one said, in the future. After all, she had no intention of giving up her hold here.

'Which one?' she asked, surveying the three.

'It shall be me,' said the dark one.

The Cailleach was pleased, for this was the strongest.

'Very well,' she said, 'let it be done. I will give you some land on the brae, between forest, river, and mountain. That will put you between me and the settlement that's growing up around the forge.'

The Cailleach had noticed the sisters held eye contact with her. Wishing to test them further she moved closer and reaching out stroked each face in turn.

'My, my, how pretty you girls are,' she hissed. There was something almost snakelike about her, with her touch, cold as a corpse and wet, that was surely the touch of death.

She tightened her one handed grip on the face of the dark one, holding her at arm's length, her long nails boring into her skull as if to impale her, and stared deep in to her captive's eyes, for surely that was what they were. They had come to relinquish freedom, had they not?

'You remind me of myself as I once was.'

There were terrible things in those eyes, things that would drive a mere mortal mad with terror. But the Cailleach for her part liked what she saw in the girl. Loyalty, strength, courage in abundance, and she was a survivor, a warrior, they all were. She knew then she'd found a prize in these young women. They would keep the people away from her mountain with their march of progress, the destruction of the natural world. And they would not be affected by that proximity to the otherworld the way that ordinary mortals were.

She released her hold.

'I could become envious, you wouldn't want that. I must try to think of you as my daughters now, my daughters of the mountain. But be warned, this deal is forever binding, you will die soon enough, and your children will take your place. They can never leave. To try will mean early death.'

And so it was done. The sisters, running for their lives, had tied their fate forever with that of the Cailleach. She was a paranormal landscape figure, the spirit of winter, immortal, shape shifter. They were healers, brave wise women from the realm of men. They had pledged themselves to her and in return they had been given a forever home, protection, and land. For this they had given their freedom. It was a good deal for that time.

But times change and people with it. They could not have foreseen. They had to live, to serve, most of all they had to survive. Over the years the conditions, like a noose, would slowly choke and in time threaten to strangle them. And their powers grew, through evolution, through struggle, and yes, even by her influence.

Eventually the deal they struck became the curse that sparked the quest. For the women who took the name Cleary, the day came when survival was no longer the main goal of life, it was freedom they wanted.

To win that freedom, the dark one would have to find the way. But curses are delicate things, so easy to deepen.

And so the quest was passed from dark sister to dark daughter, with most meeting a grizzly and untimely death. But change, while slow is sure, and in recent generations it had been noted by all that the sisters' powers were growing, their intent, deepening. By the time Ellen, Mae, and Jaen were in full force of youth, Jaen was the strongest Cleary who had ever lived.

And by the time Caer came of age it was clear to her aunts that she was even more powerful than Jaen had been. It was a shame she had to fall in love, but she was still the first and so far only one to leave. It had weakened

Bean Feasa and Cailleach alike, though not the determination of either.

A problem for Caer in her day, and for her daughter, Dara, was not only the quest. It was that the lines between Cailleach and woman were blurring, making the quest more complex, less clear, and more dangerous.

And then, there was the house. A house means many things. It can be a place of shelter, of freedom, of safety, warmth and welcoming, and it can be a place of fear, dark and forbidding. The house at *Sliabh Earrach* meant different things to different people. Everyone knew that part of the mountain held a gateway to the other world and that a Cailleach, with very great and dark power, lived there. Who would build a house in such a place? Only a witch would do something like that.

As their ancestors had hoped, the house instilled just the right amount of fear to keep people away. The women hoped that fear would be enough, to allow them to work, and to live in peace. The house was their territory, and only theirs. They'd earned it in blood, sweat, and tears. And for most of history not even the Cailleach herself could go there, but now that had changed too.

Chapter 37

In the Chapel

Seán was waiting for Caer outside the chapel as planned. She was late. Soon he'd have to go in and start mass.

'Evening Fr. Seán, that's a cold one.'

'Evening, Father.' The people filed in around him as his eyes searched the horizon, from the street lit pools of light and rain, to the forest and mountain beyond. Where was she, he thought anxiously, as he turned and went in, closing the doors behind him. He'd become more protective of late, not just because of the baby, but since they'd decided to leave a fear that something would happen to stop them had taken hold. Despite the worry, he still felt truly happy, couldn't help it. It was the happiness that comes from being true to yourself, he thought. That was something new for him. He bore no ill will towards the church, he felt it had been good to him, and his mother. It didn't change the fact that he knew he and Caer were meant to be together.

332

The ancient pews creaked under the shifting weights of the bulky whispering shapes, in an electric light glare. Here and there one coughed while others rustled their mislets or fingered rosary beads in silent thoughts and prayer. And they jumped in unison as the doors blew open with great force, and an icy wind rushed in and gripped their ankles. The superstitious among them would say it was because the front door of the chapel not only faced north but was directly in line with the Cailleach's cave on the mountain. A daily reminder, that church or no church this was still very much her territory.

Whatever they expected to see that night, it wasn't Caer Cleary. The Cailleach herself might have been less surprising. But there she stood by the door, with a look of fury. After the initial shock the whispering started;

'Caer Cleary, what is *she* doing here?'

'Never thought to see a Cleary in the chapel.'

'No doubt it's Fr. Seán she's after.'

'Maybe he's converted her!' This was met with nervous laughter.

There had been an order forbidding the Cleary women to practice. It wouldn't come to anything, but they'd decided they could use it to their advantage, to instigate a fake row. He had told her he'd need to be seen to support it, they both knew and understood that. In reality it made little difference to the women who'd had similar orders placed on them before. The people would shy away for a while but they always came back. Even the authorities turned a blind eye to these things. As much as they feared or gave out about the women they still believed in them. They had faith in the Cleary's abilities as healer women, believed in all their powers.

They'd gone over it all this just this morning.

'You brought this up at council, don't try to deny it. You've been against us from the start. You're just like the rest of them, worse, for we used to be friends, you and I,' she'd said, trying to keep a straight face.

'Don't laugh tonight, whatever you do.' He cleared his throat. 'Yes, we were friends, but we were children. This is different. Your actions, yours and your sisters and aunts could put someone in danger. It's time to move into the modern world and forget these kind of things, let trained medical people handle it.'

'And as for you,' he'd said, addressing the pretend congregation, 'you need to stop going to these women for help, for healing or charms or for god's sake, spells! You're all part of the problem. Everyone has to take some responsibility for events that have happened.'

Caer had gasped in mock indignation and they'd laughed about it all, pleased with themselves and the fiction. She'd been glowing, more beautiful than ever, he thought. Tomorrow they'd be leaving, starting their new life together. He patted the wallet in his pocket, it held two train tickets to Dublin. He couldn't wait to get them away from here. He'd found them a place in Rathmines. She'd made him tell her about it a thousand times. How it looked, what Dublin was like, what they'd do there. He'd never seen her so happy. That was just a few hours before. This was not that person.

He had felt the drop in temperature, ice on his breath, and looking around he saw something new on the faces now, fear. They were not looking at him, or talking, they were transfixed on Caer. He followed their gaze back to the figure of the woman he loved. Her lips were moving, though he couldn't quite hear what she said. He moved closer, asked what was wrong. She didn't answer.

'She's having some kind of fit,' someone whispered.

'Devil's work,' hissed another.

'Call the doctor, someone.'

The lights flickered.

He started to speak but she raised a hand and pointing at him spoke, in a voice he'd never heard before.

'May earth and worms be on you, Seán Mannion, and in your mouth, and may the curse be on your head. A bird of evil for evermore.'

All eyes turned back on him in horror, a curse. She'd cursed him, in the church, in front of the whole town. Seán had the awful sensation then of something creep over his flesh. He shuddered, almost fell to his knees.

'Caer... what is this? What's happening?'

'May earth and worms be on you, and in your mouth, and may the curse be on your head. A bird of evil for evermore.'

He felt sure this was the end. She would speak the curse for a third and final time and game over. He knew how this worked and he braced himself for the fall. But she stopped. She stopped and she turned her head as if someone had called her name. He saw recognition, awareness pass over her face, and the light come back to her eyes. Whatever she'd seen or heard had broken the spell she was under. She'd come back. She looked at him in horror, and spoke in her own voice, making his blood run cold.

'Run away. Before it's too late. RUN.' The terrible thing he feared, that would stop them from leaving had happened. Something dark and unknown to him was trying to keep them apart. He would never allow it, he had promised. This was his territory, his girl, this was his chance.

Caer had turned sharply away, and started to walk back down the aisle, but even as she walked her voice came back to him, only this time she said, 'Help me Seán, please, help me.'

'Bolt the doors,' he ordered the men at the back, who even as their hands shook rushed to do as he asked.

The men put all their weight to the heavy wooden doors, they brought the lathes down hard, turned the keys and pocketed them, then pressed themselves against the wall, as far away as they could get, and blessed themselves.

'Don't let her take me, Seán. You promised, remember? You said you'd never let me go again.'

It sounded like her voice but it seemed not to come not from her, but from somewhere far away, so that he wondered if anyone else could hear it or if it was just in his mind. He was by her side again.

'I won't let you go,' he said, congregation forgotten. 'Ever, do you hear me? Take my hand.'

Slowly she started to hold out her own, it seemed to take effort on her part, as if some part of her couldn't do it, or didn't want to. And he was loath to make any sudden moves in case she'd pull away again. But he had to get hold of her, he had to. Beside them the church doors moaned and creaked under the weight of the rising storm.

As their fingertips brushed the doors creaked and buckled with greater urgency and the wood cracked and split open. Their eyes met, and what he saw there broke him. Silent screams, with no voice, only terror. And he knew, like they always did, he knew the truth. She didn't want him to follow her. She was trying to protect him. But he'd promised. He wouldn't let her be alone again. He took her hand.

'If you have to go, I'll go with you,' he said. 'I don't care where it is.' And then everything stopped, everything was silent.

A beating of wings filled the air, crows. And death was their message. They swarmed the church, bringing darkness, and then crushing agony as he felt her hand ripped from his. Against the storm, the birds and the dark, he forced his way outside calling her name, but all that came back on the wind now was waves of sound, waves of laughter, of cries, and her voice again.

'Seán, don't let her take me, help me Seán, help me.' And then, 'It's a trap Seán, run, hide, don't follow me.'

People were rushing from the chapel now screaming and crying. He was thinking he'd go to the aunts first and was about to get in his car when he saw her again, walking down the street, and leaving the car he called out to her. But she kept walking as if she hadn't heard him. He followed her.

That was the last reported sighting of Seán Mannion. Six months later, on the night their daughter Dara was born, Seán was dead, his body found and then buried in secret by Honor and Erin Cleary.

Chapter 38

Diary of Dara Cleary – Bilberry Sunday 1985

Sheltered existence is not a feature of our family, but I've always been treated different to the rest of them. Boys, for example, were strictly forbidden, and all the more appealing for the fact. John was the one I wanted. Our romance had barely begun when the aunts discovered and just as quickly forbid it. Ellen had taken to questioning me in her usual abrasive way. I remember one exchange, I think I was about fifteen.

'Any boys sniffing about yet?'

I'd snorted with laughter.

'That's a way of putting it!'

She put down her work and stared at me in that flinty way of hers.

'Let me put it another way for you then, any one boy in particular?'

I'd been about to laugh it off but seeing the others were listening intently and watching me too I thought better.

'No one in particular, why?'

'Good,' was the abrupt and only answer I got from her.

'It's not that we don't want you to have friends,' said Mae, 'is it Ellen? Ellen? It's just, it would be better not to get serious about any one boy in particular, at least not while you're so, young.'

'Is this about sex? Because if it is there's really nothing to worry about, or friends either. I don't have any friends.'

'Surely that can't be true, you must have some friends,' said Mae.

'No, I don't.'

'But we have nothing against friends... girlfriends.'

'You've never let me bring anyone home or go anywhere, so there's no girls either.'

'For pity's sake,' said Erin, who had just come in. 'Can't you leave the poor girl alone.' She rolled her eyes and smiled warmly at me. Ellen and Mae were old and old fashioned but the young aunts were cool. Honor and Erin were my only friends really. 'She's a Cleary, isn't she? Of course she has boys, look at her!'

'Oh, we see her,' said Ellen, not lifting her eyes, 'we see her, all right.'

I don't know why I kept this thing with John a secret from Erin. It would be hard to imagine a less judgmental person, but something stopped me. It's not like it was serious, like we were in love or anything like that. Not like my parents. It was just like I'd said, I'd never had a friend, never mind a boyfriend. I was lonely, I just liked the attention. It was just a bit of fun. No one was meant to get hurt.

We had taken to meeting in secret, in the forest, or on the mountain. But even I, rebellious as I was, felt a little uneasy about that. Truthfully, I didn't know what would upset the aunts more, my meeting John behind their backs or my being on the mountain. John, of course, didn't know. I wasn't about to tell my, kind of, boyfriend, that I wasn't allowed go these places. I was a Cleary, and fifteen for god's sake.

He was nice to me, that was new, he was good looking too, and popular. If the other girls at school knew they'd be jealous, but it wasn't just the aunts who didn't know, no one knew. Like I said, this was no great love. But over the weeks we'd been together we'd become something like friends. We talked a lot, and fooled around. Even at that he was getting grief in school for being friendly with me but he took it well, had stuck up for me once or twice. That was good enough for me at the time. Given my history it would not have been easy for anyone to be with me, it was hard enough for me to be with me.

My parents, while rarely mentioned, haunted the place. Not just the house but the town and everyone in it. Everywhere I went people stared and whispered. Some even said things, and not nice things either. They talked about my mother being mad, a crazy woman. They said she was always after Seán even though he was a priest. She'd put a spell on him, seduced him. And they said he'd been swept away by the Cailleach, that my mother had given him to her, a blood sacrifice. And that her own death was suicide.

'So you're Dara,' they'd say.

'Come over here, let's have a look at you, see who you look like.'

Treated me like public property they did, and that was the adults. At school it was even worse. From the time our mother died and my stepfather brought us to live with the aunts we'd been bullied at school, me especially. We understood from the aunts it was a kind of family rite of passage, one they'd all been through. Character building was what Ellen had said, who seemed to remember nothing of her own school days.

As if it wasn't bad enough to be grieving our mother and taken from our home we'd had all of this to deal with too. If it hadn't been for my powers I don't know what I'd have done. I only used them on the boys and men, the ones who tried to assault me. Of course that was something that happened to all girls, not just witches. But I at least could do something about it. Not that I ever hurt anyone, I only used them to protect myself, or others, and sometimes to have a bit of fun. It was a comfort, an insurance policy in a crazy world, taken for normal.

Looking back, we, they, should have seen it coming. I'd been suppressed for so long, then my age, and what I was. It was inevitable something would happen. When it finally did was a beautiful Sunday in July, Bilberry Sunday. The town folk were all out on the mountain, everyone in festive mood. There'd be a feast that evening too. It's possible we were discovered accidentally but I didn't believe it. Any measure of trust I might have had in John disappeared in the moments it took for the gang to surround us. Girls and lads, jeering and laughing at me. I suppose my instinct took over. From that point I was ready for whatever came.

It was that bitch Una McGovern suggested we go to the Cailleach's cave. Everyone was on for it. I wasn't going to be the one to back down, after all, I'd be fine. I was pretty hard. I didn't care about them, or anything that might happen to them, either. As we climbed, the terrain became steeper, and more dangerous. Before long a fairy mist had fallen. The gang had been drinking and were in a jovial mood, flirting and joking around, youth making them brave. But as we drew close to the cave the atmosphere changed and even the more boisterous among us grew quiet. I'd never been here before, but I was calm and unafraid. We had reached our destination and now they stood, fearfully, looking in that abyss, the Cailleach's cave.

Finding her tongue Una dared me to enter. I just smiled and said no, suggested she go instead. She called me a coward but I could tell she was scared. She ignored me then. One of the boys had started groping her, within minutes they were kissing to shouts of approval from the others. Next thing I knew two of the boys, Jason, and another, I don't remember the name, came at me, knocked me to the ground and dragged me across it. As I struggled with the pair I noticed John standing with the others, watching.

I think we had, all of us, come under the Cailleach's influence by then, even me. A kind of trance. It didn't stop the gang from growing violent, or what happened next, and I've never been able to explain it, even to myself. This is why I write it here, and have tried to write it before. All is know is they attacked me, and when I got over the initial shock I don't know if I summoned the Cailleach or if she came of her own accord. Truth be told I don't know if she came at all, for I do think it might have been me killed that boy, Jason Spain. No one speaks his name now.

Before he fell to his death they tried to help him. When they couldn't do it, they said they would go for help. He cried, and they cried, they even asked me to help, but I couldn't, or wouldn't. I said he was past help now, they all were, that they'd cursed themselves by coming here. It seemed a long time, but it wasn't long, before he fell.

They didn't want to follow me back down the mountain but they didn't want to stay where they were either. They'd never have found their way back alone, in the mist. I didn't wait for or help anyone, I just walked ahead while they followed as best as they could. When we got as far as *Sliabh Earrach*, I left them, went inside, and I never looked back. That was the end of any life or friendship I might have had in that place.

The townspeople were apoplectic with rage. They blamed me entirely. Their young people would never have gone there were it not for me. Just like other times the guards came to the house, but this time it was to question me about the incident. In the midst of it all the detective who'd been coming to the house for years took the opportunity at last to ask Erin out on a date, and she agreed.

'Might be useful to have a guard on side,' she said to the others.

'It might, said Honor, 'but you like this one, I can tell.'

'And if I do?'

'Just saying is all. Take it easy though, this is no time to be losing our heads.'

'When is it ever!'

The onslaught of abuse rained on the house by the town after that was relentless. We were kept home from school, even the aunts stayed for the most part by the house, though Erin went out on her date with Shane. She said there were plenty of 'looks' but no one had said anything. She said that he told her he'd been 'warned' by 'concerned citizens' that it wasn't a good idea, especially now, to be seen with one of 'those women,' but they hadn't dared say more than that to him.

He himself wasn't a bit concerned, he was far too busy falling in love. The investigation of the fall was unfortunate but clearly it had been an accident. It was treacherous up there, and foggy, they were lucky no one else had fallen, that Dara had been able to lead them down. The things the townsfolk were saying and now doing were crazy, if anything they'd be in trouble with the law themselves if it kept up. It was all getting out of hand.

Little did he know. The very next day a mob came to the house, with weapons, pitchforks, hurleys, even fiery batons. We, my sisters Drew, Devin, and I, were terrified by the scene, but the aunts were stoic. They'd seen it all before.

...

'Take the girls into the house,' Mae said.

By the time the angry horde got as far as the gates, some had fallen off, lost their nerve, but others, bolstered by the crowd, were even more angry, more determined than ever to run us out. Mae was calm and confident as she planted herself between the mob and her house.

'What's the meaning of this?' she asked with authority.

There was a bit of red faced shuffling before one of the men said, 'We want ye out, once and for all.'

'Aye, that's right,' agreed others.

She laughed. 'Don't be foolish. You think we'd be here if we had any choice in it? Think we tend to you lot for our health, do you? Who would you run to for your cures and your charms if we left? You there, Jim Prior, you came to me with that problem of yours and I helped you. Would Dr Flynn have done that? Would he have been able to?

'And you, Margaret Flaherty, are you forgetting that time when you needed help? How desperate you were? You thought there was no hope, who helped you then?'

Mae went on calling out this one and that, as first Ellen, then Erin, and Honor, came to stand by her side.

'And what about herself.' She gestured towards the mountain. 'Ye want to be left alone, without us, between you and her?' She laughed heartily.

This was uncomfortable. Mae was a formidable woman, and how she'd recognised them all when some had covered their faces, they didn't know, but aside from the healing part which was true, this whole business about the Cailleach was unsettling. No one had ever spoken of it out loud, least of all the Clearys themselves. Were they willing to be left alone with the Cailleach? The young people, after they'd gotten over their shock at the events of that day on the mountain had told them something of the strangeness, how they felt as if they'd been drugged, how they'd experienced hallucinations of a fearsome woman, which they thought after might just have been Dara Cleary, not that anyone believed that.

She had told them they were cursed now, for coming too close to the otherworld. That they were bound to the

Cailleach as mortal enemies and bound to return in ten years' time. There was more to this than they could understand.

Deep down they didn't know if it would be safe for them to proceed any further with their plans, but for now they brazened it out.

'That's all as may be, but the boy is dead, no cures or help for him from you Clearys.'

'That was unfortunate, but who among you would have done what your young people did? Go to the Cailleach's cave, the mouth of the otherworld and attack my niece, a dark one at that. The same one they've bullied for years. Don't deny it.' She held up her hand, and their protests fell silent. 'The world and the crows know it's true. If you want to blame anyone for this blame those young people, for going there.'

'Aye, well, that includes your niece, doesn't it.'

'Yes, it does, but if she hadn't been there, and it was their idea to go, mind you, not one of those youngsters would have come back. She saved them, and now she's going away.'

Erin and Honor, Ellen too, exchanged looks. This was the first they'd heard of it, what did she mean by saying that?

Some of the crowd went to speak but Mae had heard enough.

'That's the end of it. Now take yourselves away from my property before something happens to you and all.'

'Is that a threat, Mae?'

'Take it any way you like,' she said, turning her back on them.

There was a lot of grumbling and stalling but they left before too long, the wind well and truly out of their sails. At least the young ones were going away, that might help cool things somewhat, that would have to do them for today. No harm to be rid of that Dara Cleary anyway, she was trouble that one.

Once inside Mae called the women together. 'Dara must leave here.'

'When?'

'As soon as possible. I'll send for Marius to come take them.'

'Because she's too close?'

Mae nodded.

'Just like Caer.'

'Yes. If she stays now, she'll be too much under the Cailleach's influence, it would undermine the quest, we could lose her.'

'But send her away, are you sure? For how long?'

'I don't know, for a long time, as long as we can manage without them.'

'Is it a bit, drastic?'

'Perhaps, but we can't afford to take chances. The fact is that while nine went up only eight came back.'

'You're thinking of Caer, after she killed Seán's father.'

'Yes, but it had started long before then, while she was still at school. She got too close. If she hadn't, who knows, things might have turned out a lot different for her, and for Seán.'

The women went on talking, making plans, and meanwhile in the shadows Dara was listening. Let them send her away. She hoped Marius would not take too long, and she hoped never to return.

Chapter 39

All Change

Journal of Dara Cleary – April 1996

The morning after I spoke with Honor about the quest and promised to stay by the house, I woke dead tired, to the aroma of decaying flesh. It was branches of whitethorn, someone had put them in my bed. As everyone knows, whitethorn is the fairy tree. It smells beautiful while it's growing. But you don't cut whitethorn, and you don't bring it in your house.

I gathered the branches and dragged them outside to burn. It was going to take more than a few branches of whitethorn to scare me. The next morning was the same. Surely this was the work of the Cailleach. There would be nothing to gain by telling the others. No, this was between her and me.

Every morning the same. I woke in my bed of whitethorn, and every morning I gathered the branches and burned them. But despite my efforts, the scent began to linger. Try as I might I couldn't scrub it from my clothes, my skin. Even my food seemed laced with its cloying sweetness. I began to feel light headed, and more inclined to dream. The sixth day dawned damp and muggy. I coughed up a fully formed flower and thorn. On the seventh day, I got caught. Erin saw me burning the branches.

Neither of us spoke, but afterwards I heard her arguing with Honor. She seemed to think Honor was somehow to blame for the whitethorn incident. She was asking if Honor had let *him* come back. Whoever he was. Honor denied it. No, he had not been back she said, and even if he had, it had no bearing on this. I'd never heard them fight before.

'You said you were strong enough. Strong enough to resist her touch, strong enough to resist him.'

'And haven't I proven that?'

'I just don't know how else to explain this. Someone let her in.' And she said something about how if anything was going to harm the quest now it would not be she, Erin, but Honor.

And Honor said, 'At least my motivation is true.'

'What's that supposed to mean?'

'At least I want it to end, at least I want our freedom.'

'And I don't? Is that what you're saying?'

'All you care about is this house.'

'That's not true.'

'But it is at least partly true.'

'Truth is it's your own freedom you're about, Honor. You're the one who wants to leave here. You're the one the Cailleach touched, here in the house, the day Caer went off with Seán. And you're the one in love with her son.'

'Very well, so perhaps the whole thing's unravelling, including your trust of me. After everything I've done, everything I've sacrificed. Did you ever consider maybe Dara is the one bringing her now? Just like Caer did. You know she's been close to the Cailleach all along, suspects us of killing Seán, she even suspected Caer. Why do you think I've been keeping her here at the house? Keeping her busy.'

'Christ, that's all we need, for them to find out about Seán next.'

'They'll have to eventually.'

After that I heard nothing more. Didn't hear Erin apologise and say no, she hadn't considered that Dara had either joined with or decided to kill the Cailleach. That that was what brought the Cailleach now. Of course, it made sense. Or that the branches were a warning to Dara, to make the right choice. And a trap, to lure her out and kill her, if murder was her choice. She was sorry, she'd been so afraid of losing Honor, especially now, when they were so close.

Find out about Seán she'd said, that was all I heard from that point. So they did know what happened him. I was not happy, I was not happy at all. Each night of the whitethorn I'd been dreaming about him, saw him lying under a whitethorn.

I desperately wanted to go there, but I had to find out more first. I didn't want to believe the Cailleach was right, that it was the aunts who had killed him, or one of them at least. That was what she'd been trying to tell me, but it could be a trap. I fought the urge to confront them directly and after dinner that evening I topped up the glasses and I asked them to tell me about my parents instead. What were they like? I knew so little about them. Strangers knew more.

I thought they might be reluctant but they seemed happy to talk, and once begun sailed off in various memory streams. I, my sisters too, were caught up in the current and we barely dared breathe.

'They were tall, handsome people. Caer with her jet black hair, green eyes, and pale skin. Seán with his white hair, sallow skin, and the lightest blue eyes.'

'You'd notice them anywhere.'

'You would.'

'They were the most beautiful couple I've ever seen.'

'Yes, isn't it funny? We only see that now.'

'But it wasn't just their looks. They radiated harmony. Even when they fought.'

'Chemistry.'

'Everyone was jealous of them.'

'Yes. Even we were jealous.' They laughed.

'Oh, we were.'

'Who could help it?'

'No one.'

'I see them still.' They sighed.

I re-filled the glasses and the night filled up with stories that had never been spoken before.

'The whitethorn was their meeting place wasn't it?' I said at last, breaking the lovely spell. 'I saw their names carved in the bark the day of Mae's funeral.'

A look of pain passed over their faces, and I was sorry I'd spoken. I had the sense then of time speeding along, like sand through an hourglass. I wanted to stop it, but I couldn't. I wanted to say, wait, go back to that summer. To when they first fell in love. Or to when they were finally together. But we couldn't go back, we had reached that part in the story, and now it must be told.

The deaths were coming. The beginning of all their pain. This was why they never spoke of it. To evoke that time was to live it again, as vivid as the first time. There had been no answers, no healing, no ending.

At last Erin spoke.

'You were born there, Dara.'

'I was born on the mountain?'

'Yes.'

'But, how? Why?'

'She went looking for him. And she didn't make it back.'

'I didn't know, she never said anything. She never told me anything of my birth.'

'You were only a child when she died. Besides, it was painful to speak of. It still is.'

'I'm so sorry, I see that now. But what happened? Who found her?'

'Well...' The aunts exchanged looks.

'We're not sure.'

'Somehow she made her way back here with you, that's when we found you both.'

'But how could she do that? Make her way back here, alone? And why was she looking for him on the mountain, in winter, at nine months pregnant? Did she have a lead in his disappearance?'

'We don't know.'

'But you must know something?'

'We don't know what happened that night, Dara. By the time we found her she was so ill, she was delirious.'

It wasn't right, how could they know so little? Or was it that they didn't want to tell me?

'The whitethorn, you say they always met there?'

'Yes, from the time they were children, right up to the end.'

She must have known he was there, I thought. That had to be it.

...

Erin and Honor

'We have to tell her everything.' It was late, the girls had long gone to bed and Erin and Honor were alone.

'I was thinking the same,' said Erin.

'I know it's been the way of our family to not talk about these things but that doesn't seem right now, especially with her. Besides, women who are looking for their freedom should be deciding these things for themselves.'

'I agree.'

'You do?'

'Of course, we're witches, witches are not followers. We want a new way, don't we? One of our own making. Besides, she's a dark one, not a child, and she's their child. It's her right to know the truth of their lives, and their deaths.'

'Yes.' Honor was surprised. 'I didn't know you felt this way?'

'These things take time, it's not easy to break from what you know. But we made a promise.'

'I remember.'

'We'll tell her in the morning.'

...

Diary of Dara Cleary

I left for the whitethorn at dawn in a crisp diamond air, determined to find the answers for myself. And waiting there for me was the Cailleach. She congratulated me on finally figuring out it was the aunts who killed my father and buried him here. My mother was planning to leave with him she said, and they couldn't allow it. Without her they'd never reach their full power, and they'd never break the curse. All this time they'd kept their little secret but she'd seen, hadn't she? In her dreams she'd seen the aunts burying Seán on the mountain.

It was true I'd had that dream. It had haunted me for years. But dreams don't have to be real. I'd hoped, still hoped, the dream was wrong.

'Just because they buried him doesn't mean they killed him.'

The Cailleach threw back her head and laughed, a laugh that rolled over the fields like thunder, bringing rain clouds and darkness after.

'Come, come,' said the Cailleach. 'You want to find him, he's here.' She steered me towards a pile of freshly turned earth, and pushed me into an open grave.

I recoiled from the earth as if it would burn me, half expecting to see my father's body.

'Dara, my dark one, my lovely one. This is a fresh grave, and a fresh grave needs a fresh body.'

This was for how I'd betrayed her. For joining with Honor, for embracing the quest to end her hold on us, for not believing the aunts had killed my father.

'Not quite, Dara,' she said.

'You women are not the only ones who see things. I see things too. I know things. Like what is, and what will come to pass, if I allow it. You were meant to be my dark one, and for a time you were. You don't quite trust the aunts, do you? But that's of little consequence now.

'I know your deepest heart, Dara, and you are not like your mother, for you plan to kill me. So let this be your final thought. It was your mother killed your father, as sure as if she drove a knife into his heart. She could have killed me, or tried to, and she could have left sooner. But no, she chose to stay, to break his heart, to let him die. Because it was me she loved. You hear that, me. More than she ever loved any of you.

'But you are different, aren't you Dara. You were different.'

Earth rained down on me, so hard and fast that within minutes I could no longer stand, could no longer breathe. And then just as suddenly, it stopped.

With effort I burst through the earthy tomb. From the almost silence of a living grave to fierce cries and shouts above. A battle. But who had dared to face the Cailleach, and her mission to bury me alive? I heard a man's voice. Whoever he was the Cailleach would surely kill him. And then I heard another, more familiar voice, that made my blood run cold.

I scaled the wall of earth to freedom and standing slowly gazed in horror at the sight before me. Two figures were lying on the ground. It was Erin's man, Shane, and Devin. The Cailleach was gone. She'd had her blood sacrifice, enough to be going on with, enough to put an end to Honor and me, and our plans.

I went to my sister in the gathering darkness. Her green gold eyes, turned to the sky, were full of clouds and circling crows, attracted by the fragrant corpses. I held her hand.

...

Sorrow

Back at the house, in the same moment Devin breathed her last, the gable wall split from foundations to roof. While at the river, Drew, who was swimming with Dúlta, saw what was happening too late, and fainted.

Returning to her lair, the Cailleach withering, withered the ground that she walked on. Better if it had been Dara as she'd planned but that would have to wait now. She was tired, she was old, and needed her remaining strength. She knew these mortals and this would set them back years, and it would slow them down tomorrow.

In town they saw the sky turn from a gentle blue with soft white clouds, to slate, then fiery red. And hearing the death sounds they hurried home, bolted their doors and closed their curtains. It was just like that other night. The night Seán Mannion disappeared.

Erin felt the foundations beneath her shake and watched the crack rise in the wall. She left the house right away and headed for the black of the mountain. The sky was crimson fire, like the blood that now drummed in her veins. And a congregation of crows ahead confirmed what she already knew, death. Had they all gone into the night? Would she ever see them again? And she thought bitter thoughts of the Cailleach. Of what she, Erin, a healer, a woman, would do to her for this. Afterwards Con Ryan told people how he'd met Erin Cleary on the road to the mountain that day.

'She had a look of murder in her eyes,' he said, 'pure murder.'

Honor was with Dealan in his cottage high on the mountain. She'd gone to him the night before, after she'd spoken with Erin. It was almost a year since they'd been together. A year in which he had haunted the air around her. And even more curious, he had stayed. She didn't need to risk going to the cottage to know that he did. Or what it cost him. But she hadn't been with him, flesh and blood, as man and woman, since the girls came the previous summer. It had been her decision, her sacrifice. She couldn't risk the success of the quest. But today was the last day of April, the last day of the quest. It might be their last time, their last chance. So she'd gone to him.

It hadn't been easy for her to admit she'd been forever changed since that first time he'd come to her door, and looked into her eyes, and touched her hand. Before then she hadn't known the weight of the loneliness of her life. The knowing, and the change that came after, only intensified after their first night together. It was an assault on her sense of self, her identity, that was frightening but needed to happen. Compounded by the stray sod incident, it disturbed her deeply. But there was no way to go back to what was. She had changed, completely, irrevocably. And now she was back in his arms again, growing in fear and joy with every breath they drew together. She felt released. She felt, free.

Happy at last and so peaceful, she almost didn't believe the creeping desolation that crept over the flagstone floor and crouched by her side.

'Something's happened,' she said. 'Something wicked. I have to go, I have to leave right away.'

'No,' Dealan said. 'Don't go back there, Honor.'

'Why? What do you know? What have I done by coming here?'

'Nothing, you've done nothing wrong. But if you go now, we might never see each other again.'

'You tricked me? She wanted me out of the way, and you helped her?'

'Lie if you must, but from the first time we met you've known the truth. What was supposed to happen, and that I loved you. Loved you too much to ever let anything happen you.'

'And my family?'

'Honor, please.'

'If you want to keep me here you'll have to kill me.'

'If you go you'll die with the rest of them.'

'I'm not afraid to die.'

'Only afraid to live.'

'Goodbye, Dealan.' She left the house, pursued by love, chasing darkness.

...

Erin

The first thing Erin saw was the ancient whitethorn, casting down blossoms. Dara. Her heart lurched violently at the sight of her. Her niece was alive. She almost burst into tears of gratitude and relief, but there were others. The first was a man, and she knew right away it was Shane. How had this possibility eluded her? That he could be taken from her like this? She should have known. She should have loved him better.

'I'm sorry, Erin. I'm so sorry, it's all my fault. I couldn't save them.'

'You're okay? You're sure? You're not hurt?'

'No, I'm fine.'

Erin sank to her knees beside Shane. It might have been just the two of them there in the cool grass, she thought, under the canopy of branches. And he only sleeping. Any moment now he'd wake, and look at her again, and smile. She stared and stared at him, willing it. She ran her hands carefully over him. Healing hands, with long skilled fingers, that searched, and found nothing. She clenched them back viciously, the nails digging into her palms, drawing blood. Useless magic. What had they done? This was what came of meddling in the quest. The sadness never ends, she thought. Never. The whitethorn waved and pitched above their heads, bringing her back to reality. And she remembered Dara had said 'them', she couldn't save *them*? She rose to her feet.

'Dara?'

'Yes, Erin.'

'You said, them.'

Dara sobbed, 'Yes Erin.'

'Is it Honor?' Bile rose in her throat, but Dara shook her head.

'No,' she cried. 'It's Devin.'

'Where?'

Erin went to where she could see the gold hair spread over the grass. A few strands were floating lightly on the breeze, a cruel contrast to the stillness of Devin herself. Her skin had already turned white, her lips to blue, her eyes from moss and gold to granite.

'It wasn't meant to be her,' Dara was saying. 'I've always known I'd be the one to go. It was me the Cailleach wanted to kill, me she tried to bury alive.'

'Sssh,' Erin said, as much to the stilled Devin, so full of life moments before, as to Dara.

'You've had a terrible time but I'm here. I know what to do. I've always known what to do.'

'What do we do?'

'Go to Con Ryan, he's the closest, make sure he brings something to cover them, don't delay.'

'What will I tell him?'

'Tell him, tell him they're dead. Tell him… to call the doctor, the guards, and Joe. Tell him to make sure Joe comes right away.'

'What about Honor?'

'Honor will be here soon enough, and then I have business to take care of.'

'What kind of business?'

'Just something needs to be done.'

'Can't I help?'

'No, this is something I have to do alone. It has to come from me, but I'll wait till you return.'

'But...'

'Just trust me, Dara. Now go.'

...

Journal of Erin Cleary

I did know what to do, I was ready. When they came back I took Joe to one side as old Con prayed, and Dara covered the bodies, and taking his two hands in mine I told him the truth. That he should sit with Devin a while, because what he'd suspected was true. He was her father. That we'd have told him sooner if we'd known. And how sorry I was it had to end like this for both of them. I waited until I heard the sirens, saw the squad car and ambulance arrive, and slipped away.

All the way back to the house my brain burned with intent. So the Cailleach thought she had us beat, did she? Thought she knew us. Could treat us like this? Well, I'd show her. I may not be a dark one but I'd show her what it meant to be human, and just how strong that could be.

It was an unexpectedly exhilarating moment, when I flicked the lighter in my hand. To burn a house, any house, is not easy. Even the oldest, emptiest houses have souls. Imprints of past joys, of life and love, good times and hardship, from all who lived within their walls we want to keep. You think it will never end. But it does. It has to.

And this house... was so much more, it was... had been, the love of my life. Light danced through the kitchen, the last of the day, the last ever day. It dappled the walls and shimmered in waves on the table. And I saw us there once more, as we used to be. Ellen and Mae, Honor, myself, and Caer. Young and happy, before all the sadness, before the quest destroyed us. And I felt such pain, such agony of longing.

'Now, now!' the house seemed to say.

I dropped the flame. And I wasn't sorry. And I didn't cry again.

'Now let the Cailleach come.'

...

Honor heard the crackle and roar of flames and saw the billowing clouds of smoke, long before she saw it. She imagined all kinds of terrible scenes. But nothing could have prepared her for the scene that did greet her eyes. The house was on fire. And Erin was standing by watching it burn, a smile on her face. She could not have sent a stronger message to the Cailleach that evening.

Chapter 40

May Day's Eve 1995

That night they spent wrapped in the arms of the forest. Summer was coming, and there was no denying the new sweetness in the earth, a softness to the air that folded in on them. The long winter was suddenly at an end.

The house, too, was gone. From where they gathered they could still see the smoke curling over the treetops. Nothing remained where the house had stood but a piece of scorched earth, and of all things the steps, a stairway to the stars. Erin had saved only photographs, not even the books.

Dara and Drew barely spoke, from grief and shock no doubt. So Honor and Erin went over what they knew. That the Cailleach renewed herself and her powers, turned from hag into maiden, and became strong again by bathing in the river before dawn. Not on Imbolc, the first of February, St. Bridget's Day, and not on the spring equinox, around the twentieth of March, but on Bealtaine, the first day of May.

The question was still how to stop her? If they had to do this alone, without Dara, they would. All thoughts and rules about the quest, all of that was gone now, gone with Shane, Devin, and the house.

'She is eternal, a paranormal, supernatural presence, she is the landscape itself. She does not rely on anything of this world, so why rely on us?'

'Is it possible she doesn't? That she doesn't need us, and maybe doesn't know?'

'And this thing of her not being able to come in the house, why is that?'

'I believe it's because she can only exist in nature,' Honor said. 'That the modern, the built world is a threat.'

'But she has been in the house, the day Caer went with Seán, when she touched you, and she put the whitethorn branches in Dara's bed.'

'It's my fault,' Dara said finally. 'Devin would still be alive if I had stayed at the house like you told me, Honor.'

'Maybe, maybe not. None of us are great for doing what we're told.'

Drew was still silent, she knew it was far more her fault than Dara's. After all, she was the one who'd had the dreams, who'd foreseen Dara, and Devin, in mortal danger. Who'd been there in the chapel when Caer cursed Seán, who'd delayed that process by speaking to Caer. Why hadn't she done more? Why hadn't she done something to save Devin? She could have warned her to stay in the house. Why hadn't she believed in her dreams? And told about them? Was it too late now? For all of them.

Dara was speaking again.

'We will have to face her in battle, you know that. A battle between wild nature and human culture.'

'With us on the side of culture?' Erin frowned. That was the part she struggled with. It couldn't be right, could it? She looked to Honor, wanting to hear her thoughts.

'Yes. I know it is strange,' she agreed, 'but the key is not society I think, it's our humanity. You're right, Erin, we are not natural enemies of the Cailleach. We should be able to co-exist. Perhaps, were it not for the curse, things could have been different. I think Caer felt this too.'

She felt sure at least part of the reason the curse hadn't been broken was this. This conflict.

'If Devin were here she'd suggest things could still be different,' Drew added.

'I think it's too late for idealism,' said Dara. 'We've become key to her yearly renewal, that's the problem. She's not going to risk that. I don't think we have any choice but to finish her. She can't be defeated by our powers. No matter how strong they can never be stronger than hers, that was proven with Caer. So yes, Honor is right, it's only by our humanity we can win. We have to fight on the side of culture, for now. One battle at a time, starting with this one.'

'All right,' Erin said, 'so we have a tool, culture, our humanity, any idea how to use it?'

'I say we go and be there when she arrives, by the river.'

'And then?'

'And then I kill her.'

'No.'

It was Drew. Looking around her she took a deep breath. No going back now, she had to speak her truth. The truth she had felt for some time.

'All right, I know this may be hard to hear but bear with me, please. I believe that if we follow this plan there are only two possible outcomes. Either we destroy the Cailleach, or she destroys us.'

Dara shrugged. 'And?'

'We don't want to destroy her. It's as the aunts have said, we are much closer to her than to society. We're women, witches, we are nature, creators not destroyers, and she is nature. What we want is freedom, the freedom to choose our own way, or make a new way.'

'Destruction is part of the creative process too,' said Dara. 'The Cailleach is both destroyer and creator, and so are we. Besides, we can't choose our own way, can we? She denies us, we are bound.'

'Only by fear and tradition. The Cailleach, she's afraid too.'

'How can you say that?' Dara was horrified.

'For how long has she been forgotten by the world? Society has declared itself separate from nature. The inevitable result of that madness is the society is going to destroy her, and itself. Meanwhile, we're in a unique position. We haunt the edges, between this world and the world inside this world, between society, and Cailleach.'

They listened, incredulous.

Now Drew had found her voice her words flowed like a river, she couldn't stop.

'The reason we haven't been able to beat her so far is we haven't really wanted to, or we have and that ends in bloodshed. Meanwhile, the divide between us and society is growing, and all the while we grow closer to her. In spite of that we have not been unaffected by cultural influence. Therefore, we do know how to destroy her. Have known for generations now. And she knows this too.'

The women were silent, she noticed. They had sunset, moonlight, and firelight in their faces, but what burned in their hearts? She couldn't say yet.

'Go on then,' said Dara, her eyes shining like stars, 'say it, say the words.'

'Honor, Erin, Dara. I have solved the quest.'

'Drew!' Honor and Erin were stunned.

'Dara has solved it too,' she added quickly. 'Haven't you Dara?'

Dara stared at her sister imperiously.

Honor and Erin looked from each of the girls to each other, wary at what was unfolding.

'I have solved the quest,' Drew continued. 'The same way I believe every generation for years has solved it. It's what Jaen knew, and was going to tell, before the Cailleach dropped a tree on her. It's what our mother knew when she left here. For God's sake, it's the reason she left. And it's simple. It's so simple. But the Cailleach, she had to stop those who chose to end her. That's why she planned to kill Dara. Still plans to.'

'And how does she fulfil her transformation?' Dara asked, in a too calm voice, that belied her furious passion.

'She has to make it to the river and bathe before sunrise. Not only that. She has to do it in complete and utter silence. Before a dog barks, or a car goes along the road, before the church bells ring, a baby cries, or the farmers are out in the fields. Before the sounds of human society, of culture, of this world, intrude. And if we were to go to her cave now and stall her, even a few moments, and if one of us was say, in the river before her and on seeing her approach strode out of that water, singing perhaps, or laughing, she would fall down, a heap of bones. Beaten, by her mountain, ringing with the sounds of this world. And that's your plan, isn't it Dara?'

'Something like that.'

'She knows that too, that's why she tried to kill you. Devin just got in the way. It was you she wanted. In every generation someone, at least one, has worked this out, this far. And when they do they have a choice. Keep quiet about it, as our mother did, though she later regretted it, I think. Keep quiet about it, leave, if you can, or plan to act on it, and die quick if she finds you when you do.'

'Ah but, she didn't get me, did she?'

'No, she got Devin instead, and Shane.'

'You know I never meant for that to happen.'

'I know, I'm sorry, that was unfair. You've done well, Dara, keeping the knowledge, and your intent, from the Cailleach for so long. It's too late for her to stop you now. I truly don't believe she can. Only I can stop you now.'

'You couldn't stop me if you tried for a hundred years. But in league with the Cailleach, Drew? I never would have thought that about you.'

Ignoring her, Drew turned her attention to her aunts. 'Honor, Erin, I know you've felt as I do for a long time. You've been safe from the Cailleach precisely because she knows you mean her no harm, once perhaps, but not any more. You want freedom, Honor, everyone knows that, but not at any price. And you, Erin, you were no threat to her, until tonight. Burning the house, it will have thrown her. Consider too that she knows so little about and has taken no interest in me. That puts us in the stronger position, for now. What's clear is Dara wants revenge, at any price. And right now, that's our weakness.'

What seemed clear was they were all in league against her, Dara thought furiously.

'All right,' Erin interjected, 'let's calm things down a bit. Drew, leaving Dara out of it please, just explain where we should go from here, in your view?'

'Find another way.'

'We're listening,' said Honor.

Dara shook her head.

'Dara, don't be troubled,' said Honor, 'listen.'

'We go to the Cailleach,' said Drew, 'like our ancestors did. To make a new bond for a new time. A bond of freedom and peace. That will break the curse and stop the quest. That will give us, all of us, the peace and freedom that we seek.

'We tell her that we only want a new way, one that will be better for Cailleach, and *Bean Feasa*. So that we can co-exist and co-create our worlds in peace. We tell her that to have this we must have our freedom. To stay or go, as we choose. To help the people if we wish, to create a better society, or to live a life of solitude, here, or someplace else.

'We tell her we will not try to end her, we will not use our knowledge to prevent her from renewing herself. And,' looking to Dara, 'we will not employ society to help us do it either.

'She can bring her storms and live her cycle of life as she has always done and we for our part will keep her alive by speaking of her, bringing her voice that has been hidden back to the world, to be seen and honoured again.

'And we too will live our cycle of life, in our own way. Not as the ancestors did, not as the society wants, but how we want. If we have to give up some of our power to do it, then so be it. I mean, I don't know we will have to, but it's possible. But I believe it's in our power, to end this today, for the good. And that is the power of our humanity.'

'Then the only bond between *Bean Feasa* and Cailleach would be one of protection,' Erin said, pleased. 'Care of the mountain, its creatures and resources, over everything. Protect the wild places, and as you said, co-create a new world. We could re-build the house.'

Honor couldn't help but smile at her sister. This was incredible. Drew had shown her true colours tonight, and the value of freedom. Of not being held back by the old ways. For all her own work, her powerful mind and intent, she had been too close to it all, and for too long. She knew, by the lighter feeling in her heart and soul, that this was right. And Erin felt it too, but Dara. There was going to be a fight there. Just not the fight they had expected.

'My turn to speak now,' said Dara. 'What if she doesn't accept your offer? She will have renewed herself, will be at her most powerful. What's to stop her from just killing us?'

'Nothing. It's a risk I think we have to take. The world of man is destroying her, and she can't stop it. But we can work between the worlds. She can't make them see, only other humans can do that, humans like us. I think that once she learns that, well then, why would she want to kill us? I believe this, I truly do.'

'I think you're a fool.'

'It can seem like that,' Erin said, 'when people act out of love. That's what Drew is doing here Dara. Love is her motivation. What will yours be?'

Honor continued, 'Drew has offered an alternative plan. It's not what any of us imagined, Dara, and it's not easy, we know that. But it *feels* right. I trust my heart on this. Can you? The old ways don't work. We can at least agree on that? And we need to make a decision, now. My hope is you'll keep faith with us. Dara?'

'You want this? After all she's done?'

'Yes, we do. Erin and I, a long time ago we made a promise. We promised we were going to end it this time, whatever that took. That's why this is the best decision. The other options mean nothing changes. And that's not something we can live with anymore.'

'But if I kill her...'

'No. It won't help. I'm telling you. It would destroy you too.'

'It's a lot to take in, I need to think.'

'We don't have much time.'

'I know that, Honor, but this was my destiny, remember? It was supposed to be my path, my choice. That's why you brought me to this god-forsaken place. To break the curse, to free us from the Cailleach. I was always meant to defeat her, or die trying. She *killed* them all, and now you want to let her go? On the chance that she might think like Drew here?

'I not only know how to kill her and end this thing for certain, but am willing to do it too. And you know that, don't you Honor? You too, Drew. You already know what I plan to do. So excuse me if I need a fucking moment to wrap my head around this new plan.'

The hurt and pain was unimaginable. How they could do this to her, to themselves? And on this day of all days. With Devin's body barely cold, and by the Cailleach's hand. But she had to be careful now. They had turned against her, were they now on the Cailleach's side? That was how it seemed.

How had it come to this? This betrayal. Was it the work of the Cailleach, even now? Some kind of enchantment. Another way to get to her? Destroy her. Like her ancestor Dea, killed at her own sisters' hands. But if she went ahead with her plan, if she killed the Cailleach, they'd be free of this madness.

They sat by the fire, surrounded in shadows, as a slender moon rose in the sky. Waiting for Dara to make her move. The only sounds were the crackling flames and snap of twigs from where she paced close by.

Thoughts of Devin and Shane filled Erin's mind, tormenting her with sorrow. The last times they'd spoken, he of his love, she denied him. Devin, of her hopes for a better, more harmonious future, and of her worries for Dara. She had failed Devin. She didn't want to lose Drew or Dara as well. Would they see the green light of summer again, she wondered? And if they did would it be dimmer now? Without Devin and Shane. And goodness knows who else. Only tomorrow would tell the tale.

Honor cradled a long cold cup of coffee and thought about how far they'd come since that night they'd stood in the garden and vowed to end this thing once and for all. Whatever happened now she was proud of them all. And she wouldn't change it, aside from the loss of lives of course. She thought of Dealan, too.

Drew had started moving about, stoking the fire, tying her hair up, watching the sky that was lightening a little, watching her sister too.

She spoke sharply, 'Dara's gone.'

'When?'

'Just now.'

'Oh no, she's dead.'

'She is if we don't stop her.'

'We have to stop her.'

The three women moved through the forest, silent as the moon, swift as the mackerel of the ocean, one with the night.

Chapter 41

Full Circle

The night was ebbing fast as Dara moved through the still dark woods. Her spirits had taken a beating but that would soon be taken care of. She wished it would rain, or the wind would blow, she wished it was cold. Where were the storms they knew? It was as if the whole landscape had stilled itself for her, the great weather deity, on the bridge between winter and summer. But Dara was neither still nor beautiful.

Thoughts of her mother and father, and Devin too, drove her. What terrors must they have known? And she felt herself growing in power. This was her land, earned in blood. She would destroy the Cailleach.

The Cailleach crouched in her wet cave, awaiting the moment, ready to strike for the river. Despite her doubts it had been a good alliance, had served her well. But a rot had set in. They wanted free of her and she'd watched them break themselves to do it. Had helped them do it.

Even her own son had forsaken her, for Honor. Though she'd punished him, punished them both for that. She'd thought this one would be different. This was the one who as a child had given her the old feeling, who wasn't like the others, the one who was closest to her. Or so she'd thought. She could feel her life force fading as she spoke to Dara.

'So you wish to meet again, and so soon. I would have thought our little grave digging session would have been enough for you. And yet, you are coming to kill me. Do you remember, when you were a child and the good times we had?'

She was speaking. *How dare she,* Dara thought. *I would trample her into the ground.*

'You mean after you killed my parents?'

'Not I my dear, not I. But I see you don't believe me anymore.'

'You lie. She was strong, and you were afraid of her strength because it was enough to end the curse, wasn't it?'

'Curse! There's no curse, your ancestors stood in my cave, they made a deal, that's all.'

'Even if that's true, you need us, our complicity in your cycle, to survive.'

'Need, I have no need except one.'

'To bathe in the river.'

'Yes Dara, to bathe in the river before sunrise. So if you'll excuse me I think I'll end this little talk of ours. You won't stop me, and tomorrow life will go on as before, at least for me. Then the hunted will become the huntress. I'll be coming after you.'

'I don't think so.'

'You underestimate me. You underestimate your sister, too.'

'Drew.'

'Yessss, Drew. Another dark sister, isn't she? But you didn't know, did you? None of you did. Gave you quite the surprise today didn't she? In league with me all this time, and you never suspected a thing.

'You know that I live, not by water alone, or your precious youth, but by death and destruction. Like the death and destruction of winter. And the next death, will be yours Dara. You tried to tell them, and they didn't believe you.'

She laughed.

'I will return in my full power today with the sun. I'll come over the hills like thunder and deal with you once and for all. Fool to think you can defeat the ancient, the everlasting.'

The night sky was no longer solid. The day was coming. The beginnings of shimmering light, when the Cailleach emerged from her lair. Conditions were perfect. Soon she would see the river, still and gleaming in the mist. That would turn her back into a maid.

Around the same moment Honor and Drew had caught up to and overtaken Dara. They were waiting for her by the whitethorn.

She didn't want to hurt her sister, her aunt, but she would if she had to. She still had time to kill the Cailleach. And she wasn't going down without a fight.

'You have no choice but to let me pass, Drew. You know you can't beat me, you know I have more power.'

'I'm not going to use magic to stop you, Dara, I'm going to use my hands.'

She meant it, Dara could see, but there was no time for this. No magic, she said. All right then, no magic. If she couldn't weaponise her powers against her, there were other things. Dara picked up a stick and rushed towards them, aiming for her legs. But Honor put herself in front of Drew, and the blow struck her instead. The crack of her arm as the bone broke, the shock of that almost ended Dara. Honor fell to her knees and the look in her eyes was more devastating to Dara than she could bear or wanted to know.

'I'm sorry,' she said, bringing the stick up again, high above her head this time. And she looked at the sky.

Fairy mist, the Cailleach would already be moving. She could bring them closer at least. Close enough for her to hear them. She dropped the stick and started to run. But Drew caught up and body slammed her to the ground. They had neither one of them ever been in a physical fight before, but were well matched in strength, size, and intent. Only Dara was more violent, more reckless, and dirtier with it. She hardly knew what she was doing, but break away she did and left Drew lying on the ground, her own sister.

The river, she had to get them closer to the river. Dara was so focused that the final blow when it came shocked her to her core. Something came hurtling towards her, something sharp. There was a sickening crack, and her hand flew to her skull. It was Erin who threw the stone. She walked calmly towards Dara as her eyes filled with blood, past where Honor was standing, and Drew half lay.

'Enough, Dara, enough. It's over. Sunrise.' And so it was. Silken, clear and brilliant.

But Dara wasn't finished.

'No. You're wrong, Erin. I sent the townsfolk to the river ahead of her. That was their vow remember? That was what I told Una, to go, not to the cave but to the river.

To wait for me there. It will have been enough. I wasn't there, but it will have been enough to end her.'

'The people never made it to the river, Dara. I met them halfway there I sent them back.'

The world started to spin and all the faces were in it, her mother, her father, Devin, Mae, Ellen. Over. It was over. The Cailleach had won, again, and they helped her, and Dara had hurt them. Would have killed them to stop her. What had become of her? They could have turned their backs on her then, but that wasn't their way.

They formed a circle around her, Erin, Drew, Honor too. A circle of protection, for her.

'There's no evil in you Dara,' said Erin, a gleam of fierce love in her eyes, 'only pain. We are *Bean Feasa*, witches, healers, sisters, but a *Bean Feasa* can't practice with pain in her heart.'

She reached out her hand, and Dara took it. And in that moment she felt only relief. Immense, earth shattering, relief. And the grief of so many years rose away on the silvery mist.

After that came the pain, and the healing. Of the day's injuries, of the life, and everything that once was buried now released. It was a difficult, necessary time. They forgave her, and she forgave them. That was their vow always they said. Loyalty, family, and the end of the quest. It was what Honor and Erin had sworn all those years ago, the night of Caer's death. There was nothing to forgive they said. It was much harder to forgive herself.

More than the Cailleach had been born anew that bright May Day. They had gone to her, Honor, Erin and Drew, broken and bruised as they were. And the Cailleach, a maiden again, agreed to the new plan. One thing about these women, after all this time, they could still surprise her.

Honor, the geis lifted, she would not lose her sight, was leaving with Dealan. It was the right thing for her then. It was only hard to leave Erin.

'Maybe I'll come back one day.'

'You will.'

'You think?'

'Yes. Because he's not the love of your life, I am. And you're mine.'

'Not the house then?'

'What is the house, without you.'

Drew had told them it was the Cailleach in Caer's image killed Seán, and not as Caer had feared, that it was at her own hand possessed that he'd died.

Dealan confirmed this was true and that Seán had known this in his last moments, moments when he as the wolf had stayed with him. That was the least he owed him he said, after all, he'd attacked Seán on the mountain that time, at the Cailleach's request, the same night he met Honor for the first time.

The girls learned from the aunts that Caer's death was not suicide as they'd always thought, but a true accident. Sadly, she'd died not knowing the truth of Seán's death. All she knew for certain was that they hadn't understood the danger for him, to be so close, even through her, to the energies of the otherworld.

Dara would heal in time, and when she did, would be stronger, and happier, than any of them. She decided to move to Dublin but first she attended Seán's funeral where she spoke with Mary. His body was found after hikers alerted the guards to some personal effects they'd found. An old wallet with some cards, an old photo of the pair, and two faded tickets to Dublin. Cause of death was deemed accidental, no foul play. Mary and Dara both felt like a weight had been lifted, a feeling further enhanced for Mary by meeting her grandchild when she had so little time left.

As for Erin, to absolutely no one's surprise she decided to rebuild the house. Drew was going to live with her, which made her so happy. She didn't think she would have been able to live alone, with only the ghosts for company. No, they never left. They roamed the hills until the walls went up again, then back they went. Drew was with Dúlta still, and Erin started seeing Joe. The loss of Devin went hard on him. He started calling and it soon became a regular thing. She looked forward to his coming, and before they knew it, it was more.

Life became good. The Cailleach agreed and this was a quiet time for her. They had the mildest winter in a hundred years. There was still the town and the legacies of the past, but even that felt easier. They too were now free of the curse, thanks to Drew, bringer of light.

Of all of them, she was not what Erin expected. And she never expected that Drew and she would be together. Just the two of them, and the new house. Though it wouldn't be two of them for long for she was pregnant, having twins.

With all the rumours of the past you'd think it would have been difficult getting the building work done but they had no problem finding men. Men who took pride, and humour, in the task. In telling their friends where they were working now, re-building the witches house. And still alive in spite of the fact. Erin oversaw everything herself. She didn't want the same house, that would have been an impossibility. She missed Honor, missed them all, but she was happy. They all were. Life was rich and full again. They were free.

...

Erin

More than a year passed. We were back with the ghosts of shimmering summer, July. Season of storms and of heaviness. I was in the garden with Drew, too many butterflies, too much gravity, and a cool glass of wine, when the black dog came shuffling up the lane with the sky on his back.

Glossary

Banshee – A female spirit in Irish mythology who heralds the death of a family member, usually by wailing, shrieking, or keening.

Bealtaine – The Celtic Festival marks the beginning of summer. What we know now as May Day, the 1st of May. The festival was marked with the lighting of bonfires to symbolise purification and transition for the season in the hope of a good harvest later in the year, and accompanied with rituals to protect people from any harm by otherworld spirits.

Bean Feasa – Wise woman, fairy woman, witch, healer, Cailleach.

Boxty – Traditional Irish dish made with potatoes and fried or boiled.

Cailleach - Witch, fairy woman, paranormal landscape witch, goddess, hag, spirit of winter, divine hag, creator deity, weather deity, ancestor deity.

Changeling – A creature left in place of a human stolen

by the fairies. It would look like the human but be different, strange in some way. Acting out of character.

Geis – **Irish for 'curse', or 'taboo'**, though in some circumstances, they might also be seen in a positive light, as a 'gift'. Almost every hero in Irish mythology has at least one. If the hero violates her *geis, some disaster will occur,* maybe even death.

Grá – Irish for 'love.'

Imbolc (Imbolg) - The festival marking the beginning of spring has been celebrated since ancient times.

IRA – The Irish Republican Army. A paramilitary movement in Ireland in the 20th and 21st centuries dedicated to Irish republicanism, the belief that all of Ireland should be an independent republic.

Milesians - The Milesians are Gaels who sailed to Ireland from Hispania after spending hundreds of years traveling the earth. When they landed in Ireland they contended with the Tuatha Dé Danann, who represented the pagan gods. The two groups agreed to divide Ireland between them: the Milesians took the world above, while the Tuatha Dé Danaan took the world below i.e. The otherworld.

The Púca – Mythological shapeshifter, may appear as a horse, rabbit, goat, or dog. Known to give advice, and warning, and to lead people away from harm.

Sliabh Earrach – Sliabh (meaning mountain) and Earrach (meaning Spring) Spring Mountain.

Stray Sod – An expression. To stand on a *'stray sod'* means to go astray. Usually someplace familiar. And not know where you are. The fairies are usually suspected to have caused this kind of mischief.

The Tuatha Dé Danann – The People of the Goddess Dana, Ireland's supernatural race, representing the main deities of pre-Christian Ireland. For over a thousand years they were central to the intellectual creativity of Ireland. Their influence is still to be found in some contemporary works. After their defeat by the Milesians they absorbed themselves into the landscape, moved to the otherworld, and eventually became the fairies of later folklore. Though they dwell in the otherworld they can interact with humans in the human world.

Turf – The surface area of soil held together by its roots, cut from boglands and dried, for burning in home fires.

The Fae – The fairy folk, fair folk, faery, faerie. Fairy men and women of the otherworld.

Pronunciation Guide

Bean Feasa – 'Ban Fasa'

Caer – 'Care'

Cailleach – 'Koll-yok' 'Koll-och' 'Kyle-och' or 'Ky-och.'

Dúlta – A boys name, pronounced 'Dool-ta.'

Geis – **Gesh or gaysh**

Grá – Graw

Seán – A boys name, pronounced 'Shaun' or 'Shawn.'

Sliabh Earrach – 'Shleeve-Arrach'

About the Author

Jane Gilheaney Barry is an author, and founder of That Curious Love of Green, a creative lifestyle blog and brand that embodies her life, home, and philosophy of creativity as a way of life. This is where she shares daily inspirations with an online following of 25,000 and growing.

With a passion for writing, creativity, freedom, and the creative path, Jane and That Curious Love of Green are becoming a go-to source for creativity inspiration. When she's not writing, Jane is in demand as a workshop facilitator and retreat host.

Jane lives outside Ballinamore, Co. Leitrim, in the north west of Ireland, with her family; husband Adrian, and children, stylist Shaylyn Gilheaney, Saoirse, ten, and Sadhbh, seven.

A keen photographer, nature lover, stylist, and artist, Jane's professional background is PR, Arts Management, Art Therapy, and Project Design. You can follow Jane at:

Follow Jane at That Curious Love of Green on Facebook: www.facebook.com/thatcuriousloveofgreen

Instagram: @janegilheaneybarry

For workshops and press email: janebarry17@gmail.com

Jane's mailing list: www.thatcuriousloveofgreen.com

Before You Go

I hope you have enjoyed this book. If you can be persuaded to write a reader review on Amazon I'd really appreciate it.

Reviews on Amazon are critical to the success of an author these days.

30526089R00242

Printed in Poland
by Amazon Fulfillment
Poland Sp. z o.o., Wrocław